Brick's *Ruin*

Lucifers Saints MC
(Sacramento Chapter)
Prequel
2ND Edition

Tonya Ink

Contents

Copyright

Brick's Ruin Prequel by Tonya Ink

Published by Tonya Ink

Disclaimer

This story contains situations and scenarios that are fictitious. Names, characters, places, and situations are fictional. Any resemblance to an actual person living or dead, events, or locations is entirely coincidental.

License Notes

For permissions, contact:
Tonya Ink
Tonya._Ink@hotmail.com
Cover by: Tonya Ink

Miscellaneous Credits:
Cover Image curated from Pexels.com

ISBN's
ASIN: B0B1W2ZQ5T
eBook:
Paperback: 9798356481215

Dedication

To all those that found love when they weren't looking. And to those that allowed their hearts to lead them in the right direction.

To YOU, thank you for being fearless.
"Every new beginning comes from another beginnings end."
-Unknown

Triggern Warning

The content is intended for mature audiences. The material contains parts that may be viewed as uncomfortable. Some scenes and scenarios include language that may be offensive to some readers. This book contains graphic violence, graphic threats of physical violence, murder, abuse/bullying, explicit language, mention of kidnapping, mention of rape but no rape occurs, discussion of loss of a loved one from murder, loss of a child, and crude inappropriate humor and sexual content, language, and situations.

This book includes minimal bondage.

This is a medium pace insta-love story. Ends in a HEA.

This story is written in the first person, and there are multiple POVs

This writing style may contain nuances and verbiage unfamiliar to the reader along with nonstandard spelling. Characters may repeat phrasing and statements specific to them such as "Oh my". This is and will be a theme throughout the novel.

These spelling and grammar choices are *intentional*.

Reader discretion is advised.

MC Members

PRESIDENT - James "Brick" Masterson
V. PRESIDENT - Tully
SARGENT AT ARMS - Slim
ENFORCER - Flick
TREASURER - Rocky
TECH - Hound
ROAD CAPTAIN - Tommy Boy
MEDIC - Doc
LAWYER - Markus *Law* Jacobson Esq.

~

PATCHED MEMBERS
Ink
Phoenix
Bandit
Zero
Fox
Ripper
Scout
Mouse

~

PROSPECTS
Cadence
Jasper

~

OL' LADIES
Nancy

~

CLUB GIRLS
Darcy
Penelope
Mandy
Manda
Penny

Mafia Members

BARONE MAFIA
DON - Elijah Barone

TOMASI FAMILY
Parents - Victor & Venezia Tomasi
Sisters
Vittoria
Valeria

SALVATORE MAFIA
DON -Stefano Salvatore (deceased)
Don - Sergio Salvatore

Translation

Italian	English
Famiglia	Family
Sorella	Sister
è morta	She's dead
sorellina	Baby sister
Madre	Mother
Padre	Father
genitori	Parents

Prologue

 VALENTINA

19 years old

All I feel is the dread and the awareness of what our lives have become. She's dead. My *Sorella* is dead. I close my bedroom door slowly behind me as I lean into it. I try to breathe, but I can't. The hot tears are cascading down my face. Their heat is all that I feel– all I *want* to feel. Everything around me *is*.

My knees feel weak, my hands flex, my eyes clenched shut, and my body trembles as the memories of what's happened over the last few months assault me: no rhyme or reason, no order, just the overwhelming assault of all the gut-wrenching memories. I can't breathe. I can't– *I can't*.

è morta

è morta

She's dead

My throat feels like it is closing as I try to hold back my sobs; my hands cover my mouth as the tears continue. Everything is so constricting. It's too tight. The leotard I wear is too much. I can't breathe. I can't. I claw at my chest as my nails dig into my skin; I can only feel the sting on my skin for a moment. Because it doesn't matter, my *Sorella* is dead. My breath comes out ragged and uneven. I can't. I can't breathe. The tears continue to flow freely and of their own accord. I haven't cried since that day. The day she was taken. That day, I forced myself to stop feeling anything other than regret and numbness. Because that was the day that I lost everything, I lost *her*...

è morta

I try to stop them... the tears. I try to hold them in; they keep coming. I shouldn't be crying. I am Tomasi, and we do not cry. At that thought, my tears fall harder. Why shouldn't I cry, *è morta?* I hold as much of my sobs in as I can. I must contain the grief. My grief means nothing, no matter how much it is trying to overwhelm my senses. I will not allow them to hear me breaking. They will never know how my heart is shattered, how the regret overwhelms me. They will never know how I wish it were me instead of her. Oh, how I wish it were me. It doesn't even matter anymore. I don't matter anymore.

My *Madre, Padre,* and *sorellina* have been through enough. The last few months have been torture, not knowing, not getting answers. I was not able to save her. They do not need my tears. But I can't stop them from coming. I can't *breathe.*

My tears fall, trailing down to my chest for a moment... just a short moment, I feel the sting from their assault on my skin. I can't stop them from flowing. I can't breathe. Unable to catch my breath, my vision goes blurry, and dots cloud my vision. She... she's *gone.*

è *morta*

My eyes flutter open, and instantly the numbness takes over, but there is also anger. So much anger. I thought when my *Padre* decided to move us and leave the Salvatore *Famiglia.* I... I thought when we came here. I thought they would help us save her.

My chest hurts, my eyes are swollen, and I'm lying on my bedroom floor. I don't know how we got here. How did we get here?

This morning's memories overtake me, no matter how much I fight against them. No matter how much I want to forget. All the sadness, all of the pain, and all the anger, it is all too much. See what I saw to know what I know after walking out of our front door.

It's too much it is overwhelming me. I try to call for the numbness that has been my companion, and I want it. I need it to come back to overtake my heart and soul. Because to feel this– to feel at all will destroy me.

Walking out to such a beautiful cloudless morning in San Francisco and seeing *that.* It was supposed to be a typical day. I was going to go for my morning run, stretch my legs and not think about her. I wasn't going to think about the atrocities she was enduring. I wasn't going to think about how she was taken. I wasn't going to consider how angry my *Padre* was with me. I wasn't going to think about how my *Madre* never looked me in the eye or how my *sorellina* barely spoke to me. I didn't want to feel. I just wanted to go for a run. My mind had other plans. Memories from the day's things began to change, and enter my mind.

It was a day like any other, returning home from our day at college. One of Padre's men was standing at the front door and told us that Padre wanted to see us in his office. I knew instantly that something was wrong. Madre was standing next to him; her lips were tight, and her eyes were glossy as if she were holding in tears. She was.

Walking into Padres' office, he was sitting behind his large oak desk, face thunderous. What drew my attention wasn't my Padre's anger, tight posture, or my Madre's scared glossy eyes. It was the vase and cardboard file box sitting on his desk. My eyes widened, and I instantly found Vittoria's wide, shocked ones.

My Padre explains that he knew because the note found with the gifts on our doorstep this morning wasn't the first. I look over at my sister, and I see her skin has gone ashen, and tears are flowing freely. My Padres eyes narrow on her, making me step closer to her to comfort her. Looking at her trying to give her as much of my strength as I could. I didn't know that she had kept them. I know that even if Padre is angry at her, he is angrier that she kept this from him. Grabbing her hand in mine and squeezing it, I can feel her trembling. We are generally not afraid of our Padre, but at this moment, I am fearful for my Sorella to see his and Madres' faces.

He explains that knowing something was amiss, he had searched my and Vittoria's rooms. He found more than he bargained for and demanded we tell him everything. I will never understand why she kept it all, I told her not to, but she didn't listen to me. She never listened to me.

There were so many arguments those last days because she was so damn stubborn. She called me paranoid, saying it wasn't a big deal and I needed to mind my business. But looking in my father's eyes the day he made her tell him the truth. He was furious at Vitty for not telling him as soon as the gifts started to come and me because I knew about them and didn't speak up. From that day on, we weren't allowed to go to our college classes or leave the house. We weren't allowed anywhere without one of my Padres' associates or himself.

Until we made a mistake.

Until that day.

Until the day she was taken, right in front of me.

Until the moment her grip loosened.

Until the door to the van closed.

Until I was hit over the head, knocking me unconscious.

I remember how she pleaded with me with her panic-stricken face begging me not to let her go. I remember the moment she realized that I had to. She fought, we fought, and it wasn't enough. They took her.

The panic that consumed me was nearly overwhelming when I awoke sprawled out on the filthy New York streets. My head was throbbing from where I had been struck, and my clothing was torn. The shock was crippling, but I knew what I had to do.

Once I could collect myself, I stumbled out of the alleyway and onto the busy New York streets. A few passersby tried to talk to me. They tried to help, which, if I am honest, isn't typical for the city. But I guess when a young girl is walking around with torn clothes crying, people will take notice, but I ignore them. I needed my Padre. When I called him from a payphone, I'd never heard my Padre so angry in nineteen years.

I could hold comfort in the fact that even though he was angry, I knew he would be proud of me for remembering the thing he always taught Vitty and me. He told us always to have a change in our pockets when we leave home. At that moment, I was happy that that lesson stuck. But it didn't last long. It's a silly thing to be pleased about. I just witnessed my sister being taken, and that's what is bringing me joy. What is wrong with me? I let them take her. I let them.

While waiting for my Padre, I tried to make myself as small as possible. I didn't want to draw any more attention to myself. I didn't want anyone to talk to me or try to make me feel better. I didn't deserve their help or pity. I let them take her.

I just wanted to cry, but I couldn't let any more tears fall. I don't remember how long from the moment Padre hung up on me until he arrived. When he came, I was sitting on the curb next to the pay phone I used to call him at home. Padre pulled up in front of me, not caring whether or not he could park where he was. A few other cars, cars that I recognized, parked in front and behind him. He simply got out of the car and asked where? I know what he meant. And I could tell by the stone-cold look in his eyes and the deep timbre of his voice that I needed to be quick about it. I told him, and he just started

8

barking orders to his men, ushered me into the front seat, and drove away.

Padre did not speak another word to me. He didn't check to make sure I was ok. He said nothing more than the question. He just stared at me with anger, disappointment, and disgust. And that crushed me. If I had known any better, that would have been a cue to how the next year of my life would have gone.

I snuck glances at him through my lashes as silent tears streamed down my face as we made our way home through the dark New York streets. His jaw was tight, hands gripping the steering wheel of his Buick Riviera, knuckles turning white at the force. I could hear the steering wheel's leather creak and...

She was gone, they took her, and my Sorella was gone.

Once we arrived home, my Padre said nothing. I could feel the anger vibrating off his large frame and was scared. So— so afraid and frightened.

Parking in the garage, he continued to sit silently, not turning the car off. I wasn't sure what I should do. I sat silently, with my hands in my lap clasped together, my head hurt from what those men did to me, but I said nothing. I knew my Padre was trying to keep it together. I knew he was trying to keep himself from throttling me at the stupid choice my Sorella and I made. We continue to sit in silence, my fear preventing me from looking at my Padre. Fear prevents me from apologizing to him, for my sister being taken, for sneaking out of our home knowing it was forbidden. I refused to make a move to get out of the car or make a sound. I sat wringing my hands together painfully, listened, and waited. I heard him taking in a few deep breaths. I could only see the profile of his face as neither of us looked at the other. What I could see from the corner of my eye wasn't shocking, not really. I never thought that... that look, that level of anger my father had would never be towards me.

He abruptly opened his door, never looking at me. He quickly got out of the car, slamming the door, and I watched him stomping his way into our home. Before getting out, I took a few breaths, preparing myself for what was to come. I knew I needed to catch up to my Padre, he may not be speaking to me now, but I knew— I knew that he wanted me to follow him. I knew the silent treatment wasn't going to last. I knew who my Padre had always been would not be who he is now. Whom he will become because of me because we chose to sneak out. Now he is a raging bull, and I know that I am the one that will be incurring his wrath.

Our home was eerily quiet, which isn't usual. There is always someone up and around, no matter day or night. But tonight, I saw no one and heard nothing. At first, I didn't know what to do with myself. I mean, I did. I just wanted to delay what I knew was going to happen. I thought my Madre would be awake and waiting for our arrival,

9

frantic at the thought of her eldest daughter being kidnapped, but she wasn't.

I knew my Padre needed to know what happened. Standing at the mouth of the hall leading to his office, tears still streaming down my face. I was unsure what to do, but I knew he was waiting for me. His office door was open, and the light streamed into the hallway. After calming down a little, I wiped my face with the sleeve of my torn, dirty shirt, my head was still throbbing, but I needed to do this. It wasn't about me but my Sorella and getting her back. That's what was necessary. I steeled my spine for what I knew would come and went into my Padre's office.

He didn't speak to me as he stared me down with fury and hurt in his eyes. He waited. I closed his door, walked briskly, and sat in the chair across from him. I didn't make eye contact with him. I just stared at my hands and tried not to let the tears fall. After a moment, I simply took a breath and told him everything that had happened that night. From Vittoria convincing me to sneak out with her, how we got past the guards, how we made our way to meet with a few of her friends, and the after.

Through it all, my Padre said nothing. He asked no questions. He just stared at me. Once I told him everything I could remember, my Padre stood from his chair, walked to his office door, opened it, stood with an iron grip on the door handle, and said, "Go to bed, Valentina," with disappointment and anger in his voice. My breath hitched, and a sob threatened to be released, but I held it in. At that moment, I knew that I had lost my Padre.

In the weeks after my Sorella was taken, I rarely saw my Padre. He didn't speak to me. He would ask my Madre to find out anything he wanted to know. But it was never anything to do with my Sorella. I knew he was trying to negotiate to get my Sorella back. I knew that in the end, my Padre decided to move our family from New York to San Francisco. And I also knew that I had to do something.

At first, I didn't understand what I was seeing. I didn't think to get my parents when I walked out of my front door. It was a morbid scene; I knew it was a warning being the daughter of a soldier in the mafia. It isn't my family's first time receiving a morbid warning like this. Sometimes, *Padre's* work followed him home. Recently all of the warnings came after my *Sorella* was taken, and they were warnings discouraging Padre from making waves within the *famiglia*. *Padre* was not deterred in trying to get her back and home to the family.

He always knew who'd taken her, but he also knew that he had to be careful in his pursuit of getting her back. Very few in the organization were willing to stand with my father against Don Salvatore. And knowing whom the warnings were coming from, the more my *Padre* dug in, the harsher and more violent the warnings became. The Salvatore family was ruthless.

It became clear that Padre wasn't giving up and was pushing to be transferred from the Salvatore *famiglia* on the East coast to the Barone *Famiglia* on the West. I can only assume it wasn't going over well if the increase of warnings we were receiving were any indication. I may be on the outside looking in, but I've overheard things between my *Padres* men that clarified what is happening.

I knew that he tried to keep his transfer request quiet, not wanting Don Salvatore to know about it until it was approved by the Don of Dons in Italy. Many outsiders and those that don't know about the inner workings of the mafia are surprised that such a thing can be done, but my family has been a part of the *famiglia* for generations; it was my Padres' choice to remain a soldier and not be promoted. For many of our family ties, my *Padre* has kept quiet not to place a target on our backs, as we have familial ties to the Dons Capo in Italy. But even still, those connections were unable to help get Vitty back.

Not many have said much about why many have requested transfers to other families. But only an idiot wouldn't recognize that it is because of how Don Salvatore treats members of the New York outfit, but it is implied. Even though the mafia has many facets, there are different Dons throughout the country based in other regions who run their territories and outfits as they see fit. They all fall under the Don of Dons in Italy, which in our situation, benefitted my father in getting what's left of our family away and safe.

Having men transfer from one *famiglia* to another is not unheard of or suspicious. The transfers are often because someone's skill set is needed in other places, though that is not the case with my *Padre*. I also heard that many American Dons had raised issues with the New York outfit over the last few years, questioning why so many have been requesting transfers, which is no secret. Many also feel that Don Salvatore has lost his mind and is out of control, yet no one is doing anything about it. Allowing him to torment the families that fall under his rule. My *Sorella* not being the first to be "abducted" under his Don-ship, other young women have gone missing, some returned changed irrevocably, and others found.

There have been talks about what to do with Don Salvatore, but nothing has been done as of yet. He is allowed to ruin the lives of those serving him and doesn't care. And no matter how much people point out his wrongdoings, no one does a thing. But that is going to change.

Padre's transfer allowed him to be under Don Barone in San Francisco. Everyone knew and respected Don Barone, even though he was considered ruthless in his reign. He was an honorable man who put caring for and provided a good life for those in the East Coast *famiglia* above all else and was not a disgusting predator.

Padre did what he had to; in the end, it wasn't enough.

When I was younger, my Padre still loved me when he looked at me. He would tell my sisters and me, "never be a stupid kitty, never be that kitty that is too curious for its own good. Curiosity killed the cat because it was too stupid to understand self-preservation. A curious mind gets detached at the neck." I've never fully understood what he meant, and I maybe still don't. Because as much as he discouraged curiosity in us girls, he also encouraged us to know our minds. At this moment, I suspect that I'm the cat. I am the curious cat.

It was a mistake to do what I did. It was a mistake to let my body dictate the direction in which I moved. It was a mistake to walk out of the door when I saw what was sitting on our lawn.

When I walked out of our front door, I cautiously walked towards the…

It was a dark omen; it was my new reality. It was my heartbreak at the beginning of the end. It wasn't that I was curious. It was because something drew me out of our front door. Something in me knew that I needed to see with my own eyes. Something in me knew that this was what I needed to see to make it all real.

It wasn't a warning. It was the end.

Her end.

It took nearly a year to devise a plan that no one would see coming. I clung to the numbness. The only emotions I allowed myself was my anger and rage. I didn't feel anything else; I wouldn't allow it. My family virtually turned their backs on me. I know they are hurting, but so am I. But it will all be ok soon.

I remember one night, when eating dinner with my family, my *Madre* just sat staring at me, and I could tell she saw the change in me, the darkness. But she said nothing, and for that, I am grateful. From that night on, she always seemed to be watching me just a little bit closer, yet not close enough.

I have accepted that I have changed and accepted the free-spirited, loving, and funny girl I was no more. I have allowed the darkness to build its home and remain unchecked. My bloodlust and thirst for vengeance and revenge are all-consuming.

With my plan in place, I knew it would work without a shadow of a doubt, and I would get the retribution my *Sorella* deserved.

Becoming someone else was never my intention, but I needed to get through this. Even though at this moment, I didn't recognize myself, knowing that I had to do things I usually would never do, something my family would disapprove of.

I had no choice in this if I wanted to accomplish my goal. I have a plan for every scenario that will play out perfectly. It has to because there is no going back. I have to do what needs to be done. And become whom I had to. I need to get the retribution and revenge my family deserves. The Don would fall.

He needs to *die.*

It wasn't easy, but I was determined. Rage and thirst for revenge fueled me. The day that disgusting man sent my battered, bruised, and beaten *Sorella* back to my family, leaving her lifeless body on our doorstep. I knew that he needed to die, and I would be the one to do it. Leaving my family, my new home in San Francisco, and returning to New York was the only way it would happen. Even if it were my last day on this earth, I had to do what needed to be done, what no one else was willing to do.

Today is the day, and this moment is the moment I will avenge my *Sorella*.

Standing in the bedroom doorway, watching the man that has consumed my every thought sleep peacefully, as if he didn't kidnap and murder my *Sorella and many others*. As if he didn't use my *Sorella* for his pleasure and discard her as if she were trash. The man that will be taking his last breaths tonight.

I stalk slowly and quietly towards the man I plan to murder, my eyes never leaving his sleeping form and silently thanking the housekeeper I paid who slipped a sleeping pill into his after-dinner decanter. She was and still is a family friend who, unfortunately, had no choice in working in the monster's home. Her father traded her to pay off his sizeable debts. Disgusting. And that is something that he will also pay for, which is why she was so willing to help me.

Once I reach him, with my gloved hands, I take the needle and cloth out of the pouch which hangs around my waste. Slowly I climb onto the bed with the fabric and needle and raise it towards where I plan to insert the deadly concoction—cringing at what I had to do to get all I needed for this plan to work. Once straddled his body, I slowly moved my hand, holding the chloroform-covered cloth towards his face. I was told I needed to be careful in using chloroform, so I am holding my breath, which I have practiced for months. I wanted to ensure that I didn't make the mistake of knocking myself out, being so close to the contents of the rag. I also wanted my face to be uncovered. I want him to see the person that stole his life from him and who will be sending him to hell. I want him to see me.

I bring the chloroform-covered rag down to his nose and mouth, ensuring that both are covered. His eyes snap open when it makes contact with his face, but it is too late. He has already inhaled it. His eyes come to me, and I smile as he attempts to struggle, but he is too weak. I have worked hard to get my body into its best shape. My thighs lock around his torso, locking his arms into place at his sides. The combination of the sleeping pill and the chloroform make it so— I jam the needle into his neck as I stare into his eyes and say the words I have longed to tell him. The last words he will ever hear.

"Marcire All 'inferno. Questo Per mia sorella, Vittoria"

He has no choice but to take in my words for him to rot in hell for what he did to my *Sorella. His* body begins to shake, and I get a sick satisfaction knowing that he will never see another sunrise. He will not live another day stealing, torturing any poor innocent, and unwilling woman. He is going to die knowing that I am the one that stole his life, sending him to hell where he belongs.

I smile as his eyes flare in rage and shock, fluttering closed for the last time, and his body stills.

I didn't know it then, but I wasn't alone in the final moments of Stefano Salvatore's life. And that mistake proved to be fatal. I thought I was avenging my *Sorella*, but I only caused the death of my *Padre* and *Madre*. Leaving me and my *sorellina* alone in the world and leaving me with even more regrets, a shattered and blackened heart.

Once again, Don Barone came to my family's rescue. He was not able to save us all, not in time. After my *genitori* was murdered, a few short weeks after I killed Don Salvatore. Don Barone was able to get me and Valeria new identities but would not let us stay together, stating that it was safer for us to be separated. Sending me to Sacramento, a town his *famiglia* had ties to, and sending Valeria to an unknown location to be raised without family.

The last day I saw my *sorellina* was one of the most challenging days of my life. I knew it was my doing. It was my fault and my decision to kill the man that killed my *Sorella*. It was my fault that my need for revenge was why my *genitori* was dead. Because of me, Valeria was going to spend the rest of her life with strangers, unable to see or speak to her only living family.

Now all but the two of us are *dead*. And my heart continues to shatter because it was and is all my fault. But if I am honest— truly honest, I don't regret it. I just regret *the after* losing my *genitori*.

Valeria has ensured that I knew she blames me for all of it. No matter how much I try to explain to her my reason. I also understand hers.

That day was the last day I was Valentina Tomasi.

Don Elijah Barone set me up with a new life and new identity after I swore myself to a vow of *omertà*..

One

VERA

21 years old

I t has been a year since my life changed, and I still have no idea how I do it. How do I get up every day? How do I keep going when the voice inside my head is a constant reminder that I am alone in this world? That I will never be happy because I don't deserve happiness. I will never see my family again. Because I am the reason my parents were killed, and I am the reason I will never see my baby sister again. I am the reason my family was torn apart. Tomasi's are no more.

"Vera, you have customers at table *sixteen,* but I can take um if ya want?" The winey voice of the one person I cannot stand in this entire building rings out, and I cringe in annoyance—deep *breaths.* Claire stares at the side of my head expectantly, swirling her damn gum around her finger.

Gross.

Claire is another one of the evening waitresses here at Patty's Diner. She claims she's the lead waitress and never lets anyone forget it. For some reason, in her pea brain, she thinks she has authority over all of the other waitresses because she banged the owner, manager, or whatever the hell Steven is. I've never been sure about that and don't care enough to clarify.

From week one, she became my work nemesis. From the very day I was hired, she's hated me. She takes it upon herself every to make working here tricky, and I wouldn't say I like it. I loathe that stuck-up lazy bitch.

I'm trying to pretend like I didn't hear her. She's coming at me, acting as if I didn't hear the bell above the door ring. Or see that my table is now filled. So she comes closer to stand next to me with her arms crossed, a scowl on her face, and popping that god-awful Bubblicous cherry cola gum.

Ugh, because of her, I now despise the once-beloved treat. Even the smell of it now makes my stomach churn.

I hate playing these stupid games with her. I turn to stare at her blankly. I honestly wish I could leave this job and do something else. *Anything* else. Unfortunately, I have bills to pay, and I am the only one to pay them because I am alone. All a-fucking-lone.

My eyes trail from Claire to my customers at table sixteen, which is no longer just a single table. The occupants have taken it upon themselves to pull tables seventeen and eighteen together. The large group of men intimidate the other customers, many scrambling to finish their meals, quickly signaling their servers for their checks.

I receive nervous glances from the two other servers, which makes no sense to me. These men have been here many times, usually sitting in Claire's section. So, I don't understand why Beebe and Mona look so distraught. Between stealing glances at me, they quickly provide their customers with their checks and clear tables along with Dan. And then it clicks when Beebe looks at me, and her eyes slide over to Claires, who is now staring daggers at me.

I get it. They are sitting in *my* section.

I hadn't had anyone in my section for some time, thanks to Claire and her bullshit. Usually, Claire is all up in the customer's faces shuffling them around to sit where she wants them to. More often than not, she seats the customers she knows tip well in her section, and if she can, which she usually does, she will prevent people from sitting in my section. Again according to her, it's her job as the lead waitress to seat customers.

The guys bypassed her to sit in my section, and she is pissed about it. Hopefully, they are good tippers. The way Claire acts when they have been here in the past means that they possibly are. Fingers crossed. A small smile forms on my lips as I know that's probably why she is being a bitch with her dagger eyes and offering to take my tables.

No dice Kemosabe.

I don't have to give anyone their check. As I said, I haven't had anyone at my table for the last few hours. I just stand and watch the men as they settle in. They are all so damn big, like huge, and from what I can tell, good-looking. I continue my perusal of the men and ignore Claire and her dagger-throwing, irritated, probing eyes.

The tension in the diner is palpable, and I don't understand why. They are a big group in more than one way, but it doesn't seem like they're here to mess with anyone. They never do. It's not like they are Godzilla coming to destroy the diner or anything. I giggle at my stupid movie reference and lame joke. I can feel the annoyance rolling off of Claire as she continues to stare daggers into the side of my head. I roll my eyes and go back to what I was doing before Claire came over like a desperate teenage girl.

Claire continues to stand beside me expectantly. I know she loves the attention they give her, so I know what she wants. Claire begins shifting her overly large breasts in her extremely tight top, unbuttoning a few more buttons as if the two she had undone weren't enough. Then she flips her head down and begins fluffing her overly processed hair. I roll my eyes so hard that they may stay that way.

It's ridiculous and desperate how she's acting. I see her do this routine at least once daily, which screams desperate and daddy issues. She is such a slut. And that's not me being judgmental. It's because I've caught her in the parking lot, bathroom, and the backroom screwing a customer, and it's happened more than once this week alone.

So... ok, yes, maybe I am judging just a little. I think you should be in a relationship when you're intimate with someone. I know that sounds old school. But that's just how I feel and how I was raised. Honestly, the bathroom, *seriously*? My body shivers in disgust at the thought of getting down and dirty in, well– the bathroom.

She is almost 30, or at least that's how old she looks; shouldn't she be looking to get her shit together? I don't know. I just know I don't want to be that kind of girl. I want– I want to one day find that one, my one and become a mother and wife. I know I don't deserve it, but a girl can dream.

I am brought out of my thoughts when Beebe and Mona walk up to the counter after clearing their tables; they have kept their backs turned to the group and never once look in their direction the entire time they have been here. I don't get what the hell the change is. What the hell is their deal? Both of their faces are set in what I'm sure is a concern for me, but I still don't understand. The men are just customers like any other, coming here to eat. So I will do my job, and they will eat and leave.

"Do you know who those men are?" Mona looks at me with concern while she leans against the counter, her small frame squeezing between Claire and as close as humanly possible to me. Her jostling causes me to drop the silverware I was holding, *merda*. I look over at her exasperated and shake my head in annoyance, answering her question. I don't know who they are, never felt the need to.

My brow furrows; she is whispering. Why is she whispering? I turn to her to ask, "Why are we whispering?" Her big brown eyes widen. Mona is the quiet one of the bunch, she generally keeps to herself, so I find it interesting that she is the one coming at me about my customers. I mean, they aren't new to the diner, they just never come in this large of a group, and they usually sit in Claire's section, whether by force, coercion, or just how it works out. Still staring at me wide-eyed, she's looking like I have two heads.

I never pay much attention to them, I mean, ok, maybe there is one that has caught my eye a time or two, and there has always been something about him. But never once has he spoken to me or me to him.

I sigh, finish my task, and set the last rolled silverware in the container. I look to Mona and answer her question because a headshake wasn't good enough for her. "No, should I? I don't know who those men are, not really. Other than them coming in here to eat. I've seen them around town riding their motorcycles, looking a little intimidating. But I paid them no real mind." I stare at her, still confused by how they are all acting.

Beebe is the one to speak up, "Those men are a part of Lucifers Saints Motorcycle gang. They moved into the outskirts of town a couple of years ago. They took over that hotel, resort, or whatever it was supposed to be." Beebe continues to whisper as Mona has been. "I have heard stories about them. They off'd all the farmers that wouldn't sell them their land. I also heard they sell drugs. They have these crazy parties where they rape women and..." And that's where I have to stop her.

"Ok..." I step back from them and look at all three of them. "Have any of you seen any of this happening? Or is it just rumors you've heard?" I look at them with a raised brow. I know what life is like for those that make their living on the wrong side of the law, and most often than not, men in that lifestyle aren't all bad. It's the rumors that make them seem worse than they are, and there are also a few bad apples that spoil the bunch. Even with my horrible, horrendous past, I know that. Hell, everyone treats me like I am made of glass, and I murdered a Don. So, who am I to judge?

They all look at me with shock, not expecting that question from me or the bit of bite in my tone. They should know better; I never listen to or participate in their gossip, so I don't get why they are so shocked that I'm not falling for the "he said, she said" nonsense.

"*Well*, I have been to their clubhouse for a few parties, and it was *wild*. They drink, *fuck*, and, oh my gosh, those men are sexy. I have been seeing their President Brick and that *man*. You never did answer me. I can take the table if you're a scaredy-cat. I am used to them, and they know me well." Claire isn't looking at me while she speaks. She's making googly eyes at the men, who have finally settled and taken their seats.

I shake my head at her and the girls. I step away from them, look up, count the number of men in the party and grab a stack of menus. Without saying a word, I walk away, shaking my head at how mental everyone is. *Ridiculous*. They are just men, big burly and, from what I can tell, good-looking men, but men all the same.

A few noticed me as I made my way to their table. I could see the lust and curiosity in their eyes as they took me in. It was an odd sensation to have their focus on me. I received passing glances but nothing more when some of these men came into the diner. I was no slouch, and I know that. So to have them staring at me now– was invigorating.

Thank goodness I have the stack of menus up to my chest. I chuckle to myself; I am blessed with *plenty* of T&A. I don't have a typical California girl body or look at five feet four inches. I am a big girl and love my body. I have green eyes, and my hair used to be much darker than it is now, but with my change in scenery, I needed a change in my look, and of course, the change helped keep me unrecognizable. Or at least, I hope it does. My dark hair used to be much curlier, but because of me having it dyed, it's not so much curly as it is wavy, people ask me if it's a perm, but it isn't. I always wear it pulled up into a high ponytail. Because I hate having it on my neck or my face when I'm working. When I first started, there wasn't a day where I didn't go home with some sort of gift in my hair because I would wear it half up, but now, I know better.

I'm far from a stick figure with my large "D" breasts and wide hips, my full *tuchus*. My mother– I shake my head at the pang of sadness that hits me whenever I think about her or my father. My steps falter, but I don't stop. My mother used to say I was built like a coke bottle, and I hated it. As I got older, I began embracing my body and loving it. Because it was me, it was also my mother. My throat starts to close, and my eyes burn, but I shake my head. I *can't*, not *here,* and *not now.*

I make it to the table, and all chatter stops; all of the men turn their heads towards me, giving me their undivided attention. But my eyes don't see them. My eyes are looking into the most beautiful and shocking grey eyes I have ever seen in my life. I mean, I have seen him before, but not this close. Not close enough to see the sparkle of danger in them. And oh my, this man is very handsome, way more than when seeing him from the other side of the diner. That's another thing Claire did or made happen. My section was supposed to be in the center, but I was changed to the opposite side of the diner from her.

I can feel the heat rushing to my face when the man catches me staring at him. I can't help. He's beautiful. Can men be beautiful because he is? That man is ruggedly handsome. He is big like the rest of the men, but not fluffy big, but I can rip a phone book in half big. Oh my.

Thank goodness for my naturally tan skin because I would be so embarrassed if he saw the full extent of my blush. His lip twitches in a smirk, and I quickly look away before embarrassing myself any more than I already have.

Before I say anything, one of the men speaks. "Well, hello there, beautiful. Why don't you come over here and take a seat while you take me and my brothers' orders?" The man that speaks. Of course, he scoots his chair back and pats his lap as if I would do that. I hear a growl, and my brow furrows as I look around. Did I hear that?

I roll my eyes as the man that spoke pats his lap again. Well, that's a hell of a way to turn a girl off. I hear a few snickers from some of the men. My mind and body snap back into the moment, and I roll my eyes again at the man as he continues to make comments trying to convince me to sit in his lap. I ignore him as I start to hand out menus without saying a word. I give them all a look that says, you may be hot, but I am not going to put up with your mess. And then I put my sweet waitress mask on my face and smiled.

Of course, I make a few attempts to get a little grabby, but I am a pro at this. I smack a few hands playfully to avoid offending, keeping my smile on full display. I don't want to seem aggressive or whatever. I continue to shuffle, smack and shift, preventing them from getting what they want.

I have dealt with all kinds while working here at the diner for the last nine months. I feel eyes on me the entire time. I don't know how I know it, but I do. I know the eyes following me around the table belong to the grey-eyed man. I do everything in my power not to look in his direction. I don't know what it is about him or why I am having this reaction. But now is not the time, and this is not the place to analyze it.

I recognized quickly that these men were dangerous, like the men in my formal life were. How they look at and watch everyone around makes it clear that disrespecting them would be bad. So far, they have been pretty tame with me. They have given a few other patrons a look here and there but nothing more.

After passing out all the menus, I pull out my pad and pencil and look up. My eyes connect, of their own accord, with the grey-eyed man. We stare openly at one another, and a few men with him stare back and forth between us. "Yo! Prez, you going to let us order, or are you going to keep on staring at your girl?" He ignores the guy who spoke and the subsequent snickers. It didn't register, and then when it did, my eyes widened a little. Oh my, what to the what?

His eyes slowly leave mine as they trail down my body taking me in fully. His stare leaves me heated and has my thighs clenching together. My eyes widen when I hear a chuckle, and he sends a smirk my way. Oh my.

My body heats even more, not in an I am sweaty kind of heat, but in an oh my, type of heat. And my lady bits are feeling every bit of it. I clear my throat, hoping that will get his attention to where I want it— off my body because this is not good at all. I am working and don't need to be a sweaty, damp mess. Oh my.

"Hello gentlemen, my name is Vera, and I will be your waitress tonight. What can I get you all to drink to start?" Of course, it can't be that easy. I hear a few snickers, which isn't new to me. I have had people comment on my accent more than once since being here. That is one thing I will never get rid of and don't want to.

"You got an accent like Rocky. Where you from, New York or something?" And then it happens... the thing most people... well, more like most men do, don't ask me why. "Adriaaaaaaan," one of the men from the other end of the table yells out in a horrendous New York accent. I shake my head and smile at him. I have answered this question a million times. I never realized I had an accent until my family moved here. But the answer had slightly changed from when I lived in San Francisco. I give a weak smile.

"Nope, not from New York, but your close. I'm from Boston." Which sounds like Bawstun, which I have practiced saying a million times. I got to make it believable because my accent is not going anywhere.

I receive a few lewd and inappropriate comments, which have me rolling my eyes, but I continue to smile at them. One of them more than once tries to copy my accent and fails miserably, which has the entire table laughing. All the while, he continues to stare at me. And I continue to feel as if my body is going to combust. I swear I am overheating even if they keep the diner damn near freezing.

Once everyone but him has placed their drink order, I look back at him, and my breath hitches at the look in his eyes. *Oh my.* Again we stare at each other longer than necessary when he finally begins to answer. Claire and her impeccable timing make her presence known. She saddles up behind the grey-eyed man wrapping herself around him and then shifting to his front so she can sit on his lap. It happens so quickly that I shake my head. Unbelievable. Something in me furls in annoyance at the sight before me.

I stand waiting for him to give me his drink order. And then it hits me. I realize he is the guy Claire was talking about earlier, and for some reason, disappointment hits me in my gut. Instantly it was as if a bucket of ice-cold water was dumped on me. My expression changes as I fain boredom, and the blush I had, is no more. I know he notices my change, and his eyes narrow on me. I am not that girl; I raise a brow at him in a challenge. Oh no, buddy, you will not have googly eyes for me and then let another woman paw all over you. Yeah, no.

"Hiya, Brick, I missed you so much, baby. You were gone so long. I didn't like going to the clubhouse and not seeing you there." Her winey voice grates on my nerves, and I am about to walk away to get the other men's drink orders. I do not need to see Claire throwing herself at another customer. Mr. President can get all he needs from her, including his damn drink.

For some reason, I am angry that he is letting her paw all over him the way she is. I refuse to show it, in any case. I raise a brow at him, and he still doesn't speak, so I shrug and walk away without a backward glance. I don't have time for this. I will get their drink orders and hope that they are ready to order their food by the time I do. We are technically a 24-hour diner; I am lucky and only need to be here until midnight, which is in a few more hours. And at this point, I am ready to go home, soak my feet and read a good book.

I get to the drink station and get the group's drinks and beers together. I watch as Claire shamelessly flirts with the grey-eyed man. I guess I should call him Brick instead of grey-eyed man. I watch as he wraps his arm around her waist and whisper into her ear. She giggles, and it carries all the way over to me.

The anger I felt earlier threatens to take over, but I shove it down. I changed. I know I am different from who I was as a child. I am far more volatile and quicker to anger. I take a few deep breaths trying to clear the haze of rage and jealousy. Jealousy? Seriously?

No

Nope

Nuh-uh

I don't know that man. He isn't mine. I don't know why I am reacting to him like this. Whatever *this* is— whatever it is that I am feeling. I need to let it go; I have to let it go.

It's clear by his good looks, attitude, and the way he carries himself that he is the kind of man that can get any woman he wants. And he isn't the only one in the bunch. I am not the kind of girl that sleeps around. I don't chase. So, Claire can have him.

I scoffed at the display; apparently, it was loud enough to be heard. Claire's eyes snap up to mine, giving me a condescending look that says she's won. Her smile widens. Then she nuzzles further into Bricks' chest. *Whatever.* No offense to him, but Claire is shameless. Any man that looks worth anything gets the same treatment from her, so he's not unique. She is just— I am not saying she's a slut, *but* if it walks like a duck. A smirk makes its way to my lips, knowing I'm not wrong in my assumption.

As I finish up getting both trays filled with drinks. I stare down at them, knowing I won't be able to carry them both. I'll come back for the other. Before I get a chance, I'm stopped by Don, the busboy. Dan is a nice-looking guy, but he is a little too friendly. I've caught him watching me a few times when we are on shift together. I do my best to ignore his lustful looks. Beebe and Mona say he has the hots for me, but I don't see him like that. He hasn't tried or said anything, and I have no plans to broach the subject. You know what, it doesn't matter. He is cute, friendly, and my co-worker. I am leaving it at that.

"Do you need help, Vera?"

His eyes connect with mine, and he smiles down at me. He steps closer. I am so close to the counter that I have nowhere to go, and my side brushes into it, trying to step away from him. My eyes trail down to where my hands were poised to pick up the tray and then shoot back up to look into his when he shifts closer to me. Something in his eyes isn't kind, which makes my brows furrow. I shake it off as his face morphs into the sickly-sweet look, the one in which he usually has on his face. *Weird.*

"*Um…* Sure." I point to the second tray, and he grabs it without a word and begins to walk over to the men. I stare at his back for a minute, feeling uncomfortable about the short interaction. I shake it off and pick up my tray and follow him. Claire is still sitting in Brick's lap and giggling, sounding like an injured hyena. The other men are having loud, boisterous conversations of their own.

Once I reach the table, I begin passing drinks out. Once I finished with the tray I was holding, I put it down on a nearby table and grabbed the tray from Dan, who gave all the men dirty looks.

What the heck is that about?

I roll my eyes at Don, which he doesn't see. I continued passing out the rest of the drinks, and once I reached the end of the table where Brick and Claire were sitting. I start to turn to walk away, but Brick's hand shoots out, grabbing ahold of my wrist, and my breath hitches at the sensation I feel from his skin touching mine. Ok, is it weird to feel sparks shooting up my arm? I am even more shocked seeing how he has Claire on his lap, and the move seems disrespectful. Can he not use his words instead of touching me? The electrical pulse and tingles continue to shoot through me. My brows furrow, and my eyes narrow, as I jerk my hand away and look at him.

Claire stops the conversation with one of the men when she notices Brick and my interaction. She turns her body, and in true Claire fashion, she shoots daggers at me. I don't respond as I watch her from the corner of my eye. I continue to stare Brick down, daring him to try me. Then one of the men on the other end of the table calls out to Claire and says something to her; with a huff of annoyance, she gets up from Brick's lap, but not without giving me another one of her dirty looks. She sashays her boney ass to the other side of the table, and I watch for a moment shaking my head.

I look back at Brick, and something crosses his face, and it seems he's made a decision. One word comes out of his mouth, and I'm…

- B R I C K -

The waitress serving us tonight is too damn beautiful for her own good. I can guarantee I'm not the only one that notices the sexy little pixie. Her body is one made for sin. She's sexy as fuck, and my dick gets hard every time I see her. Fuck.

Every time we enter the diner, my eyes find her, no matter where she is. I have no damn clue what it is about her, but something unfurls within me more and more, making me want to know her in a way I have never wanted to know any woman. And after the run we just had, I am ready for something new– different. The same old snatch at the club is getting boring. I have a feeling that she is going to make me work for it. And I am damn sure up to the challenge because I need to get her out of my system.

I've seen lust, annoyance, frustration, and anger in her eyes during her interactions with me and my brothers. I have seen a hint of interest from her towards me in the past, but fuck if she does anything about it. She is nothing like the women I've dealt with in the past. Even though I've caught her eyes on me a few times, that has been the extent of our interactions. I hope that changes tonight. She seems a little standoffish, not stuck up but nothing like the women I am used to. Nothing like *Candace, Casey, Cassidy* or whatever the fuck the waitress's name is that we usually have when we're here. The chick is like a dog sniffing out a bone; she doesn't understand what she is. She doesn't get that me fucking her doesn't mean shit to me and never will.

Not many, including the staff outside Steve, the manager, know that the MC owns this place. And we like it that way. The people in this town are still wary of the club, not sure what to make of us. So, instead of making it known that we own this place, we keep that shit to ourselves. This place is a money maker, so ownership is on a need-to-know basis.

The girl in my lap clearly sees something going down between the other chick and me. I believe her name is Vera, and I have been staring at one another for too long, enough to annoy the girl in my lap. She is doing everything she can to keep everyone, including me, attention on her. And for a short time, it works.

Once this chick planted her ass on my lap, she hasn't stopped talking and groping me. I've banged her a few times during open club nights, but I won't be doing that shit again if this is how she will continue to act. I don't need this kind of shit happening whenever she sees me in town. And it *has* more than once. I know what the fuck she's doing. She's angling for the ol' lady spot. It isn't going to.

I don't have an ol' lady, and I don't want one, at least not yet. I shake my head, thinking back to the conversation Pop and I had had when he visited the club a while back. He has been on me about how we treat our club girls. It's not that we disrespect them or anything, but we treat them like they are just holes and leave it at that.

He wants me to settle down. And I get it. I'm not getting any younger. I told him something which had him looking at me a little differently. A little like he understood where I was coming from but still wanted me to put myself out there. I told him that I got it.

"Love isn't something to be searched for. Love finds you. Love, if you are open to it, has the ability to be the best thing that will ever happen to you or the thing that ruins you."

And after that, he has been less pushy about the *find a wife and pop out babies* kick he's on. And for that, I am grateful.

As I said, the girl in my lap will never get the distinction as my ol' lady. She's slept with just as many of my brothers as our club girls have. I don't want that type of girl as my forever. My brothers would not respect her or me in any way if I did. I am the damn President of LSMC and am held to a higher standard. So, this little thing is good to get off and nothing else. I need a woman with a bit more self-respect. Don't get me wrong; I respect a woman who loves sex as much as I do. But a woman that throws herself at every man that looks at her, intending to get something out of him, is not the kind of chick I want on my arm. When it's about what you can get and the status of who you bag, I am all set with that kind of chick.

The cackling hyena hasn't shut up, and a few of my brothers can see it on my face. I am about to lose my shit. Before I shove the girl off of me, I take a quick look over at our waitress *my waitress* I see the fury in her eyes, and my lips twitch. Seeing that look makes me do something that is either really smart or really dumb. I know it's dumb because this chick will get the wrong idea. But I can't help myself. I lean in and whisper some nonsense into the girl's ear. Of course, she lets out a very loud and very obnoxious giggle. The fire that was burning in *my waitresses'* eyes, the fire that was dissipating, comes back in full force. And my smile widens. Why do I keep calling her *my waitress* when I damn well know her name, Vera. Beautiful sexy as fuck Vera.

My smile fades, and my eyes narrow. When I see the busboy, Don, walks over and stands way too close to her, my eyes narrow further at their closeness. Is she into him? Are they together? And then, I see it. Her face, as I said, shows it all; she is not into Dan even a little. *Good.*

I lean down and talk into the girl's ear. "Hey sweetheart, don't you have some work to be doing? I am about to order and need two hands to eat my food." Doing my best not to be a dick to the little thing in my lap, she may not be ol' lady material, but the bitches' mouth is fucking legendary. She giggles and looks over her shoulder, not answering me, and it pisses me off. Because I know she knows what the fuck she is doing. I'm sure my face shows that I am at the point of no return with her games. I shouldn't have done what I did. *Damn it.*

I look over to Tully, my VP, who sees it too. We hate shit like this; desperate girls like her never last long around us or in the club. What we've suspected is true. We have heard some shit around town, hence why we didn't and will no longer be sitting in her section when we come here. We don't play games and can't stand girls that try to lay claim on us when we don't want to be claimed. Before I can shove her off, Dan comes over and stands near our table with a tray of drinks. He doesn't try to pass them out. He stands staring at us as if we are scum.

Yeah, ok, Donny boy, I see he is still a little bitter because we shot down his prospecting request for the club and told him to come back when he grew a pair. And it's the truth. The little weasel is too damn scrawny and wouldn't make it a damn week in the pit with the brothers.

Vera finally makes it to the table and starts passing out drinks. She doesn't make eye contact with me at all. It's pissing me off even more– I know she's digging me like I'm digging her; from the moment our eyes connected tonight, I knew it. Then I feel the girl squirming on my lap and realize. Yep, I fucked up. Well, I'll be damned.

She finally gets over to my side of the table and passes out the remainder of the drinks except for mine. She didn't take the order because *Candace, Candy, Caydence,* or whatever her name is, has been trying to monopolize my time and attention. In true dumb-ass fashion, I snag her wrist, which stuns her for a moment, and she turns and looks at me. At the contact, my breath hitches. What the fuck? The girl on my lap turns to watch the interaction, and I can see the dirty look she's giving my girl from the corner of my eye, which angers me even more.

"Hey, Claire, come over here, sweetheart. Let me talk to you for a minute." Tully knows what's going down and knows that what this little girl is doing is pissing me off. He's being a good brother and is trying to save her from herself and the embarrassment that will surely come if she doesn't skedaddle. She finally gets the hint, and with a huff and another dirty look towards my girl, she gets the fuck off of me.

My eyes never stray from my girls, though, not entirely. And I *know.*

One look and one moment are all it takes to realize that I was fucked from the beginning. And that she, my beautiful waitress, my beautiful sexy as fuck Vera, is the one that will ruin me. The thing is– I will let her ruin me every damn day for the rest of my days.

For a guy who wasn't looking for an ol' lady five minutes ago. I'm sure as shit about to have one. I don't even know her, but I do know thus far *she's.*

"MINE"

Two

VERA

Over the last few weeks, Brick and his club brothers' have been coming into the diner more frequently. I am not complaining because those boys know how to show their appreciation. They always leave excellent tips. They've also continued to sit in my section, which has pissed Claire off. And in pure Claire fashion, she's been an even bigger bitch to everyone, especially me.

If I'm being honest, Claire thrives off the attention she receives from men, good, bad, or indifferent she doesn't care. The woman is the poster child for daddy issues. She spreads her *love* openly for any man who sneezes in her direction. Receiving every man's attention is what she feels she deserves from all men, no matter their status. Brick and his brothers are very much included in her delusion of every man wanting her and only her. Poor thing just doesn't get the hint nor has a clue.

Claire *loves* to boast and brag about her daily exploits with different men. Like it's some great accomplishment, which I can assure you it's not. I am honestly tired of her shitty attitude. I am so close to—

"So you're his new flavor of the week, huh?"

For weeks, Claire's comments have come more and more frequently, and I genuinely have tried to ignore her. I can see that she is desperate beneath all of her caked-up makeup and teased hair. She is a woman that simply doesn't know her worth and thinks throwing herself at every man in her path will fill some void. It won't.

She is standing next to me as she usually does, popping her dang gum, and I try to tamp down my annoyance. I know that she is trying to beat me down with her words. It's her way of making herself feel better. It won't work.

None of the brothers from the club pay her much attention. And why would they? Her display weeks back would turn anyone off if they had good sense. I also heard she had been going around town saying she was Brick's, ol' lady. And that… that did not go over well. That is one of the quickest ways to be blocked from being a part of the club.

And yes, I have learned a lot about the club, which isn't a gang, as the girls called them. I've learned quite a bit about them and some of the members over the last few weeks. I have learned about how they work and how they live by their own set of rules.

I try to keep things simple, not wanting to learn too much, nothing too personal about the club, more surface stuff, enough to understand they aren't that different from the mafia. At first, it scared me a little. But getting to know them, they are different in many ways. They don't hide their true colors. They are who they are, and either you like them or you don't. They don't give a shit. I found out that no matter what club you are in, it is said that women and children are off-limits, which earned them the utmost respect from me. I also found out that even though they are a one-percenter club, which is a distinction that means they aren't entirely legal, they also own a few legal buildings and businesses around town, which is impressive.

"Claire," I say in an exasperated voice. More than once this week, I have had to walk away, biting my tongue, but today my annoyance with her is at its boiling point. From the minute she walked in for her shift, she has made comments not just to me but to some of our patrons about me, and I am sick of it. I'm sick of the looks I get from the men.

I turn my body fully in her direction, smiling sweetly at her. "Claire, sweety, let me make something clear to you. I am *not* now, or will ever be, someone's favorite of the week. I, unlike *you,* am not built that way. I have far more self-respect than that." I can see her going cherry red like the bubblegum she's so obsessed with, but I am not done. I continue to speak calmly to her. I need her to understand that this… whatever she thinks she is doing is done. I will no longer put up with it, and she needs to get over it.

"You've made an absolute and utter fool of yourself in front of members of the club and customers in the diner. And for what? You were trying to prove you got one over on me that night. You were trying to prove you are better than me and everyone else here. You were trying to prove that Brick was your man. What is it, Claire?

Yes, you slept with Brick. Kudos to you. Good for you.

But the thing is, that is all you did. He slept with you and sent you on your way—no promises for tomorrow, no commitment, nothing. You were trying to make it seem like your relationship was more than it was with him, his club, and people out in town. He and his club didn't like what you were doing and have made that clear by their actions. I say again. You made a fool of *yourself*.

If you want to continue to be a bitch to me, that's fine. At least acknowledge that the rejection is of your makings. *I*, nor has anyone else had anything to do with it. I will not lower myself to your level or continue to allow this childish behavior. I am better than that and have a whole hell of a lot more self-respect. I know you didn't get it the first time. I will not, now or ever, fight another woman over a man, no matter how good-looking and successful that man is. If you kept your legs closed, ears open, and brain on, you'd realize a few things.

Men do not want a woman who is clingy and desperate. Men do not want a woman that throws herself at anyone that looks her way. So, what is it you want from me, because this…" I point between the two of us "…is getting damn old. I don't want this negative energy when I come to work. I don't want to hear snide remarks from you. I am over it, and I am over you, just like the motorcycle club is." I throw the towel down I was using to wipe the counter and stare at her. She struggles to come up with something to say as her mouth opens and closes. I shake my head and walk away.

I did not want to say all of that, I didn't, but she is ridiculous. This scorned, jealous ex-lover thing she has going on, and this made-up rivalry she conjured up in her head, which she can't seem to let go of, is not just affecting me but everyone. I didn't ask Brick or his club to stop talking to her or sitting in her section. I had nothing to do with that at all. Outside of working and seeing them ride around town, I don't interact with Brick or his club. So, I cannot understand how she came up with all of these assumptions about me being Brick's flavor of the week or whatever. He barely even speaks to me when he comes into the diner. He places his order and just watches me interact with his brothers. There is no flirting, no asking me out or inviting me to one of their clubs' parties, at least not on his part. A few of his brothers have, but I am not that kind of girl. Ugh.

I am pacing the parking lot on the diner's side parking lot, not realizing that someone is watching me. I don't care, as I feel like I want to spit fire. I am so angry and annoyed. My frustrations about what has been going on since I started working here have worsened since the whole situation with the club. Maybe I need to find another job because I don't think I can handle any more of this nonsense every shift.

"So, you think I am good-looking and successful?"

I am startled at the deep timbre of the voice that just spoke. I spin around so quickly that I nearly lose my footing. I let out a squeak, and my nose slammed into a wall. Wait, I was nowhere near the wall while debating and cursing my life choices of continuing to work at the diner. Two large hands band around my hips, and I don't know who, well yes, I do. My body knows precisely whose hands I'm in.

The lot is not entirely shrouded in darkness, so when my eyes trail from the hands holding me to the broad leather-clad chest and stubbled chin, and finally up to steely grey eyes that are swoon-worthy. My body reacts in ways it never has to any other man. And again, it shocks me as it does every time, I see Brick.

"You didn't answer my question, sweetheart. You think I'm good-looking and successful?" His voice tells me that he finds my earlier words amusing, and a smile makes its way to his face. I'm so enraptured by the dimples that make their presence know that I forget the question as I strain to continue to stare up at him. Goodness, how is this man so damn beautiful? I get why Claire's panties are in a bunch about him. And tall, so dang tall. I guess anyone is considered tall compared to me, but Brick and his muscles are a whole nother ball game. Oh my, he could so snap me in half. And I would love it. But I would love to lick every last one of his tattoos on those beautifully muscled arms and anywhere else.

"Oh yeah… So I take that as a yes, then?" He chuckles. And my brows furrow. Oh no…no, no, no, no, no… Did I say that out loud?

"Crap"

He chuckles at my obvious distress and realization as my eyes snap to the ground when I step back from him. He places his thumb and forefinger on my chin and lifts my head; the embarrassment is too much for me to bear.

"Don't be embarrassed, sweetheart. I think you are the most beautiful woman I have ever seen. And I have been around a lot of beautiful women."

At that, I stare at him, and my eyes narrow. But he ignores my narrowed eyes.

"I would like nothing more than to let you lick every last one of my tattoos." He chuckles, and I gasp. He stares down at me with lust and amusement in his eyes. I know that even with my tan skin, my blush is furiously showing itself. I swear his face is getting closer to mine.

Oh... oh my, it *is*.

Bricks lips slowly descend, and I'm frozen in place. I have no idea what to do. The way he moves his lips slowly but so reassured against mine. The pressure and warmth of his kiss were not what I expected. His lips are soft, and he's being so gentle. Everything in this moment slows down. My rapidly beating heart gallops in my chest. I don't hear the cars driving or the typical sounds always around. It's all just–quiet. The only thing I can hear is the sound of my heartbeat.

His lips continue to caress my own. His tongue sweeps against my bottom lip. Then I feel his hands leave my torso and come to either side of my face. And oh my, my breath hitches and my mouth tentatively opens. He takes full advantage. I did not expect Bricks' tongue to do. *Oh my.*

At this moment, I feel as though my world expands, my senses heighten, and I feel everything, every stroke of his tongue, the brush of his fingers on my cheeks, the hair on the back of my neck rises and not in a bad way, my core clenches. This kiss, my first kiss, is one of passion and need. My hands go to his chest. My body is begging for the closeness, closeness that feels right. I know it shouldn't– I shouldn't. Am I supposed to feel this way?

As if something snaps in him, Brick's hands leave my face and grab ahold of my thighs. He unceremoniously lifts my feet off the ground. He detaches himself from me for only a moment, and a needy whine leaves me. And my eyes pop open at the sound. He notices and chuckles. He begins nipping and licking the seam of my mouth, allowing us both a much-needed breath. But swiftly attacks my mouth again. My legs and arms automatically wrap themselves around his torso and neck. I feel us moving, but I pay no mind. I have become consumed by this man's kisses. His need for me and my need for him is overwhelming my senses. I don't care what is happening with the rest of the world. This moment may never happen again. So, I'll relish it.

I feel something cool and rough on my back and recognize it faintly as the diner's wall. Bricks kisses become *more,* it is if he were to stop, his life would be over. My body has a mind of its own and begins grinding against him. My core is dampening with every movement. I can feel his manhood and am shocked to know I did this to him. He wants me, and I moan into the kiss.

Brick stopped as quickly as it started, and my breaths came out heavy. He pulls away, looking into my eyes. His forehead slowly comes down and connects with mine, and we both struggle to catch the breaths we've stolen from one another. My lips tingle, and I can tell they are swollen. My core is damp and aching. Surprisingly, I am not embarrassed by either.

"Go out with me?" His voice is so gravelly with need, and my brain doesn't understand what he is saying.

"*What?*" I whisper out.

"Go out with me... Like on a date. I know you have felt this." He kisses my lips gently, only shifting his head away from mine for a moment. "This needs that we have for one another. The moment I laid eyes on you, Vera, I knew you were... you are something special. I know you've heard rumors about my club and me. And I..." He trails off and looks up at the sky. "Shit" He shakes his head and looks down at me again. "I want you to get to know me. Not the President of Lucifers Saints MC, but James Masterson." And at his name, I can't help; I start to giggle.

He must take my words wrong because he abruptly pulls me away from the wall. His hold on me loosens, which has mine doing the same. He guides me, disconnecting my body fully from his, and a coldness I have never felt before washed over me. He sets me down, allowing my feet to touch the ground. He does it gently enough to ensure that I am steady on my feet. He steps back, and his eyes narrow on me.

"What the fuck?"

My eyes widen at his abrupt change and the anger in his voice. "Oh my, no, I am sorry, no, you are amazing, Brick. I *just*..." I giggle. "I just found it funny that your first name is James and my last name is James." He looks at me for a moment before he starts to chuckle. I don't like the distance between us, so I step closer to him. I wrap my arms around his torso and rest my chin on his chest, looking up at him and his mesmerizing eyes that glint in the moonlight. He looks down at me. My smile widens and is bright. At least, that is what I am trying to convey to him. Happy, open, accepting, and encouraging. I can do this. I can let myself have this, even if it doesn't last.

"Yes, James Brick Masterson. I, Vera James, will go on a date with you."

"Thank fuck, because if you said no, I would kidnap you and make you go out with me." He says with a smirk on his lips.

I know he doesn't mean anything by it, by the look on his face, but I can't help the memories that assault me. Memories of *that* day and the after. My arms around him loosen, and my body goes rigid of its own accord. Try as I might– try as I might to stay in this moment. Those memories threaten to take over. I know my smile drops because there is concern on Bricks' beautiful face.

"Hey– hey– hey, I didn't mean anything by that, sweetheart. I promise you." His voice is soft and gentle when he speaks. He gently places his hands on either side of my face, his eyes looking into mine with concern. "I would never do anything like that, and neither would anyone in my club. We may not be law-abiding citizens in other ways, but we would never–ever do something like that. Do you understand me, my sweet Vera?" Now, I can nod my head and give him a small smile. I take a few deep breaths as I know his words are honest. I can feel it deep in my bones. Brick may be many things, but I don't think he is a liar.

"Good"

His mouth comes down on mine again, a quick and gentle kiss. But it also holds a promise. His hands leave my face, and I immediately miss their warmth. He steps back slightly, but not too far, where he can't grab ahold of my hand. He begins to walk with me; hand in hand, we make our way back to the diner entrance.

"Now let's get you back inside, beautiful, so that you can finish your shift, and I can take you home. And yes, I know all about you taking public transit to and from work, and that will not happen anymore. You understand me?"

When I say nothing, I am still in a daze from my first kiss, and I am shocked that he knows I ride the bus to and from work. Brick abruptly stops, spinning me to face him, placing his other hand on my hip, and stares down at me expectantly. I realize he is waiting for an answer. I smile up at him because I see someone who wants to take care of me for the first time in a long time. I may not know what this is or where it is going, but I know that I will go with it and hope for the best.

"Yes, Brick, I understand."

He studies me for a moment, brings my hand he's holding up to his lips, kissing it, and pulls me towards the diner entrance. He looks down at me, smiles and winks when he grabs the door handle. "Good."

-BRICK-

I have no idea what I'm doing when it comes to her. I've spent the last few weeks watching her every move. I watched how she interacted with my brothers and the customers in the diner. I watched as her smile lit the room. I watched her and saw how kind and caring she was. But I also see that when needed, there is an edge to her. She doesn't take shit from anyone. She's a conundrum, sweet, innocent, but fierce and protective.

You can call me a stalker, but I have followed her home several times to ensure she's safe. The war between my head and my heart has been raging. I didn't think I was ready for what she made me feel. But I know that I don't have a choice. Every day that I am around her is *just*– What I want to do with her and what she does to me is— I can't explain it. All I know is that she will be mine. She is mine. Fuck, fate has gone and done it. She is going to be my ruin.

That kiss was like nothing I had ever felt before. I can admit that, at first, it threw me. I wasn't expecting it to feel the way it did. I didn't expect it to consume me and have me wanting more from her. I had to pull away from her when she moaned because my dick was rock hard and raring to go. If I didn't stop myself, I would have stripped her bare in the parking lot and had my raw cock in her. The thing is, though, I don't think she would have stopped me. I don't think she would have with the way her body responded to mine. And when I finally get into her warm heat, I know I will never want to leave; I will never let her go. Fuck, she is turning me into a pussy.

"What's that smile about, Prez? You finally get in that girl?" Tommy Boy says with a smile and a knowing glint in his eye. For a moment, I forget he is my brother and punch him in the face. I haven't even been with Christ, and I'm already ready to rip my brother apart over her.

"Fuck you, Tommy Boy, she ain't that kinda girl." I narrow my eyes at him, and he sees the warning. Realizing he's walking a dangerous path and talking about her the way he is the quickest way to get his ass beat. Tommy Boy is a good brother and Road Captain, even with the whole free love thing he's got going on with his ol' lady Nancy. That girl is so in love with him that she will take whatever she can get from him, even if he can never keep his dick in his pants.

"Aww, now come on… Prez, I meant no disrespect." He raises both hands. I stare him down a little longer until he gets it and turns away from me. He's smart enough to start a conversation with Hound, our clubs' information guy.

"So, she's it. Huh?" Tully leans over to me and gives me a head nod. I look over to Vera. She is taking the order of one of her customers and smiling down at them. I narrow my eyes at the interaction. I don't want to share her smiles, and I don't like to share her. I know I am being an irrational dick. I just kissed the girl for the first time, and already I am laying claim to all that is her. I don't care. Something about her makes me want to wrap her up and keep her safe and far away from the rest of the world.

"Yeah, she is."

"Well, all right then, brother. You want me to have Hound do some asking around on her. I know you are already claiming her as yours, but with what's going on with the club, I want to make sure she's on the up and up."

I know he's right. We can never be too careful; I give him a nod. My eyes leave my girl to connect with Tully's so he can see the truth in them. And at that moment, I know he sees that no matter what we find if anything, she will be mine.

Vera James is my woman; that kiss sealed her fate and mine.

Three

BRICK

I am fucking pissed the fuck off. "How the hell did that happen? Talk to me, Tully." My body slams down in my office chair. We just got back from a run that went to shit. How in the fuck did those fuckers know our route? And why in the actual fuck did we take it?

"I have no fucking idea, Prez, and we were all set for that drop with the Italians. Tommy Boy ran the run last week and didn't say fuck all about us running through their territory. That little shit fucked us. Fortunately for him, I don't think he did the shit on purpose. We are all still trying to determine the borders between clubs, gangs, and other groups in the state and outer areas." Tully growls out. He is just as pissed as I am about what went down. Fuck.

My hand smacks down on my desk, sweeping everything onto the floor. This shit is not good, and it shouldn't have happened. Now I have a pissed-off buyer whose order wasn't delivered completely. The fucking Keepers, that fucking club has been the bane of my existence since we moved here a few years back. Fucking Pyro and his little shit stain of a club. They had *years* to take Sacramento and make connections, but they didn't. Now that we have the city under our thumb and our relationships are solidified, their club wants to start acting like a bunch of winey bitches. Why is he acting like such a prick? We did our groundwork. We are cool; with many of the operations in town and others in the surrounding area, we don't step on anyone's toes, and they don't step on ours. What is his fucking game?

"Fuck"

"We have some supplies, but..." He trails off, and my eyes narrow at him. "But what? Tully, spit it the fuck out." He knows I am not pissed at him, but the fucking situation we're in. That run was supposed to be a quick drop. That's not what went down.

We were on our way to the drop, a half-day ride up to Washington. We were barely out of Chico when shit went down. The Keepers came out of fucking nowhere. They had a fucking blockade on the backroads road we were using. I had no intention of being taken for a ride, but bullets started flying after some threats were thrown back and forth. In all the chaos, we lost one of the trucks we used for transport. I am livid. Fortunately, none of our brothers were seriously hurt, just a few flesh wounds, but that's beside the goddamned point. I am happy that we could take out a few of their guys. I am thrilled I got a shot off and into Pyro, that slimy fuck. How fucking dare he and his fucking little band of idiots think he could take me on.

"If we make this delivery for the Italians, with what we have…" He begins to rub his hand on his stubbled chin. "We are going to run into problems down the road. We will be short on the remaining deliveries for the next few weeks. Using our supply is not ideal. But I would rather that than go to Barone and tell him we lost his shit."

"Damn it, man… Get fucking Tommy Boys' ass in here. I need answers to find out how he didn't know. The damn road was supposedly their territory. What I want to know is HOW IN THE FUCK DID THEY KNOW WE WERE USING IT *TODAY*. Somebody is going to die, brother." I train my furious glare at Tully. He takes no offense.

Tully says nothing and walks out of my office. I continue to fume. I need to see my girl. It's been a few days since our kiss in the diner parking lot. I never got her home number or her pager. Does she have a pager? I know that's the new shit. If she doesn't, I'll get her one. I don't like not being able to contact her and for her to be able to do the same. Shit, I should've had one of the brothers keep an eye on her before we left for the run. Fuck.

A knock sounds at the door, and I yell for whoever is there to enter. Tommy Boy comes strolling in like the run wasn't completely fucked, and another club didn't jack our shit. I want to punch him in the fucking face. You know *what?*

I get up from my desk, and before a word comes out of his mouth, I lay into the incompetent fuck, punching him right in the fucking jaw. Good on him, the stupid cocky fuck doesn't crumble completely, but he falls to a knee with his mouth busted and bleeding. Good.

"How in the fuck did this happen? Tommy Boy, you told us the route was secure, and no other clubs were within a hundred miles. THE KEEPERS WERE WITHIN FEET, YOU STUPID FUCK." I leer over him as he looks at me with trepidation and a bit of anger in his eyes. I swear if this fuck doesn't give me a goddamn answer, I will strip his fucking cut and kick his fucking ass until he is a fucking memory.

"Fuck Prez, I didn't know it was their territory. That route was supposed to be neutral. I asked around. I talked to Butch, and he told me no clubs run that road. I ran that shit myself more than once and never saw fuck all of them, Prez. You got to believe me on that. I wouldn't fuck the club like that."

He looks up at me, and as pissed as I am, I can tell he is telling the truth; fucking guy can't lie to save his damn life. He may be a prick of an ol' man, but he is a good club brother. Arrogant and cocky as hell but a good brother all the same. If he thinks he's getting an apology for clocking his ass, he can think again. Fucking hell, I need to see my girl. She calms me the fuck down how I don't fucking know, just know she does. Cause if I don't, I am liable to lay more than one of my brothers out on their asses for looking at me wrong.

Tommy Boy looks between Tully and me and starts to stand slowly. I can see he's still unsure what else to do or say. "I'm sorry about this shit, Prez. I sure as shit don't know how they knew we were going to be there. I didn't tell anyone about the route we were taking until the morning of, so I don't know how the fuck anyone beside you and VP knew."

I stare at him for a moment because we are in the same boat with that. I have fucking questions, and the main one is…

Is there a fucking rat in my club?

Because if there is, they will die a traitor's death.

- V E R A -

41

I haven't seen or spoken to Brick or anyone from the club for a few days. None of them had been in the diner since Brick and I kissed. I am not sure how to feel about that. On top of wondering what's going on with Brick, Claire still keeps up with her crap, but she's gotten sneakier about it even after our talk. I noticed some changes.

I know what's been going on is somehow her doing. I've noticed I've been getting more male customers in my section from the beginning of my shift until the end. Most people wouldn't think much of it. But for the first nine months of working here, Claire made sure I had very few customers in my section if she could help it, especially customers of the male variety. Now I am run off my feet damn near every night. At first, I thought nothing of it and never mentioned it to Steve when he came in to ensure we were doing our jobs. And because none of the customers ever did much, at least nothing I couldn't handle. I just gritted my teeth and pushed through.

When there have not been any club members eating in the diner, some of my male customers make inappropriate comments and are far worse than I have dealt with in the past. I found one waiting for me when my last shift was over the night before. He kept trying to get me to talk to him and go out for a nightcap, and it was creepy as shit. I was able to get away from him when I got on my bus home. I got pepper spray yesterday before coming to work. I was that weirded out.

I need to find another job.

It's final. That is what I am going to do for the next few days off. I am so sick of dealing with Claire. This new influx of male attention and the whiplash I am getting from Brick is too much for me. I am finally starting to feel normal, and all this stuff is *just*.

"Hey girl, why don't you come over here" a few snickers are coming from the guys sitting with him. I roll my eyes; this guy has been here for a half-hour and has propositioned me more than once. I take a deep breath, steeling my spine, readying myself to deal with him. Can't he and his friends eat their food quietly and leave?

I plaster my best fake smile on my face before turning around. "Yes, Sir, what can I do for you? Is your food ok? Can I get you a refill on your coffee?" If I can steer the conversation, I'm hoping he won't say anything else that makes me want to cringe, poison, or punch him in the face.

"Naw darlin', I was just wondering…" And then he stands up, grabs my wrist, and to my horror, pulls me to him and sits back down, pulling me so that I slip and fall into his lap. And for a moment, I was so shocked that this creep touched me that my brain didn't register the bell above the diner door ding. I calmly but quickly try to get him to release me as he wraps his arms around me and pulls my back to his front, and I can feel his– ewe gross.

"Oh, come on, darlin', your *friend* told us about you and how you like it."

I don't stop struggling to get out of his hold. Am I at all shocked by his words? Or what some supposed *friend* said, no. What I need to do is get my ass away from this prick. Because I fucking knew it, I knew it. I am going to lay that stupid bitch out.

I seethe and struggle as the prick and his friends keep talking and telling me all they want to do to me. I don't hear half of it. I'm too busy trying not to let my anger get the best of me because if I do, I know I will pick up a fork and stab him in his eye.

I don't have friends outside the diner, and I don't trust people that easily. I know, for a fact, Mona and Beebe would never say something like that. They may not be my best friends, but they are trustworthy enough. I don't consider them enemies, unlike I do that bitch, Claire. I try to pry his arms from around my waist. I don't want to make a bigger scene than we already have. I need to get away from this guy. Because I am most definitely going to maim the evil bitch.

I don't notice when a dark shadow looms over the table. I'm still shifting and struggling to pry Mr.-I-don't-know-what-personal-space-is hands from around my waist. But I do feel the change in the air, and I don't see the face of the man behind me. Or the fact that the prick had gone pale.

"You mind getting your hands off *my* fucking girl."

My head snaps up at his voice. Oh my, he's here– he's back. But my excitement about him being here dwindles when I realize where I am and what's happening. Oh my, I was so busy looking down, trying to figure out how to get this man's hands off me, that I didn't see Brick and his brothers walking over to the table.

"Aww, man, if you want next, no worries, biker boy, there is *plenty* to go around." I can hear the false bravado in his voice. But he squeezes my ample thighs, and his friends chuckle at his obvious joke about my weight. I gasp, and for some reason, him saying that makes my eyes sting. Never in my life have I've never felt so disgusted in my life. Not because of my body but because of these men's reaction to it. I can feel the man's tiny little dick digging into my ass, and I feel sick. I look up to Brick, and I can see that he is seething; Tully and a few other brothers flank him, and they all have the same look on their faces, one of pure rage. When Tully shifts, my eyes go to his briefly, and he sends a wink my way. I hear a growl, and my eyes snap back to Brick's; his eyes are boring into the man who still has me in his lap.

"I'm going to say it one more fucking time. Get. Your. Fucking. Hands. Off. Of. My. Girl." His tone leaves no room for misinterpretation. Brick is fucking livid his face is set in a deadly scowl. I would shrink away as quickly as possible if I didn't know what and to who he was directing his anger. The diner goes quiet. Brick just stares the man down; I feel a little tremble from the man holding me. But then his hold tightens.

I groan quietly to myself. I know he will try and be a big man and say something stupid.

Please don't be stupid.

Please don't be stupid.

"If I don't... What are you going to do about it? This slut will take whatever my boys and I give her. When we are done... well." He shrugs and a chuckle leaves him and his friends follow.

And, of course, he's stupid.

He and his friends sitting at the table chuckle. And I can tell he isn't done. The idiot keeps talking, *idioti*. "Don't worry, big boy; we'll leave her somewhere. You 'biker trash can find her and take your turn."

Wait, did *he*– did this idiot just say he was going to... Oh, hell no...

This prick doesn't know who he is talking to. Even *I* have heard stories from the guys about their exploits. And not to mention my mean streak. But the idiot doesn't recognize the charge in the air. He stands me still in his arms. He shifts so that my body is reluctantly plastered to his. He locks his arm around my shoulders so I can't get away from him, and I am half tempted to elbow him in his balls.

That's when an idea hits me. You don't get raised by a mafia soldier and not learn a thing or two. At that thought, my chest begins to ache, and my throat gets tight, now is not the time to think about them.

I rear back and slam my head it into his chin, simultaneously stomping my foot down onto his. It may not do a lot. But it's enough to make his grip loosen. I quickly hall ass over to Brick. The prick collects himself and tries to reach out to pull me back, but Brick grabs ahold of me and pulls me towards him, shifting me behind him.

"You fucked up. Now, I will give you and your boys one chance to walk the fuck away."

"Or what? That slut…"

And that is when things went from bad to fuck shit up. Brick rears back and punches the guy in his face hard; he falls into the table behind him and is out for the count. And *I'm– Oh my.*

That was hot.

Someone grabs ahold of me and pulls me into a hard chest, and I start to fight them off as hard as I can. Because at this point, who gives a fuck about making a scene, a scene has already been made, and I am fucking sick of men manhandling me. "Calm down, darlin', I got ya." I look up at the man holding me and recognize him as one of Brick's brothers. He carries me over to the diner counter, ensuring I am safe behind it. He lets out a breath and shifts his head back and forth, cracking his neck, and takes off back into the fray.

Beebe and Mona are huddled behind the counter, watching shit go down. The cooks are staring wide-eyed out the order window. Claire is standing on the opposite side, shooting daggers at me, looking back and forth between me and the carnage in the diner.

"You think your something special, got all these men fighting over you. Fucking *slut*."

"What in the actual fuck is your goddamned problem? You are such a bitch, Claire. I didn't ask for *this*." I wave my hands around. My eyes narrow at her. "I know it was you somehow. It was *you*, saying shit and causing men to talk to me the way they have been lately. You are mental if you thought that was a good idea. You're such a stupid bitch. I am so far from a fucking slut, you dumb whore." I seethe. Clapping my hands at her stunned face,

"Good job, pot calling the kettle black, *slut*." I step closer to her. I am so fucking done with her and her shit.

It was one too many insults for her because she took a step closer to me with malice in her eyes.

Oh… please be stupid…please be stupid.

And she *is* very, *very* stupid. She rears her hand back, slaps me, and starts screaming like a fucking banshee. I hear none of it, though. The anger takes over. My body moves without thought. I end up on top of her punching her in the face with all I've got. All my anger and frustration from everything she has done to me since I started here is coming out. Everything that I have bottled up inside comes out of me.

Arms wrap around me and pull me off of her. I am not done, and I struggle to get back to the object of my frustration. The arms around me tighten, and whoever it is, starts talking to me, and I don't hear what the person is saying.

"Where is her stuff? Someone needs to grab all of Vera's shit. Vera ain't fucking working here no more." I catch the gravel in his voice. I recognize it. I am still struggling to get back to beating that bitch's ass.

I look around and see Beebe and Mona staring at me wide-eyed. And a few of the brothers are looking at me with something akin to respect in their eyes. I get a few smiles and winks. Looking around a little more, I see the diner is virtually empty other than the bodies littering the floor. Holy Wow, they destroyed this place. No other customers are around, which I think is a good thing given the state of oh *wow*.

My body is trembling not from fear but from anger. I'm being pulled through the diner, out of the door, and into the parking lot; my body starts to feel heavy from the exhaustion of kicking that stupid girl's ass. Oh my gosh. I just kicked Claire's ass. Oh– I am so getting fired for this. Damn it.

"No, sweetheart, you ain't getting fired. You quit." Wait, what? I look over my shoulder and realize Brick pulled me out of the diner. My hands start to throb, and I step out of his arms and look down at them in embarrassment. I can't believe I just did that. My hands start to shake.

"Look at me, Vera…" Brick says softly, softer than I've ever heard him speak. When I don't immediately follow his request, his hand comes to my chin and lifts my head, so my eyes are now on his.

"Sweetheart, she had it fucking coming. I know that she has been needling at you all because of me. She had that shit coming. You do not need to be embarrassed about how you reacted. You reached your limit; we all do. We all have limits. Sometimes people need to know how far they can and can't push you. I bet she learned her lesson tonight" Brick chuckles and winks at me, and I give him a small unsure smile. He leans down, gives me a peck on the lips, and stares into my eyes. "Missed you, sweetheart. I'll take care of all this shit. Don't you worry? I got you. I will always have you."

Oh *my*. Wait. Am going to go to jail? I am going to go to *jail*.

"You ain't going to jail, Vera" he chuckles and shakes his head at me. I need to stop saying my inside thoughts out loud. My cheeks heat up when another wave of embarrassment hits me.

"Yo, Prez? What do you want to do about all the... *trash* in there?" We both look over to see one of Bricks brothers standing at the diner door, holding it open and pointing inside. Brick takes a breath and pulls me into him hugging my front to his.

"Call the clubhouse and get one of the prospects to bring a club truck. One of the shit ones, have them take the trash out." He gives the guy a look.

He looks back up to his brother. "Then have someone take care of the girl and make sure she knows to keep her mouth shut and not to come back. She's fired." I blink up at him.

Wait, what? How can he fire Claire?

He looks down at me and sees the confusion on my face. "It's not well-known, sweetheart. You know the club owns a few businesses in the area. Well, this is one of them. The club owns this place. Steve just runs it for us." Oh my, my brow goes to my hairline. I was always under the impression that Steve owned the diner because he acted like he did.

Bricks eyes leave mine and return to the other men. "And Flick, make sure you compensate the staff and apologize for the trouble. Hopefully, no one will call the pigs. If they do, you know what to do. Get the place cleaned up as much as you can, and we'll get the Prospects over tomorrow to fix what got fucked up. Also, give them the rest of the week off. We fucked shit up in there. Cleanup will take a few days. Put up a sign saying we are closed for construction or some shit. I'm taking my girl to the clubhouse."

Oh my, my face must be saying way more than it should when Brick looks down at me and chuckles.

"You got it, Prez."

"Come on, sweetheart, take a ride with me."

Oh   *my…*

Four

BRICK

I need to set eyes on my girl. After taking care of business and sitting down with Tully, Slim, Hound, and Flick, we discussed what I was thinking and how I had a few suspicions. We set a plan in place; I don't want to stick around the clubhouse. If I did, I would be clawed at by the club girls. I have a girl of my own to get to, and no one and nothing will stop me.

I had no idea I was going to walk into what I did. When I made my way into the diner. I was excited to see my girl. After the shit that went down with the club and the drop, I needed to lay eyes on my sweetheart. I didn't think shit would go down the way it did. I've never seen red so quick. My body vibrated with fury when I saw what was going on. I could barely restrain myself, asking *nicely* for the shit-stain little prick to let my girl go. When he decided to mouth off, he got to put the fuck down, not permanently but close e-fucking-nough.

Now that we've put a bunch of yuppies on their asses, I'm holding my girl in my arms, and it feels right. Before laying eyes on Vera, I was dead set against having an ol' lady or any women attached to me for many years. Hell, a few weeks ago, I was on the fence about it. Not many of the presidents in LSMC chapters have 'um. I think we— well, they agreed this life can be pretty taxing on a relationship. One, because we can't share anything about club business, which rubs women the wrong way. They don't get that we do it for their protection, not to be dicks. And two, women don't like that sometimes we leave and can't tell them where we are going or what we are doing. Again, it's for their protection, and they don't like it. I've watched a few of my brothers put through a lot of shit, and that shit was deterrent enough for me. The prospect of having something, someone permanent, was not for me until now.

Now though, with this little bit in my arms, I *don't, I can't,* and *I won't* see a future without her. My little ass-kicking spitfire is a forever kind of girl. After the brothers and I took care of those pricks, I instantly looked for my girl. And what I found made my cock so damn hard. I wasn't as shocked as my brothers, but damn, it was a sight to see.

Vera was straddling that Claire or Candy girl or whatever the fuck her name is. And she's pounding into her like she was nothing but an annoying nat. Flick told me that he overheard some of the shit Claire was sewing. She has been sending or encouraging men to harass Vera, telling them shit about my girl that ain't true. That on its own had me seeing red, but my girl had that under control, and I will make sure that bitch is sent packing. We don't put up with shit like that.

As we stood out in the parking lot. I could tell immediately that she was embarrassed by her actions, and I wasn't having that. I ensured she understood that she did what needed to be done and necessary. My brothers told me Claire had been giving my girl hell. It may have been a dick move not to step in or have Steve step in. I wanted to see how my girl would handle it when she reached her breaking point because *everyone* reaches their breaking point. And she handled it beautifully, and I could see her claws, which solidified what I already knew. My girl was made for me. Once we talked and I told Flick what needed to be done, I needed to get her out of here.

When we reach my bike, Vera tugs my hand to stop me. I look down at her as her face morphs into one of concern, and my brows crease. I smile down at her. Vera lifts her hand to my face and wipes something away. Then she lifts onto her toes. And she is too fucking cute because even on her tiptoes, she doesn't reach my chin. I show a little pity and bend my knees. She kisses both my cheeks and then my mouth. That beautiful soft mouth connecting with my own is always incredible.

I swear that the world fades with every kiss and touch from her, and my body goes into overdrive. My cock instantly gets rock hard, which makes me groan. It will be a bitch to deal with when riding, but I'm not complaining. My girl will be on the back of my bike for the first time, and after the day we've both had, I know we'll find peace on the ride.

This kiss is desperate and tells me everything I need to know. She wants me as much as I like her, and like before when she lets out a low-keening moan, I know we need to stop. I swear I will take her now if we don't stop. My need for her is that great. I know that if I were to take her out in the open, I would rip the fucking eyes out of anyone that looks at her. Yes, I am a fucking caveman. But damn, this woman is doing things to me. No other woman has, or ever will, and my control is slipping like a motherfucker.

I growl into her mouth. We *need* to stop. I grab her by her hips and shift my hard as fuck cock away from her, reluctantly extracting myself from her. Fuck, these damn lips feel too damn good. I slowly start to nip and place a few pecks on her lips. I don't want her to think I don't want to keep kissing her. But we need to stop. Fuck we *need* to stop.

"Sweetheart." I peck her lips, but she moans again.

"Fuck"

I pull away and shake my head a little before putting my forehead against hers. "Sweetheart, we have to stop. If we don't, *fuck*. We need to stop. Are you ok with coming home with me? I need you near me. It's been too long, and I need you close. And we have had a hell of a day." I look at her and into her eyes. I can tell that she is unsure. I grab her hands, putting them together and placing them over my heart.

"When I was a little boy, my father told me. That there will come a time when I would find the one. He said you would look into her eyes, and you will *know*. You will know she was meant for you and you for her. She will be the one that consumes your thoughts. She will be the first person you think about when you wake up. And the last person you think about when you close your eyes at night. The one you dream about…."

Her breath hitches as she looks at me with a sheen in her eyes. I need to get this all out. I need her to know how soul-deep this is for me. In the short time I've known her, I fought my mind, and my heart won. "I never wanted *this*." I point to both of us, and she starts to pull away. I won't let her. She begins to struggle in my arms to get away, misunderstanding my words and meaning.

"Listen to me, sweetheart, that night. The night I finally saw past my nose and saw *you*, truly saw you, not just the other waitress, but my Vera, my sweetheart. That night you walked up to our table with that damn smile of yours. You became my everything. You became my future. Sweetheart, we may have just started getting to know each other, but that can be remedied with time. And we have time– a lifetime to learn. And I want to learn you, my sweet Vera, from the inside out. And I, for one, can't wait."

The smile she brings out of me is not one many see. My brothers say I'm a surly bastard, but for her... for my girl, I can't help but let myself enjoy what she makes me feel. She deserves every smile and happiness I, along with this world, have to offer her.

She relaxes, and her face softens. "That night I truly saw you, my soul bound with yours and yours with mine. I may not be a good man to everyone else. I've done and will do bad shit. Not all of it will be on the right side of the law. But I want– I *need* you to know That even if I am a bad man out there...." I release one of her hands and point to the road, and she looks to where I'm pointing, her beautiful brow creases. She smiles a little when she looks back at me. Yeah, she gets it.

"...I will be the best man. I will be the man that holds you when you are sad and lifts you when you need it, but call you out too. Sweetheart, I will be the man who stands by your side and defends you with all I have and am. I will be there for you for all of it... all the good, bad, and the ugly. I could never see myself happy if you weren't a part of my life. Because you have so quickly and frankly without my permission become my world." I let a small chuckle and a smile when I hear her gasp and giggle. I am laying it on pretty thick, and I may sound like an idiot, but every word is the truth.

"Today, I am making you a promise, a vow. Today I promise to dedicate myself to you because no matter what my head may have thought before you. Now that you are here and in my arms. I know– I *fucking* know you are and will always be my everything. I promise I will do everything I can to keep you happy, healthy, protected, respected, and hopefully soon loved." I stare into her eyes, making sure that she sees the truth.

"Do you understand me, sweetheart?"

Usually, I would lose my shit or run when a chick cries. I know chicks say they look ugly when they cry or use that shit to get what they want from you. But she– my girl is the most beautiful woman I have ever seen in my life. And I am so entranced by her beauty. Staring into her eyes while her tears flow so freely and unbridled. Her hands were still in one of mine over my chest. I am sure she can feel how steady my heart is beating for her. She is my calm. Without another thought, I wipe her tears away with my thumb and kiss both of her eyes.

She lets out a little giggle shaking her head, and smiles at me; I smile in return. I remove my hand from her face trailing it down to her shoulders and back up to her hands that still rest on my chest. I intertwine my fingers with hers and start walking backward to wear my bike is parked. Without saying a word, I release her hands, open my saddlebag and pull out a helmet. One that I picked up specifically and only for her, handing it to her. It's Black with purple and glitter stripes along its bottom half. Even under the dim light of the parking lot, it shimmers. It's a full-face helmet with "Bricks Sweetheart" written on its back.

Yeah… yeah.

I'm a pussy for knowing that her favorite color is purple. But when you realize that you have found your one, you notice everything about them. You learn the little things, nuances, likes, and dislikes. I smile as she stares in awe. She takes it from me and turns it every way to see what's written on it. She looks up at me in question. I say nothing. I lean down and gently kiss her lips.

Moving closer, I lift the helmet from her hands and secure the neck strap, flipping the visor up. I turn, reaching back into the saddlebag. I grab the leather jacket I got for her. It has her name on it, it isn't quite a property cut, but we'll get there. Once I slide the jacket on her, she stares wide-eyed at me. I put my hands on her hips, lifting her and placing her on the bike, and she lets out a little squeak. Which makes me smile and chuckle. I tap her on the top of the helmet and wink. I hear a muffled *thank you*. I give her a wink.

I step closer to her to explain what she needs to know about riding on the back of my bike. I explained to her about keeping her feet on the pegs and watching out for the pipes that could burn her beautiful legs. I tell her to lean with me in turns and hold on tight. That part I am going to enjoy the most. I can see the concentration on her face as she gets situated. Once she signals, she's heard and ready. I flip her visor down and swing my leg over, saddling my other girl and starting her up. I hear a squeal, and I can't hold it in. I let out a bark of laughter at her excitement.

She's sitting too far away for my liking, so I wrap my hands around her calf, squeezing it and pulling her closer to me. Her pussy nestles into my ass, and damn if the heat doesn't make me even harder. *Fuck.* Her arms come around me, and I have to breathe. I lean back into her for a moment, preparing to deal with a very uncomfortable ride. Once I'm calmed enough, a feeling of contentment washes over me. My hands go to hers, pulling them a little tighter around me. I can feel her helmet resting in the middle of my shoulder blades, and *damn* if I don't want to always feel this. I tap her leg, put my hand on the throttle, and take off from the parking lot heading home. For the first time in my life, I have a woman on the back of my bike, and it feels fucking good. Her warmth on my back *is*. Yeah, I'm never letting her go.

I took the long way back to the clubhouse riding through town. She squealed, seeing her lift her arms in the air every now and then. My woman didn't mind the long ride one bit. The last time she raised her arms in the air, she quickly put them back when I hit the throttle.

Pulling up to the gate, I see Cadence manning it, seeing me coming. His brow furrows when he notices I have someone on the back of my bike. He is quick to school his features when he sees the look I'm giving him. He nods in understanding and steps back into the guard shack after closing the gate behind me.

It's Friday night, so everything's a little crazy around here with the brothers, and club girls, especially when we figuratively open the gates for outsiders.

Hang-arounds and outsiders flock to the clubhouse to get their fill of the *dark side* and need a taste of being around the outlaws. Something I will never understand is that they often come here with their wide-eyed curiosity like we are a circus exhibit or some shit. I don't mind it. Some of the reactions we get are fucking comical and entertaining as fuck.

We may be outlaws, but we still have a few rules that must be adhered to, or perpetrators will be out bad and banned. I am far from an idiot; I know some clubs leave their gates open and unmanned on open club nights. That practice never sat right with me, so that is not how I do things, and it helps to keep the riff-raff out, and from anyone we don't want in, out.

I turn my bike, so I can back into my spot, looking around and trying to see the club as Vera would. I shut my bike down. The place is large, it was supposed to be some upscale resort and hotel, but the folks that started the project ran out of money and tanked. They filed for bankruptcy, and I was able to snatch it up at auction. The main building is set up like a hotel because that's initially what the place was going to be. The main entrance is mostly glass. There are several levels or floors, the structure is massive for a biker clubhouse, but it works for us. I plan to make this club one of the West Coast's largest. This space will accommodate my brothers and their families now and in the future. We have outbuildings that we have done upgrades to and others that we are still upgrading as we continue preparing to expand our club numbers. There are already several family homes built, not many but enough. Once this place is complete, it will be something else—our little town, created for us, by us to grow the brotherhood and our family.

I get off of my bike. There are a few brothers and hang-rounds milling around. I shake my head as I see a few half-clothed and fully nude girls running around giggling and some being chased by brothers' *shit*. I suck in a breath when I see my brother Crank getting a blow job from one of the club girls on a picnic table. I run my hand down my face. Maybe I should have warned Vera that shit is a little different around here, double shit. I quickly get off my bike, realizing my mistake of bringing her here on a Friday night. I turn around so I can see her reaction. I pray she isn't disgusted by what she sees, it may not be what she's used to, but this is the life we live. It would crush me if she couldn't or wouldn't accept me.

Shocked at what I see when I look down at her as she straddles my bike, she's looking around, but I can't read her. It's not like she doesn't see what is going on. She seems utterly unaffected by it. She shakes her head and looks up at me as she looks around the yard. I can see a smile on her face through her helmet. She lifted the visor at some point. I lift her off the bike. Her legs start shaking, and she grabs onto my forearms as she lets out a squeak, cute. I feel like a dick because I didn't warn her about sea legs after your first ride. I hold onto her for a minute until she's steady. Good fucking job, Brick, oh, for two. Oh, for fucking two, I'm killing it with trying to be a good ol' man. Guess I can only go up from here. I shake my head at myself and my stupidity.

She steps back from me when she's steady on her feet before I'm ready to let her go. She shifts, bending down, taking her helmet off. I have to bite back a groan when she flips her hair back up. She holds the helmet she uses her open hand to run it through her beautiful dirty blond locks. She then hands me the helmet, takes her jacket off, and hands that to me without a word. I step over to my saddlebags and put them inside. I turn around, and she looks around again. Stepping behind her, I wrap my arms around her middle, pulling her back to my front. Her head rests on my chest. She chuckles and shakes her head again. I look down at the top of her head, and I rest my chin on the top of her head as she continues taking everything in.

Shifting, she bends her neck so she can look up at me. "Just so we are clear…" She points to where Crank is still getting a blow job. "I am too much of a lady for that shit. So, get that out of your head."

She giggles, turns, and wraps her hand around my neck, smiling at me. "I am far from a prude, but I will always be a one-man kind of girl. Public displays to that extreme are not for me." She lifts on her toes and kisses me on my chin. As quickly as she was there, she was gone. She saunters her sexy ass off as if she didn't just blow my damn mind. I watch as her ass sways, and she's walking away from me. I know damn well she doesn't know where she's going, but damn if I don't love watching her walk away. I quickly snap out of my ogling and shock before I take a step.

Out of fucking nowhere, Penny launches herself into my arms, and before I can say or do anything, she pins a kiss on my lips. *Shit.* I pull away from her and shove her the fuck off of me. She stumbles but quickly recovers. I look up to see if Vera has witnessed any of this shit. I don't see her; Penny didn't get the memo when I pushed her desperate ass off me. "Hey, sugah, I've been missing you lots, Prez. Like totally." Penny giggles, grabbing my arm and...

Shit, fuck, damn it.

"Not the time Penny. Maybe later, I'm...."

Fuck

"Maybe later... You'll *what?*"

Fuck, shit. I freeze for a split second, slowly extract Penny from my arm, and push her away from me again. Being the ditz she is, she doesn't take the hint or acknowledge the woman standing a few feet away from us, my woman who is giving both of us a death glare. I am so fucked.

"I guess we never made anything clear about what this is– or was supposed to be. I am not that girl. I will never be the girl that looks the other way. I will never, ever grin and bear it..." She rubs her hand across her forehead, shaking her head and chuckling, not the cute kind of chuckle, but the annoyed, loaded with disdain and disbelief kid, damnit. She shakes her head again, turns on her heels, and walks away. For a second, I'm again stuck on stupid and shocked at what just went down. Where in the fuck is she going? Again fucking, Penny has latched onto my arm; I try to detach myself completely from Penny, but this bitch is fucking relentless.

"Penny, I swear to *fuck,* if you don't get your fucking hands off of me, I will take back everything I have ever said about not hurting women. I will rip the fuckers off and hang them up in the clubhouse, so all of you whores learn to never touch a fucking brother without GOD. DAMNED. PERMISSION. Fuck."

She looks at me in shock, and fake as fuck tears glisten in her eyes. I don't give a fuck if I hurt her feelings, bitch knows damn well I don't like her or any of the other club girls touching me without permission. She steps away slowly and runs like her ass is on fire without saying a word or looking back. And that is my cue to go search out my girl. Fuck, where the hell is she. A few brothers give me looks as I pass them by but don't say anything as I'm far from approachable now. Fuck.

I spend the next hour searching all over the clubhouse and can't fucking find her anywhere, I am constantly getting stopped by brothers and groped by some of the townies, and it serves to piss me off even more. Goddamn it. Where in the fuck did she go? She still has to be here. We are too far from town, being on the outskirts. There are a few ways to get from here to there easily, not unless you drive or get a ride. I drove us here, and she didn't know anyone to get a ride back to her place.

Fuck. This was not how tonight was supposed to fucking go.

Five

I have absolutely no fucking idea how I got here. Friday night was not supposed to go down the way it did. After shit went down at the diner, we got the situation handled and cleaned up. So, I thought– I thought that was a fire I put out, and it would be smooth sailing from there. The plan was to bring my girl to the clubhouse and introduce her to the brothers and my family. But fuck if that's what happened. When Vera and I got to the club and shit went wrong and fast. One second, Vera was there being her usual cute self, shocking the shit out of me with her reaction and acceptance of what was happening around her. And the next she was gone; a misunderstanding and she skedaddled. I haven't seen hide or hair of her. No one has.

What went down had my blood boiling. I am not angry at her, not really. I fucking get her reaction; I wish she would have stuck around to hear me out. I get why she didn't because I know myself well enough to know. I would have lost my shit if I saw another man touching her, let alone having his mouth on hers. Fuck, somebody would die, and I am not just talking; I *mean* that shit. I can admit that I'm irrational as fuck when it comes to my girl. Hell, the only reason those yuppies at the diner weren't put down was because there were too many damn witnesses who saw us going at it before my brothers and me and shut their shit down and beat their asses. otherwise, well…

I spent the rest of my night searching for her. Tore through every room of the clubhouse. I even checked the rooms in the unoccupied wing, tearing them apart, and she was nowhere to be found. I even went to her place and no dice. I've had the prospects looking for her, and no one, and I do mean not a single person, can tell me where she is. This shit is starting to fuck with me. She's unfamiliar with the area because we are outside town and surrounded by farmlands. But still, she could seriously get lost trying to make her way back home on foot if that is what she did. Fuck

I have a prospect posted at her place. No one's been there all weekend. Not once has she gone back nor been found. Living in Sacramento is not like living in a small town. There are plenty of places to hide and not be found. Is she that pissed at me that she would just up and leave? I run my hand through my hair, thinking about the possibility of not finding her or seeing her again.

The tightness I've been feeling in my chest with worry for her has been painful as fuck all weekend. There is no way– none, that I'm giving up. I will find her. I'll tie her ass down and make her listen to me. She will let me explain what went down and what she would have seen if she stuck around long enough to see me lose my shit on Penny. I refuse to lose her when I just found her.

My patients with my brothers, the club girls, and everything else has me at my limit and testy as all hell. The shit with the Keepers. We are figuring out that, with what went down, we have a snitch in the club. People outside the club already know that her disappearance is fucking with me. I can admit I lost my shit Friday night in front of the townies and hang-arounds partying with the club. So, it's not inconceivable that if she were to be found by someone other than my club and me, they could use her against me.

Shit.

Fuck.

Damn it to hell.

Suppose she doesn't let me explain and doesn't want me in her life. I am *not* ok with it, but I would deal.

Nope.

Fuck no... who am I kidding? I'm not ok with letting her go at all. No fucking way in hell will I just let her walk away from me, from us.

"Any news about your girl, Prez?" Tully slides in next to me at the bar. I have been sitting here thinking about my girl and where the hell she could be for far longer than I thought. Looking up at the clock hanging above the bar, I see it's nearly noon. I let out a deep breath, taking a drink, wincing when I get a mouthful of my cold, bitter-tasting coffee. I stare into my mug, trying not to let my emotions show before answering my brother.

I shake my head, rub my hand over my two-day-old stubbled face, and look over to my best friend, righthand man, and the club's VP. "No, I haven't. Prospects said there hadn't been movement at her place. I did a drive-by over at Beebe's and Mona's, but no luck. Fuck, man, that shit was fucked. The shit that went down with Penny." I let out a growl and ran my hand down my face. "On top of that fucked up situation, I didn't get to explain shit to her before we got here last night. And now I'm regretting the fuck out of that. And with shit with the Keepers. I'm... fuck..."

Tully puts a hand on my shoulder, squeezing it. I take a breath, trying to keep my shit together. My brother knows me well. I am never like this ever, not over some snatch. But when I recognized V was and could be to me, he and I discussed it at length. Damn, that fucking woman has me. She has me completely whipped over her.

"Prez, that girl had stars in her eyes just like you've had over the last few weeks. It was a shit situation, and the way it played out was suspicious even to me. I know we'll find her; folks aren't watching us like that." My eyes snap to his. Damn, my brother knows me well. Because he knows where my head's at and why I'm so damn wound up. "The Keepers shouldn't know about her or what went down last night. Her coming here with you wasn't planned. Nobody knew till y'all got here. I am saying; everyone saw you drive up with her and the kiss she laid on you." He takes another drink of his coffee. I look down at mine, wondering if I should just get another cause my tastebuds are not willing to be sacrificed for more bitter shit. I know I need more coffee; I haven't slept for shit since Friday night. I signal for the prospect to bring me a fresh cup.

"The club girls have been squawking about you being turned off and pushing them away for a while now. Penny must have got the short straw; she may have been the sacrificial lamb to their bullshit and plotting. You know how territorial and conniving those bitches are. You see how they act whenever a new chick comes around sniffing around you." Tully says, which makes us both chuckle because it's true. They are always trying to mark their territory and have been warned many times about that shit. They are club girls, holes to be used. And as much as they want, it's doubtful they will earn a spot as an ol' lady no matter what their delusional minds conjure up.

Tully continues, "I guess the shit they pulled last night was a preemptive strike. Those girls are quick to check out when their territory is being encroached on. You and I both know that since that first night you saw her, you haven't touched any of 'um or townies when we've had party nights. This is an obvious clue that you're about to be off the market or seeing someone outside the club. Those bitches are fucking bloodhounds. Last night made it all real to them. Them being the territorial bitches seeing her on the back of your bike, they were ready and wanted to scare her off. But your girl is reasonable, Prez. She'll let you explain shit. Just don't fuck it up." He gives me a look. I nod my head in understanding, and my blood begins to boil.

He's right. I haven't been fucking with none of the girls. I kept busy with club shit and took every opportunity to go and eat at the diner when I could, so I could see and watch my girl. Fucking hell.

"Get all those bitches down here in the next fifteen minutes. They are about to get a rude awakening." Tully just smiles at me. Well, as much as the surly fucker can smile. He taps the bar top before he gets his big ass up to leave.

"And Tully, make sure Slim and Flick are here too."

Those bitches are about to get their asses handed to them, and they're about to learn a valuable lesson about playing games and being mental around this club. I don't discipline them often for the shit they stir up. But their little plan could cost me, my girl. And I can't have that. It makes me understand why the ol' ladies from other clubs and Nancy, the only current ol' lady here, despise their asses so much.

- V E R A -

I haven't run across a single person the entire weekend. Granted, I've been hiding out, holding up here and keeping a watchful eye in my current little hideaway. Somehow, I'd made my way to one of the buildings that seemed to be a recreational space. I figured someone would make their way out here at some point and find me in my hidey-hole, but they haven't.

This place has everything a girl would need to survive, and not a single soul has come here. Not once over the weekend is a plus. There are bedrooms, a kitchen, TVs, food, and an out-of-this-world game room with all kinds of arcade games. It surprises me even more that no one has come here. Because I could so live here, a giggle bubbles out of me because I've been living my best life.

I wonder if there are kids here, I am assuming by the sheer size of this place, everyone in Bricks club lives here. I saw a few houses on my walk while trying to calm down. The weird thing is, though, the further I went, the less populated it became; the places didn't seem occupied. I haven't seen anyone at all, all weekend. That's neither here nor there. At the ripe old age of twenty-one, I'm having the time of my life. I even got the highest score in the block-building game. You know, the one where you have to fit all of the little block thingys together to make straight lines. Ok, I know that is not some great accomplishment, but I am a simple girl enjoying throwing her tantrum and hiding out. But whatever, I have spent more time watching my shows, playing games, and stuffing my face with all the snacks and non-perishables they have stocked, than I should have. But I don't care. I am having a blast; I could live in this bubble forever. It's not like I have a job or anyone to get back to.

Ok, yes, maybe staying here the *entire* weekend was not a nice thing to do and childish. But when you *see*. Nope, not going there.

The reality is, who would be worried about me? Brick, yeah, right. He has plenty of women waiting for him to get home every night. Figured he's too busy to worry about little ol' me. So, besides that ass, there is no else, not really. I have *no one*. I suck in a breath at the crassness of my thoughts, tears begin to sting my eyes, and my throat gets tight. I am alone in a world where I am now jobless and soon will be homeless. I know I shouldn't be throwing a pity party this. This is a life of my own making, and it fucking hurts– and it sucks. No one, least of all him– cares about where I am. I chuckle. Anger bubbles up in me for how stupid I was for believing *that*.

I was thinking about Friday night because *why not* torture myself a little bit more? The guy I liked brought me to his home, and not five minutes later, he had his hands and mouth on another woman. Yeah, not cool. So, I have a right to be a little irrational and angry. I am permitting myself to wallow in my one-woman pity and sorrow, and it's a party of one.

My intentions were simple. I was only going to take a walk to calm down before demanding that he take me home. Being in a new place, around new people, and not knowing or having a way to get back to my apartment was– rough. As I said, I had every intention of telling him to take me home. I am so fucking dumb for *thinking*.

Seeing Brick with that girl was a lot, and it cracked something in me. I had to get away. And oh did I, I stumbled upon this place, and my brain was like, meh fuck it, why not enjoy this little bit of peace and get my mind right. I had no intention of it being an all-weekend thing. But here we are.

I'm walking around in my freshly washed clothes. Thank goodness I always have an extra set with me. Working at a diner, you never know what could get spilled on you, so I am glad to have options tucked away in my bag. This place has a freaking washer and dryer, which is pretty dang fancy if you ask me. And it's very convenient since I'm hiding out like I stole something. I probably should make my way back to the building Brick called the clubhouse. I have been lolly-gagging enough. And should stop being such a baby and face the music. Brick wanted a good time, girl, but that's not me. I was dumb. He said all the right things but read me all wrong. I take in a breath and hold it for a few seconds. I need to get this over with.

Stupid man and his grey eyes.

Stupid man and his sweet words.

Stupid man and all those muscles.

Stupid man and all his… all his… ugh

Stupid, stupid man.

Do I want to go back there, however? I'm not sure if I can face him. Suppose I want to face him. I still get a pang of hurt in my chest whenever I think about what could have been. I wish he were a guy like my father, a man who was faithful and devoted to one woman, my beautiful and fantastic mother. My parents had a love story to be envied, and my father was completely and utterly devoted to my mom, who was the same as him. I have always wanted that. I may not deserve it for all the bad I've done and caused, but for a while, I thought that maybe, just maybe, I wouldn't be alone anymore.

"Stop, Vera, you have to stop thinking about them. They are gone, and…". My tears begin to fall, and I become angry with myself all over again. How am I supposed to do this, to be the one that lives knowing I will have to hide for the rest of my life because of what I did? Do I regret killing that disgusting man? No. I regret the after. I shake my head at where my thoughts are taking me. I have to stop this. I have to move on. I have to let go, no matter how heartbreaking it is. I have to allow myself to live, even if my living is a solitary existence.

For the first time and in one night, I felt something other than pain and sorrow. I felt happy and was looking forward to the future. A future where I wasn't this sad, pathetic thing that grief wouldn't let go of. I was going to have more; I was going to be more. I know he and I don't know each other. But I felt things for Brick that I never once felt for any other man. Was I a fool for thinking that a man like that, a man in his position, a man with power, would settle for a simple girl like me? I don't know, but I hoped he would. Ugh, whatever, at least I found out sooner rather than later the kind of man he is.

I pack up all of my belongings and put them in my tapestry tote bag, the few things I had with me over the last few days fit snuggly, but it works, for now. I clean up any mess I create because I may be sad, but I'm not a savage. I mentally prepare to face him and the people in his club. I have no choice in the matter. I need to get home and prepare to start over again. I have to figure out how to get back to the clubhouse. Then I have to figure out how to get a ride home. It's time to pull up my big girl panties.

I *sigh*.

On top of it all, I have to find a new job. Damn it. Urgh,

- B R I C K -

I sit at the bar *waiting, seething* and thinking about how these bitches think they have power. Power to claim me or any of my brothers. Power to dictate who we spend our time with. Control of who we let into this club, *my* motherfucking club. No, these bitches don't have power, and they never will. It takes a certain kind of woman to handle men like us. They must be strong, accepting, and, most of all, loyal. These bitches are anything but that. They are snakes in the grass. Many come looking to sink their claws into a brother, looking to be taken care of, and are unwilling to do the work to earn the devotion we give to our ol' ladies.

Ol' ladies are to be cherished; they are most often the backbone of any club. A good ol' lady, one worth a damn, can be a balm to the soul of a broken man. To have someone solely dedicated to us, no matter who we are, how hard we are, how broken we are, it's everything. There is something to be said about the type of relationship forged by a brother and his ol' lady. So, when you find your one, you damn sure hold on for dear life. The fact that I have found my one and these bitches thought they could run her off.

Fuck that

There are fifteen club girls we house and provide for. Club girls choose to provide a service for the brothers. And as a club, we provide them with a roof over their heads, protection, and food in their bellies. Our girls are here of their own free will, they choose to fuck and suck, and we don't force anything on them. Everyone knew the score when they signed up to be a club girl. But from what went down Friday night with their plotting, they have forgotten their place.

A few of the girls have been up for a while. They're on a rotating schedule, responsible for cooking breakfast and cleaning the place up. I'm sure they can feel the annoyance and rage rolling off me. They are smart enough to keep their distance. Smart enough not to say shit. Good.

The weekend's debauchery always has this place destroyed afterward. Even though I wasn't into partying like I usually am, given the situation, I didn't fault my brothers for enjoying their time. And by the looks of this place, they did. I watch a few prospects clean up the bar area and common room, doing shit to put this place back together.

Along with bringing Vera here, we celebrated patching in a few of the prospects. Patch-in parties always last all weekend before everyone gets back to work on Monday. And the brothers part damn hard, and it shows.

Flick comes to stand next to me, leaning his back into the bar top, staring me down. I can feel the heaviness of the questions behind his eyes. He and the brothers know what went down, especially after I lost my shit. My brother has taken a liking to Vera, which is surprising, given our history and his general distrust of women. I know his stare is probing, he is trying to figure out what this little impromptu meeting is about, but I ignore him. He'll find out soon enough.

I love my brother; he is one of the few men besides Tully. I know, without a shadow of a doubt, will always have my back. He is also one of the few that can call me on my shit, and I won't shoot him in the face. Not many outside our circle know he's my blood brother. My mother was a rolling stone. That's a story for another day.

Seated at the bar, I stare into the mirror above the bar with my back to the room. I watch the club girls come sauntering in as if their shit doesn't stink, as if their plotting asses haven't been found. My eyes narrow on a particular few. I can feel it coming. I know that my brother has something to say. I wait for him to say what he needs to say.

"You know… I never thought that I would live to see the day. The day when my big badass brother would find a woman, one that he would want to stick his dick in for the rest of his life." He stares at the side of my head, waiting for me to react. I don't, at least not yet. I wait because I know he has more to say.

"Brother, I saw it the night you met her. I knew then that she's your balm. And watching that little lady of yours, I can tell you she isn't some delicate wallflower that will get swallowed up and spit out. She is a keeper, and I would be proud to lay my life down for hers. She will be a good first lady for this club, more than that. She is going to be good for *you*. She is family now. I only know what I heard about what went down, and I'm hoping this little meeting…" He waves his hands towards the club girls. "Is to set these leeches straight. Or… I will do what needs to be done if you don't set this shit straight. I just may steal your girl and show her how a real man can treat her, right" I growl at that last part. He smacks the bar top, not waiting for a response, then stands at his full height. Well, I'll be damned. I know if he is saying this shit, my girl has left an impression, but I'll be damned if anyone takes her from me.

I quickly grab ahold of his shoulder before he even takes a step, and I turn my narrowed eyes on him. "She's mine," I growl out. "I get it, brother. The warning noted, but if you even look at my girl in any other way than with brotherly love, I will end you." We stare at each other for a few minutes before a huge smile breaks out on my brother's face.

"You sure can try, don't let those two inches you got on me fool you. I'm a squarely bastard." He chuckles, as do I because he is a squarely motherfucker. "But I hear you, brother, she's *all* yours. When you find her, that is," I growl again. He steps out of my hold, sends a wink, and walks away.

Fucker

I look up to see that all the club girls are now seated. A few look nervous as hell, others look bored, and some barely have their eyes open. And then there are the few who think they are above everyone else. I narrow my eyes at them sitting at their table.

"So, Friday night… One of you dared to make me look like a liar." I say with a booming voice which makes a few of them flinch. My back remains to them as I stare in the mirror and speak. I am pissed, and I know… I just fucking know one of these bitches is going to piss me off even more. I don't hurt women, but I don't have to. I have young sweet Magda for that. A lot can be said about Magda. She came to the club when she was only fifteen years old. She has a way about her that scares the shit out of the other women. She's not a whore or an ol' lady, but she is a part of this family. Everyone thinks she's my sister, she'd not, but no one needs to know that. At the age of twenty-three, she is a force to be reckoned with and a force this and many of the other chapters use to our advantage, and she loves that shit. I cringe thinking about her last job. Yeah, she loves doling out justice.

"Some of you decided that you were not happy with me. Believing I wasn't giving your cunts the attention you felt they deserved. You decided to not only make me a liar but have *my* fucking girl run from me thinking I am a lying, cheating piece of *shit*. AND I CAN'T HAVE THAT."

"*Well*, we can't have some outsider coming in here taking *our men*," I narrow my eyes and let out a growl at the offender. The bitch doesn't shrink back, even after she catches my eye in the mirror and even after seeing the fury on my face. Oh no, She sits up, staring at me with a self-satisfied smug look on her overly made-up face. If I wasn't pissed off *before*, I'm pissed the fuck off now.

All the girls sit at *her* table and shift nervously in their seats. That bitch is the bane of my fucking existence and has been for years. She's a good lay and can suck rust off a bumper, which I can't deny. The thing is, she thinks because she's had my dick along with every brother in this club and *all* the brothers in the mother chapter, that she owns us. She doesn't, not in the least. Like every club girl, she is a hole, no more, no less. If it weren't for the by-laws and needing to vote to kick out a club girl. I would have kicked her ass out a long time ago.

Darcy followed us from the mother chapter, and I honestly wish she hadn't. If I could send her ass back if Mad Dog would take her ass. I'd send her in a heartbeat, but even he's sick of her shit. The fact that in her mind, she truly believes that being an ol' lady is owed to her. She thinks she deserves it, deserves to be *my* ol' lady, and tries to make everyone around her believe it. But that shit needs to stop. I know that she's devoted and loyal to the club, and I respect her devotion, but the shit she's been pulling lately is out of line, even if, up until now, I haven't called her out on it. She will learn what happens when you poke the bear one too many times. Oh no, I am not even broaching the subject of kicking her out of the club, at least not seriously, because that would be too easy. I am going to do far worse.

I look around the room, with my back still facing it. I zone in on my brothers and see the fury in Tully, Flicks, and my silent guardian Slim's faces. I guess they heard her talking her shit, as well. I begin to laugh. A full-on belly laughs bubbles out of me because this bitch should have known better. She should have sat there quietly, but since she didn't...

"Is that *right?* Your *men,* hmm, Darcy?" I smile wickedly at her, and her eyes widen as she realizes she just fucked up. I shake my head as I think again that she should have sat there quietly and taken my wrath like the rest. I stand and turn entirely to face her and the other club girls.

"If we're *your men,* do me a favor. Go and get your 'property of' cut. Better yet, show me where you hide your 'property of' tat.' I know I haven't seen one on you. Maybe I'm mistaken." I stare her down and then look over to my brothers, and they all send smirks, knowing I'm being a dick but don't care. They are just as tired of her shit as I am. "How 'bout you boys? You see a property cut or patch on Darcy here?" Pointing back to the bitch, raising a brow, and waiting for an answer. She huffs, puffs, and stutters over her words, but she doesn't give up.

She's never one to give up.

She stands holding my eyes, and she starts sauntering toward me. I can tell that whatever her plan is, whatever she thinks she will accomplish with her self-serving display, she's going to put on. One thing is for sure she is going to piss me off more. I watch as she walks across the room, trying to use her feminine wiles to entice me into letting this shit go. I won't. I will let her dig her own grave.

I already want to wring her neck. All the other girls sense the danger and look at her with wide eyes. A few even try to warn her off. I raise my hand to shut them down and for them to let this shit happen. She's bold, clueless, or dumb, and having a sense of self-preservation is not her strong suit. Her priority is being labeled an ol' lady or securing her spot as the top girl of the club girls. She doesn't realize that she is just making this shit far worse for herself. She doesn't know she is on a razor's edge and pushing me to my limit.

She reaches me, and as predictable as she is, I'm stunned at her brazen behavior. She wraps her arms around me and purrs like that's supposed to do something, but it's not. She isn't getting the reaction she wants, so she starts rubbing her tits against my arm. Then she gets bolder and starts to run her hand along my chest. I look down at her, and my blood begins to boil. I want to rip her arms off her body and toss her nasty ass away from me. As I try to rain in the beast, the back door to the clubhouse opens.

All heads, including my own, snap over to the intruder. Tully let the brothers and prospects know that we were meeting' and to stay the fuck out of the common room. So, whoever it is, isn't going to like the consequences of interrupting me when I am laying down the law.

Once my eyes clear from the shock, light changes in the room. I see a shadow standing at the open door. The sun surrounds whoever it is like a halo. The person takes another step in, and I– my heart starts to beat, and my eyes connect with the beautiful moss green ones of my Vera's, my sweetheart, and it takes a moment for me to realize.

Her eyes fill with sadness. Her eyes trail from my own, down my chest, and then back up to my eyes. For a moment, I stare at her, not understanding. Then I see flashes of resignation, acceptance, and then nothing. Her face goes completely blank. I hear a throat clear, and my brows furrow. I look over to see Flick staring at me with a raised brow, and then his eyes trail to my chest.

Motherfucking, fuck, shit, damnit. Not a-God-damned-gain. Son of a bitch.

I groan when I realize, yet again, that I've fucked up. Shit. My eyes snap back to the door. I now understand the emotions that crossed her beautiful face and why she is now staring at me with a blank closed-off stare. Damn it to hell.

"Um…" She shuffles further into the room, looking around, unsure where to focus her attention. One thing is for damn sure. She doesn't give me a second glance. She looked everywhere around and passed me. Hell.

Something shifts in her as she realizes no one is answering her. Everyone is staring, some in anger, annoyance, and others in curiosity. She snorts and a slight chuckle, seeming to make a decision. I see it in the change in her demeanor. She looks up, squares her shoulders, and looks at me, her face void of emotion. "You brought me here, and I couldn't get back home. So, I kind of found your recreational building or whatever it is and stayed there. That place is nice. I am sure you already know that." She chuckles, but I can tell whatever bravado she has is waning. "You don't have many kids around to use it because I spent the whole weekend there. Sooooo, uh…" She fidgets a little when she hears a few giggles from club girls. "If you can send me the bill for the food I ate, I will pay you or your club or whomever back. I still need to get my last check from the diner, and then I have to find another job. Crap." She takes another breath, probably realizing she's rambling and rubs her hand over her face. Everyone in the room is staring at her, but her head doesn't lower, even if she is a little embarrassed. She stares blankly at me.

"I need a ride, I don't care who gives it to me, but I *need* one. Being that I am now jobless because of *you*. Jobs pay bills. I don't want to lose my place, so yeah me. It's all I have left since my family died and moving here alone." She sucks in a breath, realizing what she let slip. Her hand runs through her, and her eyes begin to mist. She quickly focuses on something on the ground. Fuuuk. My heart hurt for her. How fucked up is this? The shit that went down Friday, then me standing *here*.

"So I need to go and find another job; I need to be able to pay my bills and such. So, can someone give me a ride to town?" She looks up, licking her luscious lips and the question she asked hangs in the air.

Damn it, why didn't I check the outbuildings. I told the dumb ass prospects to check the compound. I guess I wasn't fucking specific enough. I should've told them to check the entire damn compound, not just the clubhouse.

She's had an entire weekend to stew on this shit, to shore up her defenses against whatever she felt for me. And this moment doesn't help matters. I stare at my girl, trying to figure shit out, trying to figure out how I will explain all this shit to her. And yes, I am still a dumbass because I still have.

"Um, not likely. That's *totally* a no. You got your ass here. You can get your ass home. You are not welcome here, bitch. So you can find your way out. We are busy and…" I can see. Vera is so done and about to snap and take off again. There is no way in hell I am letting that shit happen again. I spent the whole damn weekend going out of my mind, stressed, worried about, and looking for her. Fuck that.

Before she bolts.

"Don't you take a single step out of that door, Vera." I stare her down, realizing, too late, that my tone could be taken wrong. She looks at me in disbelief and hurt. Fuck me, shit, damnit. I still have this bitch, pawing at me.

I look down at Darcy, pissed this bitch thought it was a good idea to open her fucking mouth and speak to my women the way she did. I look back at Vera, pinning her to her spot as I do. My hand goes into Darcy's hair, and I grab a handful of it. Tully, who had been standing next to the door Vera, entered steps over, blocking her from leaving. My eyes find his for a brief moment, and I give him a nod of appreciation. My eyes quickly return to my girl to ensure she is paying attention. The bitch at my side starts writhing and rubbing on me more, acting as if me holding her by her hair is the best thing ever, and the stupid bitch begins to moan. I pull her hair harder and yank her off of me, and she squeals, realizing I am not fucking playing with her dumb ass. I stare at her with anger and fury in my eyes.

"You have got to be kidding me."

I hear her soft voice and want to go to her, but I need to do this. My hand tightens even more in the dumb bitch's hair, and I twist her and wrench her head back so she is no longer touching me but looking at me. She cries out at the action and tries to take my hands from her hair, causing her to fall to her knees, but I don't let go. I stare at her for a moment, putting the full force of my anger in my stare, she's clawing at my hand, and tears are glistening in her eyes. I know her– she won't let them fall. She won't allow herself to be seen as weak, even if I treat her like shit right now.

Releasing her hair, my hand goes to her neck, and I pull her close to me, staring into her eyes. I squeeze her neck, letting her know this isn't a fucking game. She tries to get away, scratching and pulling at my hand that is not so gently preventing her from breathing freely. The bitch is finally getting it, as I hear a whimper coming from her, and she pleads with me with her eyes not to embarrass her in front of the others. At this point, I give two shits about her pride; she deserves everything she's getting.

"Not only did you come up with some fucked up scheme to stake claim to me. You and the other bitches decided to try to make my girl believe I'm a liar, but you also tried to make her believe I'm a chump, a cheater, and a piece of shit. You thought that if you could scare her off, I would let what– end up back in your beds?" I'm seething. Darcy shakes her head. I know she has something to say, some excuse to make, but she had her chance. It's my time to talk now and make things clear.

I'm shaking. The fury within me grows the longer I'm around these bitches. Darcy finally lets the tears fall. I bend down and stare into her eyes. The other club girls are either crying themselves or looking anywhere but at me. They know they have awakened the beast, and he is hungry for retribution. I shove Darcy away; she falls flat on her ass. I look down at her and see the hurt in her eyes, and I may be a dick, but I don't give a shit. She knew they *all* knew the possibility of us brothers finding ol' ladies were there, and them making plans to stop us is straight bullshit. Right now, today, at this moment, it needs to be nipped in the bud before they get too far out of control. If I lose my girl because of this shit…

"You bitch's went to fucking far. You are not ol' ladies. You will *never* be ol' ladies. You knew what you signed up for when you asked to be club girls. So, why in the *fuck* did you suddenly think the rules would change. Your stretched-out and overused cunts are not so magical that this would go unnoticed or unpunished." I smile at Darcy. "Oh, I know you think I will kick you and Penny out. I am not. Oh, no, ladies…" I choke on those words; these bitches are far from ladies. "You two are now banned from any of the brothers' beds, and during club parties, you are to be in your rooms until I deem you repentant enough to join the fold once again, if ever. You will be responsible for cooking and cleaning the clubhouse, rooms, kitchen, and brothers' rooms. You'll be responsible for doing laundry for all of us and the restaurants and bars. You'll no longer be working at the garage as a receptionist, Darcy. And Penny, I have already called the clinic. Manda will replace you because she has completed her coursework." Both women begin to sob, and I don't give a shit. I stare down at Darcy. She wails on the floor, acting as if I hit her. She's clutching her neck as if my hold were anything but restrictive. It could have been worse., much fucking worse.

"You may have lost me the best thing that I."

I try to rain in my anger. "You bitch's and your games pissed me the fuck off and have me at my fucking limit with your asses. All this shit

72

because I won't touch you, you didn't know why and it fucking wasn't your business to know…" pointing to and looking at my girl. I stare into her eyes as I say what needs to be said, part of which she may not like. "You have no fucking clue, no idea what you could have cost me. Vera is one of the most amazing, kind-hearted, honest, loyal, and strongest women I have ever met. The first and only woman that I have ever wanted by my side. If she doesn't forgive me, Fuck." I pause, still looking at her.

"You better hope she forgives me and hears me out because if… Just know I will do everything in my power to make your lives a living hell here or until we kick your asses out or you leave if you think about pulling shit on a brother in front of his ol' lady. Be warned because no one will save you from me. Test me if you want." I say nothing else. I don't look at those bitches for a reaction. I know Tully, Flick, and Slim will ensure that my message was received loud and clear.

I turn on my heels and walk straight to my girl, bending down, putting my shoulder in her stomach, and lifting her. I hear her breath hitch, and she squeals, making me chuckle. A smile breaks across my face. Oh yeah, baby, you are in some shit. As my hand comes down, I lightly smack her ass, which has her wiggling.

Smack, for good measure.

I'll be damned if I lose the best thing that has ever come into my life. Time to show my girl *who* she belongs to. Before walking out of the common room, I bellow out for the second time for all to hear.

"Mine"

Six

BRICK

Wordlessly, I stomp my way through the common room and to the elevator. If she thinks for one solitary second that she's leaving without talking to me, she's got another damn thing coming. I can feel her squirming, and I have to stifle a groan, Fucking-A, my dick is hard as fuck. I have to calm my shit down *before* we go there. And as much as I want to rip her clothes off and spank her little ass for disappearing on me without talking shit out, we've got to talk about what went down. I refuse to give in to her acceptance that we are over. Because fuck if we are. We will *never* be over.

My floor, the Presidents floor of the clubhouse, is on the upper level and is dedicated solely to me. Well, at least my suite is. My suite takes up half of the top floor. My suite has four bedrooms, three bathrooms, a kitchen, dining room, game room, theatre room, and office. I designed my suite to house any family I have, visitors, and guests. There are a few smaller suites between mine and my officers. Usually, other MC Prez stays with their VP or other high-ranking club members.

On the other side, suites are dedicated to my officers. So yeah, it's my primary residence at the moment. I figured, why build a house on the property if I am the only one that would be living there? So I've made this floor my home. When I have a family, which will happen sooner than later, we'll still stay here if the club were to go on lockdown or for any other reason, I deem necessary.

I'm sure Vera will soon want to build a home within the compound for our little Mastersons. At that thought, my dick hardens even more damn. Fuck we need to get this talk over with, so I can get into my girl. I let out a groan thinking about her swollen with my child. Something I'll be working on real damn soon. She's going to hear me the fuck out. I know she thinks

I'm going to give her a choice. I'm not.

Once the elevator reaches the top floor, wordlessly, I stomp to my suite. Usually, the door is locked, but with me not in my right mind, it isn't. And thank fuck for that. When I get to the door, Vera struggles harder than before. The entire time I have had her in my arms, she'd been struggling, screeching, and cursing me out for all she's worth, but now she is giving it her all. And it's clear she needs another–

Smack

She lets out a squeal, and her wiggling stops. Once we make it through the front door, I head straight to the main bedroom. I have no plans of leaving it anytime soon, and by the end of our talk, I plan on making up for the last few days. The days I could have been working on the little Mastersons.

I let out a chuckle. Before...

She lets out a surprised yelp as she flies from my arms and into the bed. She bounces a few times, and I can see the fury in her eyes and the uncertainty on her face. I can't have that. I follow her body down, holding my body weight off her as I box her in with both hands on either side of her head. Shit, maybe I didn't think this through. I shift, pushing her legs apart, and now my body and, most notably, my dick nestled between her spread thighs and searching out her heated core. Regardless of how pissed she is at me, I know this attraction between us isn't one-sided. I smirk because as I look into her eyes, I can see she is trying damn hard not to show what I know to be true. Hot damn.

I am a good foot taller than her and a whole lot heavier. For a moment, she stares at me, and I can tell she is trying her damndest to fight her body's reaction to me. I can see the war raging within her. She's unsure if she should feel the way she is or if she should hold onto her hurt and anger.

I lean my head down to kiss her, but she quickly turns her head to the side, and my lips press against her cheek. I chuckle at her and lift my head, and hers whips back so she can look at me with narrowed eyes. She starts to struggle to try to push at my chest, which only makes me chuckle even more. Then she shocks when she goes to...

"Oh no, you don't not unless you want me to tan your ass." I grab ahold of the hand that was poised to slap me. I continue trying to keep my full weight off her when I lift her arm over her head. Grabbing the other arm and doing the same, just in case she gets any other ideas. And because both her legs are outside of mine, her only other option is to buck. And boy does she, while she again curses me out for all she's worth. I let her, at least until she tires herself out.

"No"

Her struggling loses some of its fire, and I can tell she's tired as she shakes her head back and forth.

"Sweetheart, you *are* going to listen to me. You had me losing my mind all weekend. I had a man at your place and tailing your friends. I have been looking all over for you. I didn't know what I would have done if you hadn't walked in that door today."

My voice is softer than it has ever been. I tried to show her everything I felt, all the worry for her and the fear I had of never finding or seeing her again. She needs to know that I mean it.

"Wh… what do you care? *You– You–*" She harrumphs and looks away from me.

She stares at the wall, and I can see the tears glistening, and it fucks with me that I did this. She takes a deep breath as I stare at the side of her head, and she slowly turns her head back to look at me. I can tell she is trying to assess me and whether or not I am being genuine. I am. I was losing my fucking mind, and I nearly took out more than a few of my brothers for some of the shit they were talking about. And there may or may not be a few walking around with bruised ribs and broken noses. The fuckers should have known when to shut the fuck up.

"You need to understand something, sweetheart. I never, and I do mean *never,* say things I don't mean. I don't make promises I can't or don't intend to keep. I've never told another living soul what I told you that night. You are all I think about, all that I dream about. You are all I want, and you are all I *need.* You, just you, sweetheart." My head dips so that it is nestled in the crook of her neck. Allowing me to breathe her in, she has a sweet and subtle scent of citrus and lemongrass. How in the fuck do I know that shit? Fucking-A. What is she doing to me? I've never wanted to smell a woman. Never wanted to be this close for this long. It's always been, get in, get off and get out. And now here I am deciphering her scent. Being here in this moment, her scent envelops me, and I just want to bury myself in her and never leave.

"Bu— *but* you, you *had*– those girls" Her breath hitches, and fuck if I don't want to go down there and throw those bitches out for causing all this shit. I fucking hate her feeling like this.

"Sweetheart, I am not going to apologize for my past. It happened. I have been with a few of those women downstairs, and I won't deny that," I say softly.

She sucks in a breath and the tears she's been fighting back begin to fall. Fucking damnit. I know this shit is hard for her to hear, but she needs to hear it. I lift my head and look into her eyes.

"I've never wanted them the way I want you. I never saw them as anything but stress relief. Does that make me a pig? Yes. But they knew the deal when they shared my bed. You would *never* be that to me. You *could* never be that to me. You've quickly become my everything. When I was on that run…" She looks at me with tears in her eyes, confused. I shake my head; I have to remember that she is not from my world, so she has no idea what I am talking about. "When the club has to go out on business, we call it a run." She nods in understanding. I smile down at her and continue.

"I fucking hated having to deal with club business. Being unable to talk to you, see your beautiful face, and not be near you killed me. But– I knew when I got home. I would see you, hear you, and hopefully feel you. And then Friday night happened, and after that shit show, you *disappeared*." All tears on her face dry up as I mention the incident. I shake my head, lean in, and kiss her teary cheek. Turning my eyes back to hers, "It was unbearable not to know where you were if you were safe. I will never let you out of my sight again if I can help it. Fuck, I am being such a pussy right now." I drop my head back into her neck and feel her body shake. I look at her and see a smile as she laughs at me.

"You think it's funny your man was losing his shit?" And at that, her face blanks. Shit.

"I want *you* and only *you*, sweetheart. I was shocked as shit Friday night when Penny jumped on me. And I am so sorry, baby, that I didn't push her desperate ass off me fast enough. I mean it. When I say– I only want you, I mean it to my core. Today when you walked in looking adorable and saw another one of the girls pawing at me, I wanted to punch myself in the face." She giggles at that, and that giggle goes straight to my dick. Fucking hell, I need to hurry this shit along.

"Darcy, the bitch from downstairs. She was trying to use her feminine wiles or some shit to get her ass out of the trouble she's in. She and a few other girls are butt hurt. I've not touched them since meeting you. They didn't know or understand how serious I was about staying away from them until they saw you riding in with me on the back of my bike. Being on the back of my bike is a statement in my club and with my brothers. It says to everyone that I am serious about you, that you are important to me. It tells them that you are mine and I am yours." I lean down slowly, hoping she doesn't move her head this time. And thank fuck she doesn't. I give her a quick peck on the lips. I want to go further, but I need to get it all out.

"That shit show was a setup. From what I gathered, they had been biding their time, waiting for the day I brought someone here. And they planned to do some dumb shit to try and claim me. And care off whomever I brought into the fold. They knew when they saw you on the back of my bike and that kiss in the lot. Darcy was the ring leader. She's always the fucking ringleader. She was the one that was on me like a fly on shit. But, like I told her and all of them, I am done with them. That is a promise I am making to you. I will keep that promise until I take my last breath."

At that, Vera narrows her eyes at me, and for a long time, she stares. I show her the truth in my eyes. I bare it all, never wavering. She needs to know that I am all in with her. I am in this for the long hall. After a time, her face softens, and I want to leap out of this bed and do a happy dance or some shit. Thank fuck, we are getting somewhere. I lean down and kiss her jaw on both sides, her nose, and her lips. And again, I look into her eyes.

"Say that you're mine. I can't take for you not to be all in with me. Because I am all in with you, sweetheart… And from now on, you, Vera James, will let me explain *before* you take off or write me off as a liar or a cheater. I will accept if you don't want to be with me."

I choke out that last part. I am trying to convince myself it's true, even though I know damn well it's not. But for the sake of wanting to work shit out with my woman…

I continue, "I won't like it and don't want you rejecting me— us because of those dumb bitches trying to stake a claim on me." Yeah, nope. I can't; there is no way. I cannot have her thinking I will accept her not wanting us.

I let out a growl.

"Fuck that. I'm lying. I will definitely not accept it. I will fight for *you*. I will fight for us because I know we are worth it. I know that you are my end game, my *everything*. *You* will be my ol' lady, my wife, and the mother of my children. I will always fight for you. *Always*."

"Always," I hear whispered.

She continues to stare at me, assessing me with those gorgeous moss-green eyes of hers. And the damn tears come, and I fucking hate it. I'm hoping they aren't tears of sadness. I can't take this shit. She says nothing for a long while. So, I take matters into my own hands, and I lean down and kiss the sides of her mouth on both sides. When she doesn't immediately jerk or pull away, I make my way to her mouth full-on. She doesn't kiss me back at first, and then her kisses are tentative. But that won't do.

I deepen the kiss, and instantly it becomes all-consuming. My already hard cock gets even harder, and I try to calm my shit down. I damn near cum in my pants when she moans into my mouth. She begins grinding her core on me, and I am about to fucking lose it and rip her and my clothes the fuck off.

I lift my head after forcing myself to slow the fuck down. I stare down at her, and the lust in her eyes is– *Fuck*

"Sweetheart, I need you to use your words. I need you to tell me if you want this because— if I start, I'm not sure I will be able to stop. You own me. Every part of me is yours. I don't want to scare you, but if we do this, you are MINE, which is forever. Ain't no taking that shit back because you get pissed at me. No taking off without talking to me. You. Are. Mine."

I continue to stare into her eyes as she stares into mine, and I see so much there. There are so many emotions, but the one that has me questioning if I am pushing her too fast, too soon is the look of fear on her face.

"Talk to me, sweetheart."

I release her hands and pull myself up and off her, sitting back on my haunches between her spread legs. Shit, I grab her around her hips and lift her, sit her on my lap facing me. Her legs wrap around me, and I feel her heated core against my denim-clad cock. I let out a groan when she shifts her body. Fuck

She looks down at my chest and takes a deep breath. Her beautiful tan skin has a tinge of pink. You wouldn't see it if you weren't paying attention, but I know, my girl. I have watched my girl and learned every inch of her. I smile down at her. Is she embarrassed? I put my finger under her chin and lift it, so she looks at me.

"Do you not want to be mine, sweetheart?"

For a second, her eyes go wide, and it dawns on her that her hesitation has me doubting whether or not she wants this or us. She shakes her head as her eyes tear up, and I am about to *fuck*. She bites her lower lip and stares into my eyes. I see lust reflected at me. Fuck me. She takes another deep breath and steels her spine, and I wait patiently because as much as I want her, I need her. I also need her to do and feel the same way I do.

"Um.... I... I uh..." she pulls out of my hold a little, leaning back and placing her hands between us. Not the most comfortable of positions, but I hold her to me. Her head lowers, and she looks down at my chest again. "I'm a virgin," she says quietly.

I just stared at the top of her head for a moment. My girl, my beautiful amazing girl, has never been touched by another man. No other man has ever been given her gift. I am— Fuck me.

"Baby, look at me" I wait because this is a meaningful conversation, and I need to be sure I respect her and her choices. It takes her a minute, but she does. And I smile a reassuring smile at her.

"You have no idea how happy that makes me. To know that when you decide. When and if you decide to let me, I will be your first, but I am telling you now that I *will* be your last and you mine. You are it for me, and I don't know how often I will have to say this. But I will say it as often as I need to ensure that you understand that I mean every word. This is a gift— the gift of being your first is a gift that I will cherish for the rest of my days. To know that the woman I am falling for is willing to trust me. To trust me to give her the pleasure and love she deserves..." I rub my hands through her long hair and bring my lips to hers, giving her a small kiss.

When I pull away, the fear and embarrassment are no longer on her face, and I smile even bigger, ensuring my dimples are on full display. "There is no rush, sweetheart. I am your man and only your man. My hand will do just fine until you are ready. But I promise you that when you are ready— *truly* ready for me, I will cherish you like the goddess you are. I will worship you in the way you deserve. I vow always to protect you and your heart." I lean in and kiss her lips. What I didn't think would happen does, she deepens the kiss, and I am trying my damndest to slow it down. She won't let me.

Fuck

- V E R A -

I don't know what comes over me. I know we still have things we should talk about. I haven't said much that'd made a lick of sense since Brick brought me to what I assume is his room. I cringe at the fact that he now knows I am a twenty-one-year-old virgin.

The thing is, I believe him, and I believe that he didn't initiate anything with those women, which means at some point, I *know*, I will have to put one or all of them in their place. I know, just from the looks I was getting even when Brick was laying into them, that they will give me shit. I will be ready for it if I want him. If I want to be with him, I have to lay it out on the line and put them in their place. Not looking forward to it, but a girl has got to do what a girl has to do.

As the president of an MC, there will always be women out there throwing themselves at him. I mean, the man is hot. So, if I do this, I will channel my heritage of being a strong Italian woman and be who and what he needs. I hear a growl coming from him. Not sure if it's a good or bad thing, but his–

I can tell he's trying to slow our kiss so that he can hear the words. The words that my brain is screaming at me to say. The words that will make this all make us *real*.

I am his, and he is mine.

For a minute, I don't let him slow down the kiss. I can't. I spent the entire weekend thinking that this was never to be. I am going to enjoy this moment and every moment after. Being here in his arms brings me peace. Even when I was lying down, staring at him with fire in my eyes, I still felt at ease.

He tries again to pull away from the kiss, and I let him. His breaths are coming out in pants, as are mine. He rests his forehead against mine, which seems to be his favorite position. He closes his eyes as I watch him.

He goes to speak, but I put my finger against his lips to stop him. It's my turn. He needs to see that I will try. I will give him this. I want this— us.

"I believe you. I mean, look at you, you're hot. Of course, women will happily throw themselves at you, hoping they will be the ones to stick. Hoping to be me," I smile. "Am I angry and hurt it took you so long to knock them down a peg or ten? Yes. The minute those parasites latched onto you. You should have been Flash Gordan and hiyah'd your way out of there. Because you and I both know if it were the other way around, it would have been a *situation* like at the diner, fists flying, and you lose your shit. And since I am a lady, I walked away, but don't get used to that" I narrow my eyes at him. "I get it. It takes time to retrain your caveman brain to realize that no woman wants to see her potential partner cuddled up with another woman. Hmm. Here is a thought, maybe I should give you a dose of your own medicine so you can…"

Before I finish my sentence, my back is on the bed, and he is hovering over me. And I let out a giggle, he lets out a growl, and there is mock fury in his eyes.

"Mine"

"Yes, I am yours."

He looks down at me and something akin to— No, it's too soon for that. We are still learning about each other. "You mean it?" The vulnerability in his voice makes my eyes soften, and I lift my head and give him a small peck on his lips.

"Yes, I mean it, James. There is something about you. From the moment I looked into your eyes, I have been drawn to you as you have been drawn to me. I have never been drawn to another man like I am to you. That is why I was so hurt before. Accepting your apology means that you and I will be something that people say is once in a lifetime. I know it. I can feel it. As long as those bitches keep their hands off you, and you do the same. *This*–" I point between the two of us. "Will be a forever kind of thing." I lean up again and kiss him.

As it always does, things become heated between us. My body responds to him, and my nipples tighten, my breasts become heavy, my core slickens, and my clit throbs, and without even thinking, my body moves to rub against his hard denim cover cock, and he growls into my mouth. My hands go to his hair. Once again, he tries to pull away. I let him, and I say the words I know he wants to hear and I want to say. My eyes are on his

"I am ready. I want you, James. I don't want to wait a minute longer. You made a vow that I am it for you, that you will care for my heart and mind, you will be faithful to me in all ways– I am ready to be yours– all of yours."

I say the last part on a whisper. I lift my hands, placing them in his hair over my head and stare at him, showing him the truth through my eyes. He stares down at me. I see the moment he finds what he's looking for, he realizes I am serious, and I am all in. He goes into caveman mode, the good kind, not the dumb kind.

"Mine"

With that, his mouth crashes down onto mine in a bruising kiss. His hands make their way to my shirt, and he slowly starts to lift it. I know he is going slow to give me time to stop him. But I won't. He lifts my shirt over my torso and up and over my breast. He sucks in a breath when he realizes I'm not wearing a bra. I guess he overlooked that until now. I let out a giggle. His eyes shoot to mine.

A mischievous glint is in his eyes along with lust, and I shudder. He rips my top completely off me, instantly attaching his lips to one of my bare hardened nipples. And he is none too gentle, but it feels so good. My hips continue to rub against him even more, searching for release. Searching for him, wanting more, needing more.

He continues worshipping my breast, eliciting sounds, moans, and feelings I didn't think possible. He laps, nips, and twists my nipples. And I feel like I am going to explode. Between his tongue, teeth and fingers, I am becoming incredibly sensitive. As if he realizes, he begins to make his way down my body kissing both of my swollen and sensitive buds. Kissing me between my breast. He begins to trail kisses down my abdomen as he makes his way down my body.

James makes it down to my hips, looking up at me. I know what he wants. He slowly undoes the button, pulls down my zipper, and inhales a deep breath. His hands go to either side of my hips, and he grabs ahold of my pants. He begins to pull them down, taking my underwear with them. Once he reaches my feet, he lets out an annoyed growl when he realizes I still have my shoes on. I giggle at his frustration. Moving quickly, he removes my shoes, throwing them over his shoulder with a flourish, a smile, and a wink. He returns to my pants and slides them the rest of the way. He gives me a lust-filled satisfied look at his accomplishment, and I giggle at how ridiculous he is.

He throws the discarded pants behind him in the same direction he tossed my shoes. He climbs back into the bed, slowly raking his eyes hungrily from my spread thighs to my hips, up to my breast, and then to my eyes. He sits between my spread legs on his haunches, still completely dressed. My legs are spread wide, and he sees everything. All of me. He stares at me for a moment taking all of me in, and it is taking everything in me not to cover my naked form. I am not a twig. I am a woman with a full body, breasts, and wide voluptuous hips. As I said before, I am not the typical California girl, and I am ok with that. I love my body. And I will never want to change a single thing about it. But I am still a girl. I am still nervous about the man I am giving myself to seeing me, seeing all of me.

His eyes return to my core, and the lust I see scorches me. He licks his lips shaking his head. He lets out a groan. I can hear his breathing become heavy, and I can't help but spread my legs wider as my lower lips spread. I can feel my juices spill out of me and down my center. I hear another growl I am quickly starting to love, mainly because it makes my core tighten in anticipation. I watch him watching me, and I love it. He's taking his time without touching me, and I know he loves what he sees by how he looks at me.

Once his perusal of me is complete. With his eyes meeting mine, he stands, and without looking away from me, he begins to take his clothes off. First, his vest— or cut, as I was informed by one of the guys when working at the diner. He doesn't look away from me as he steps to the side and puts his cut on a chair near the bed. He steps back over, and his eyes are filled with lust and need. I return his heated stare with one of my own. Am I really doing this? I blush. He notices and smiles down at me.

His hand goes to the hem of his shirt, and with no hesitation, he rips it off, and I, holy mother of– wow, he *is*– wow, there is a reason they call him Brick, he has muscles on top of muscles. His broad chest on display and tan skin has my core clinching even harder than before. Brick isn't as dark as I am. I think his tan has more to do with riding than heritage. He is a work of art with dark hair and grey eyes. His stubbled jaw ticks, not in annoyance but in anticipation and need. His arms are massive, and his muscles bunch and release. He is tatted up on his arm, there are beautiful designs displayed, and I want to lick every last one of them and commit them to memory. His smile turns into a smirk as he sees what he is doing to me.

His hand goes to his jeans, and he slowly undoes his belt letting it hang, doing the same with his button and zipper. Pushing his jeans down, letting them fall to the floor. I try not to look, but I can't help it. His big— *Oh my*, he is encased in tight black underwear with white lines that outline. *Oh my*, they hug him *and* him. I can see everything. My eyes are showing my shock and intrigue as I hear him chuckle. My eyes fly back up to his. There is still lust, but there is also humor in them, and I blush furiously.

My hands go to my face in embarrassment. I feel the bed dip near my feet. I'm so embarrassed at my reaction to seeing *him,* and my hands don't leave my face. I feel warm breath on my foot. He kisses it. He kisses both of them. He kissed my feet. Oh my. He begins to kiss my leg, making his way up, trailing warm wet kisses up my legs, and I am–

His hands trail up both of my legs when he reaches my hips. He begins to kiss my hip bone. Oh my– He kisses my inner thigh, grab both of my legs, pulls them open and over his shoulder, and stares at me, all of me.

And I hold my breath.

Seven

BRICK

I didn't expect her to tell me she wanted this, wanted me after everything that went down. I figured she would need time to process shit. I would accept waiting as long as waiting led to– an us. Don't get me wrong. I am a man, I have needs and all that, but I'm ok with waiting for her. It wouldn't have been a hardship because I would do anything for her. My dick would be rawer than it already is, but I'd deal.

I have spent more time with my hand over the last few weeks than I have since I was a teenager. It's not that there wasn't anyone available and willing to get me off. Or that fact that it is technically not considered cheating. From the moment I laid eyes on her, I knew that I couldn't and wouldn't let another woman touch me, and it didn't feel right. A few have tried, but I just couldn't get into it. My dick didn't even twitch. It helped when those dumb bitches attempted to cop a feel, realizing they weren't doing a damn thing for me.

A whimper brings me out of my thoughts, I stare down at her heated and glistening core, inhaling her heady aroma mixed with her already intoxicating scent of citrus and lemongrass, and I groan, and my cock jumps. I saw her eyes widen slightly when my pants fell to the floor, so I left my underwear on. I am not usually one to wear them, but for some reason, today I did, and I'm glad for it. She was not ready to see all of me just yet. I smile to myself. I'm not a small man and don't want to scare her off before we even begin.

My hands trail up to her breasts, and I squeeze her nipples, tweaking them. Her hips lift, offering up her beautiful pussy to me. And I will take her offering willingly and with fervor. Lowering my head, my mouth latches onto her clit…

Her taste explodes in my mouth. I can't help myself. I attack her pussy like it is my last meal. Her body begins to writhe and twist. She tries to get away from me and push herself into me further. It only takes a few swipes of my tongue over her sensitive nub, and she explodes without warning.

But I'm not done.

I smile into her core as her hands go into my hair.

- V E R A -

Oh my, I've never felt this before. I have touched myself, but it has never felt... like this. Never– ever like this. My orgasm hits me so hard that my legs shake. He is back at it without giving me a break or reprieve. He is doing things to me that– oh my, my hips lift off the bed, my hands pull at his hair, and I don't know what I want, to push him away or pull him closer.

His hands leave my aching breasts and wrap around me, resting on my lower belly, holding me down as he licks and sucks my core. His tongue is magic, it enters me, and I start to see stars. One of his hands leaves my belly and– his thumb goes to my clit, and I know I will explode again, but he pulls it away along with his tongue, and I whimper at the loss. I look down at him, so overwhelmed with the sensations I'm feeling. I am so needy for him and don't feel bad about it. Our eyes connect, and he smiles at me with a mischievous grin.

His head lowers again. I feel a finger probing my entrance. I hold my breath, doing my best not to tense up. There is a slight pinch, but the pleasure eclipses it. Slowly his fingers pump in and out of my tight core. With a few pumps and the attention his tongue is giving my nub, I explode harder than I did before. I scream his name chanting it and writhing from the pure pleasure of what he is doing to me.

He's not done. Oh my, I am not sure how much more I can take.

"James, please"

How many orgasms does one girl need to have? His finger pumps in and out of me slowly as he continues to swirl his tongue around my clit. He slowly places another finger inside of me, and my hips rocket up at the intrusion pushing him further in, there is another twinge of pain, but the pleasure is intense that again I focus on what he is making me feel.

He curls his fingers up, and I explode, screaming his name; I know my voice will be hoarse, if not entirely gone, by the night's end. My lungs are screaming at me as I pant for breath. Every part of me is sensitive yet so needy for him, needy for more. My moans and his growls are the only sounds to be heard.

Once my latest release wanes, he removes his fingers from my core and kisses my hip bone. I am panting and feeling every brush of his skin against mine. I can feel him shifting. My eyes are closed, and tears burn behind my lids as I try to get my emotions and breathing under control. He slowly works his way up my body kissing and nipping at me on his way up.

Once he reaches me, I can feel his eyes on me, which prompts me to open my own. My breath hitches at the look on his face. He wipes my juices from his stubble, a ghost of a smile is on his face, and I return it with a sated smile of my own. He leans down with the softness and kindness I've known him for, something that I think is only reserved for me. He never takes his eyes off mine as he leans down and kisses me. I taste myself on him and can't help but relish the taste. My core is sensitive, but it doesn't stop my body from seeking him out and wanting him closer. He pulls away, staring down at me.

"Please"

"Please what, sweetheart" His eyes crinkle with amusement and lust. I am far too needed for his games. I need him. I want him, all of him.

"James, please"

He seems to get the hint and rests his forehead against mine. Both of our breaths come out labored. He reaches down between us and shifts so that he can remove his dick that has been confined in his underwear. He shifts his body and positions himself at my entrance. His breath hitches, and he lets out a groan. As he slides himself between my folds, I swear I will cum again. His body shutters as he looks into my eyes.

His eyes show me everything, every part of him. He takes a few breaths. "Are you sure, sweetheart, because once I do this, you are mine and mine alone. Are you ready for that? Because I will *never* let you go; I will do everything in my power to consume you as you've consumed me, from the moment our eyes connected in that diner. I will never leave, lie, cheat, or betray you. I will be yours as you are mine. This is forever, and I will never have anything between us."

"Yes, *James*. Make me yours."

Without another word, he begins to push forward, making me his. I can feel how wide he is as he stretches me. It is slightly uncomfortable; the pain is not as terrible as I've heard it could be. He stops and takes a breath when he is halfway in, and I can see that he is straining. His eyes are tightly closed, his jaws clenched, and his breathing becomes even more ragged.

"Sweetheart, this is going to hurt, and I'm so sorry, baby. If I could keep the pain away, I would do anything. I am going to make you feel so good. I will give you all of me as I take this cherished gift you are giving me. You are...." He takes in another deep breath.

"*Mine*"

With that last word, he slams into me, breaching my virginity. The pain is momentarily overwhelming. My breath hitches for a moment. I want to push him away, and a tear leaks from my eyes. Taking a few deep breaths, he remains motionless above me. He bends down, whispering how sorry he is, kissing me all over my face. I breathe through the initial shock of pain, holding him close to me. I breathe him in, taking in his fresh ocean and musky scent, as another silent tear slides down my face. His kisses reach my mouth, and he continues to hold steady until he feels my body relax. I don't trust my voice, so I slowly lift my hips to encourage him to move. The pain is no more. All I feel now is fullness. The fullness of the man that has so quickly become my everything.

Slowly he begins to move, and I am not sure if this is how it was supposed to feel after the pain dissipated. It is more pleasure than anything that I have ever felt before in my life. I feel like this moment, the feeling of him connected to me in the most primal way is joining us in a way that is more than on a physical level. I feel at peace in his arms, and I feel whole. The numbness that has consumed me since losing my family disappears, and warmth fills my heart in a way that I haven't felt in a long time. It is a feeling I never want to let go of.

Our combined breaths mingle as he lifts his head and stares into my eyes. I can feel the words I know I shouldn't say wanting to escape my lips. I desperately try to keep them in for now.

"You are my everything. It may be too soon to say this…." My eyes widen slightly. He kisses me gently on the lips. "Vera James, I am falling for you. And I know it won't be long until I fall completely and utterly at your feet."

He whispers the last part into my lips as he kisses me. I couldn't stop the tears from falling. That was the most beautiful thing anyone has ever said to me. The kiss is all-consuming. I feel it down to my toes. This moment— this is a moment that will seer itself into my mind. This memory will last me a lifetime. This is the moment I realize that even though I don't know him, my soul does, and I am irrevocably in love with James Brick Masterson.

"Don't cry, my love" He wipes the tears from my eyes with his thumbs and kisses both of my eyelids. My breath hitches. Slowly, so slowly and gently, with so much passion, he starts to move again. "Just feel me, Vera, my sweet girl. Feel everything you do to me. Feel how we fit so perfectly together. You were made for me. You are whom I've waited for. You are my everything."

"You" thrust "are" thrust "mine." Thrust

"I… I am yours."

At my words, something changes within him, and he begins moving his hips; they piston in and out of me with reckless abandon, and I can feel another release coming. My hands rake down his back, allowing this feeling to consume me. I am sure that will leave a mark. I smile up at him. He begins to move faster our combined moans of pleasure and bliss become more desperate. And then it hits me. I scream out his name as the intensity of my release converges. At first, there is a bright light, and then stars dance behind my lids; my body shakes, and I yell out again.

"*JAMES*"

It only takes a few uncontrolled and jerky thrusts for him to find his release. His warmth spills into my channel, and he pulses within me. His thrust becomes erratic but slows down as if trying to prolong his release. His lips return to mine for a kiss as he looks down at me.

"I'm more– so much more than halfway to falling for you."

He pulls away, and his lips connect to my forehead, cheeks, and then my lips. Both of us were still breathing hard from our combined release. I feel a release sliding out of me, down my core, and down to his bed sheets. My breath hitches…

"I am not on anything, and we didn't use *protection*. I…" He leans down and kisses me to stop my musing.

"Sweetheart, I meant what I said. You are mine, and if we made a baby, then" he shrugs and smiles. "Our son will be loved and cherished just like his mother." I stare into his eyes for a few minutes and can see the truth in his eyes. He is *very* serious. I am not trying to ruin the moment. Before I can say anything, we moan as his softened manhood slides out of me. He shifts away from me, getting out of the bed, pulling me with him. And because apparently, that's all I can do when he manhandles me, I squeal.

This man– this beautiful, gorgeous, talented man just destroyed any chance of me walking straight for the next week. I can feel a slight twinge in my lower region, but I'm not complaining. I can't believe I just lost my virginity. My cheeks heat. I wabble a little as he places my feet on the floor, and he looks down at me, smiling widely, kissing my forehead. He holds me up, so I don't end up faceplanting.

"Come…" My legs are jelly, and I don't know where he thinks we are going. There is no way I can walk after *that*. He's crazy, and he just gave me like five orgasms in a row. If I try to take a step, I will fall on my ass. He releases me and takes a step away from me. I narrow my eyes at him playfully, and he just chuckles. He freaking chuckles. And now my narrowed eyes aren't so playful.

When he sees the look on my face, he sobers, stepping toward pulling me closer to him. "I want you to soak in the tub for a bit, you are going to be sore for a day or two, and I want you healed and ready for me sooner rather than later." He smiles as he bends down and lifts me; he carries me bridal style to the bathroom. I squeak and wrap my arms around his neck, and he buries his head in my hair, kissing me behind my ear, and I swear my lady bits have a mind of their own because–

Oh my

James walks into his huge and impressive bathroom. And I can't help but take it in. It is beautifully simple. Like in his room, the floors are wood. On the right side, opposite the door, shelves are built into the wall. They are filled with towels and other things one would need in a bathroom. It is all organized in little containers, and it's impressive. The counters that he put me on look like black marble. On either side of me, there are sinks with silver accented nobs. The cabinets and shelves are the same color as the floor. Everything is so clean, not what I expected. Looking around a little more, the walls are painted a deep grey. He says nothing as he stands between my legs as I look around the space. He pulls away after kissing me. He walks over to the tub, completely naked. The tub is the same as the counters; it sits in the corner of the room and is enormous. It looks like it could fit several people.

My face flames as I watch his firm ass, as he bends over to turn the water on and place something in the tub, and my breath whooshes out of me and the very sexy site. "See something you like, sweetheart?" he says with his back still to me, and my face heats even more.

He turns around, and his eyes connect with mine. His smile is broad and mischievous as he stares at me. My breath stalls as I watch as he walks back over to me and steps between my legs. He leans down and kisses me so passionately that I get dizzy. Can you get drunk off of kisses? Because I definitely think you can. Yes, you can get drunk off of kisses.

He wraps his arms around me while kissing me. His hands grab ahold of my very bare ass. And *again,* I squeak, wrapping my legs around him when he lifts me from the counter. He chuckles, releasing my lips, sauntering to the bath. He urges my legs from around him and shifts me away from him, setting me on my feet. My legs are still a little wobbly, but not as bad as before. He steps away from me, and my brow furrows.

Smiling down at me. "If I get in with you, I guarantee that we won't be leaving this bathroom without me making you scream my name over and over again. I want you to soak for a little bit, I am going to shower and get dressed, and I will wait in the room for you. I'll put a towel over here on the hook" He points to what he means. I watch him as he walks over to the shelves that hold the towels, grabbing me a body towel. When he walks back over, he places the towel on the hook. He stares at me for a moment with a contemplative look in his eyes.

"Also, we will go to your place and pack your shit. I don't like you so far away from me."

Before I can process everything said, he winks at me as he quickly steps over to the shower. And before I can even respond, he is in and out of the shower before I can utter a word. I am sure I didn't hear him correctly. Right? He... Nope, that isn't.

I pull my long hair up, twisting it into a loose bun. I don't want to deal with it if I don't have to. I slip into the tub, trying not to think about what he said. My eyes are closed for a moment and snap open when I feel a hand on my shoulder. James is holding out a washcloth and bar soap. I take it, and my face begins to flame... I snatch them from him and look down at my wet hands holding the items.

"Cute"

He leans down, kisses the top of my head, and again walks away and leaves the bathroom without another word. I giggled because I could see his cock becoming ready to go again. My core begins to pulse. Oh my.

"That– really just happened?"

After washing my body and sensitive lady bits, I rest my head on the back of the tub and just think about everything that has happened over the last few weeks.

Meeting Brick, the electricity I felt when I looked into his eyes for the first time, feeling like I couldn't breathe on the days I didn't see him. My irrational anger when seeing women throw themselves at him while he was at the diner. Felt things for him I have never felt before, feelings that very well scare the absolute shit out of me. Then the kiss and the fights, his and mine, and I chuckle because I still can't believe I beat Claire's ass like that.

My mind then goes to Friday night and my rogue weekend hiding out. My face heats in anger when I think about those women. And then lust hits me thinking of the after... that hole debacle downstairs, and when he brought me to his room. All the words he's said to me, things he has made me feel. I know that in the few months I have gotten to know him, Brick is one of the good ones, even if I am not supposed to say or think it.

"I am in love with James Brick Masterson."

Maybe I shouldn't have been standing outside the bathroom door. But I couldn't help myself. I'm drawn to her when we are in the same space. My mind reeled at what I overheard. I may have said I am more than halfway in love with Vera, but I know after what we just shared. The feeling of sinking into her bare for the first time, I knew at that moment that she was and is meant to be mine forever. I felt it before, but making love to her made it so fucking real to me. I felt it soul deep. It's scary as fuck, but I know that this— us. This is going to be something else.

Vera James has become my ruin. She has ruined me for any other woman completely and utterly ruined me, down to my soul. I will never let her go in this life or the next. I will grow old with her and watch as she swells with our children. I will protect her and cherish her always.

"I am in love with you too, Vera James.

Eight

CLAIRE

I cannot *believe* this; I cannot freaking believe this. He chose her— *HER* over me— *ME*! I am a knockout… Like supermodel beautiful. I keep my feathered Farrah Fawcett-esk-styled hair long, blond, and big. I have a killer body that I stay nice and tight. I have been told all of my life how gorgeous I am. So, for me, a *ten*, to be discarded like I were a two, or something. I let out a scream, yanking at my hair. I am so pissed off.

For me to be discarded by the president of LSMC for *her*, that frumpy waif of a thing. I am livid. I am furious that I have put in so much work, and she gets him.

Grr

It's bad enough that I had to fight against those stupid women at the club. I got into it with them constantly, they wanted me gone, and I wanted them to stay the fuck away from my man. They hated spending time with their president, and they hated that I was all he saw when I was around. But I couldn't make it easy for him. I may or may not have shown up a few times on the arm of a brother or two to show Brick I had options. He needed to know that if he didn't play his cards right, someone else would get all that is me.

I put in a lot of damn work to get and keep his attention. I spent countless hours at the salon making sure my hair was perfect. I did the stupid workouts to keep my tits perfect. I made sure I stayed thin and perky. Maybe I may have missed a meal or two, but you have to do what you need to keep your man wanting you. I did everything he wanted in bed, nothing, and I do mean *nothing* was off-limits. But it wasn't enough, that stupid girl swooped in, batting her hideously ugly swamp green eyes, and he and the entire club were putty in her hands, defending her, treating her like she was better than me. She's *nothing*. *There* is no way she can handle a man like Brick, not like I can, not like I have.

I am so freaking pissed as I pace my living room floor, thinking about what happened at the diner. Those stupid idiots messed up; I told their dumb asses to wait to do anything. They were supposed to wait until after she left for the night, but they didn't. I watched them all get beaten to a bloody pulp for daring to put their hands on precious defenseless Vera. Fucking Danny and his grabby hands.

I fucking hate her. She ruined everything. But I'm going to make a plan. She is going to pay. I will make her regret how she treated me, how she stole the life of being the club queen, and how she took Brick and all of his connections and money from me. She is going to pay for nearly destroying my beautiful face. And Brick is going to pay for turning his back on me. They will pay for everything I am going through, no matter how long it takes.

They.

Will.

Pay.

- V E R A -

I feel a hand brush across my face, which is so warm and sends tingles down my spine. I lean into the touch. "Sweetheart, you need to wake up. If you don't get out soon, you'll become one of those singing California raisins." He chuckles at his joke with a shake of his head. I'm sneaking a peek at him through half-lidded eyes; the man is beautiful. My eyes shutter closed again, and I am sated and comfortable. I never want to leave this tub. I hear something and feel something brush against my foot. I hear a gurgling sound, and the water slowly starts to drain, and I groan.

"Well, I guess if I want something done, I'll do it myself." I squeal. Brick wraps his arms around my back, under my legs, and lifts me out of the tub. I giggle and open my eyes as he sets me down on my feet.

"I'm going to get you all wet," I squeal.

He chuckles that sexy chuckle of his. Without saying a word, he leans over, grabs a towel, and starts to dry me off. Of course, I swoon at how sweet he is being to me. I stretch my arms above my head and let out a big yawn and a squeak. I'm not ashamed to say the man wiped me out; all I want to do is climb back in his comfy bed and cuddle. Does he cuddle? I hum, thinking about cuddling next to his naked hard, and warm body.

I hear a growl and a curse. I look at him and notice his eyes are honed in on my pebbled nipples. His gaze is heated. He's fighting against the lust he feels. I smile a little to myself. I do this to him.

"If you don't cut that shit out, I will take you again. You are still sore, sweetheart, but if you keep moving around like that and making those sounds, I can't be held responsible for what I do. Damnit, woman, you are fucking perfect, so damn perfect." He wraps a towel around my body and grabs the other, stepping behind me. At some point, my hair had fallen from the bun I'd put it in, and it's wet on the ends; he attempted to dry it but gave up wrapping the towel haphazardly in my hair. Men. I feel the heat coming off him as he leans down and whispers in my ear.

"When you are all healed up, I will sink into you over… and over… and over again until you beg me to stop, and even then… I won't. I will worship every part of you and have you screaming my name, so everyone knows who you belong to. I'll ensure that every ounce of my cum paints your insides and delectable body. No one will ever have doubts about who you belong to." My breath hitches.

"MINE," is growled out as he nipped my ear stepping around me and walking away.

I watch as he walks out of the bathroom, my body heats at his words, and I can feel my arousal begin to dampen my thighs. And for a moment, I stand stunned. Maybe teasing him with my bare body wasn't such a good idea. Technically, I wasn't doing it on purpose, but I wasn't *not* doing it either. My stomach decides to make itself known at that moment and lets out a thunderous and prolonged growl.

James walks back into the bathroom with my discarded clothes in his hands, chuckling, apparently hearing my very loud stomach amuses him. He pulls me into his arms, kisses me quickly, and steps away. Even that little kiss was dizzying. Yep, you can get drunk from James' kisses.

"Saved by my sweethearts' need for food."

He lets out a shuttering breath, and he's as affected by me as I him. He makes a show of stepping away from me and shaking his head in amusement. He walks to the sink, pulls out a toothbrush for me, and sets it on the counter. I try not to look up again as I shuffle around, but I feel his eyes on me as I dress. I try to ignore him because he's not the only one that is all hot and bothered.

I hear another chuckle. He knows exactly what he is doing to me, just as I know what I am doing to him. The only difference is that I am not as confident as he is. I should feel insecure about that, but I don't. I know that what he said to me earlier is true. I know my confidence will grow in time. And when that happens, he better watch out.

Once I'm dressed, I walk over to the sink where he's standing, staring and watching me. Sliding next to him, I pick up the brand-new toothbrush and begin brushing my teeth. I try to make it look sexy. Can brushing your teeth be sexy? No, that's just weird and awkward. My eyes connect with his in the mirror, my mouth is full of fuzzy toothpaste, and I know I look ridiculous. James is watching me with amusement in his eyes. Thank goodness he can't read my thoughts because...

I finish rinsing my mouth, and he grabs ahold of my hand and starts to lead me into the bedroom. "Come on, let's get fed before we head to your place to pack your shit." I pull my hand out of his, which makes him stop. He spins around and stares down at me with a furrowed brow. He then schools his features, locking eyes on me and giving me a stare that says this decision, the decision he's made for me, is not up for discussion. But a girl has got to try and maintain a sense of control in their own life. I've already been told I no longer have a job. I'm not saying I don't like the idea; I have to ensure he knows that bossing me around will not always get the response and cooperation he wants. Got to keep my man on his toes.

"Now, Brick. You and I...."

He leans down and kisses me, and I forget any argument I had filtering through my head. He starts walking me backward, and I am so caught up in the kiss. I don't know what he's doing. He releases me from the kiss, pushing me towards the bed where my bag is now sitting on the fresh, clean bedding. Aww, how sweet, he changed the bedding after we... My blush heats my skin, but I push it down.

Since he wants me to eat dinner with the rest of the club, I want to make a good impression on them. I can't go down there looking like... looking like we did what we just did. I blush again. I am determined not to be such a girl and make a fool of myself or look it. I pull out my brush and a hair tie and put my hair in a high ponytail. It will have to do for now. I can feel him watching me as I adjust my clothing. When I am tucking my shirt into my pants, I realize it is all stretched out and falls awkwardly on me. I guess he was a little hasty when taking it off of me. I stare down at my stretched shirt for a moment.

"Wear this. I want everyone to know that you are mine."

His eyes shine with possession, and I smile at him. Taking the shirt out of his hand. If I am honest, wearing his shirt is no better than wearing my stretched-out one. I have to tie it on the side; otherwise, it would hang down to my knees, and that's not the look I am going for. The t-shirt is a black Tee with the LSMC club colors on the back and Brick's name on the breast, it's soft and comfy, and I already know I will keep it. I do a little curtsy and smile at him when I am dressed and ready to head downstairs. I know I need to address the whole going to my place and packing all my stuff. As I said, I have at least to put up a little bit of a fight.

"Seriously, James..."

"Nope. You are mine. That means I take care of you in all ways. One thing you have to know about me, sweetheart, is that I am the kind of man who is possessive and will always take care of my woman. I take care of everything from where you lay your head to who is protecting you when and if I am not around. I will never tell you what to do, as long as what you're doing isn't something that jeopardizes your safety. And *this* is very much about your safety, sweetheart. Also, I am a selfish prick. I couldn't handle it this past weekend, not knowing where you were or if you were ok and safe." He looks at me with determination in his eyes and a tiny bit of fear. I don't like that at all. I don't want him to fear something happening to me. If I am honest, I don't mind that he wants to protect and provide for me. I just don't want to be reliant on him for everything. I've gotten on pretty well on my own and enjoy a certain amount of independence, but I get it.

"And If I am honest, I know damn well that if you went home at the end of the day, you would always wonder if I was stepping out on you. Not saying that I would. I would never do that because I keep my promises. And I am determined to protect your heart, sweetheart. Also, you are now

99

the President of Lucifers Saints MC's woman, and its own set of dangers comes with that. Plus..." He steps closer to me, resting his hand on my stomach and my eyes wide. Oh my... He leans down, and his lips are a hair's breadth away from my own.

"You are already carrying my son, and if you're not... Well, I want you here so we can make sure that happens sooner rather than later." He winks, grabs my hand, turns, and pulls me out of the suite. I am not sure what to say. A few hours ago, I was trying to figure out how I would get home. Now, I am with a man who has claimed me in all ways and wants to try to have a baby actively. A baby, like an entire human being. And I realize something...

"James, um... How old are you? Where were you born? You're making all these plans, and we don't even know the basics about each other. Don't you think we should slow down a little?" I stare up at him biting my bottom lip. I am being ridiculous because, honestly, I don't want to slow down, not even a little, but I'm a fucking lady and have to give the illusion of putting up a fight.

- B R I C K -

To be honest, I didn't think about that. I already know how old she is, along with other personal information. Since she was an employee of my club, I had bare-bones info on her. I did, although, get a little more news from Hound. I know that her family was killed in a home invasion, that she was the only one to survive and that she has no family in the states. Her only living family is in Italy. That crushed me to know she was here and alone.

I pull the button that stops the elevator and look down at her. "I'm 26 and was born here in Sacramento. I was raised with my brothers by our free-loving hippy mother until I was five. My ma was a free spirit, never wanting to settle down in one place, always moving around with us. She, of course, would always come back to my Pop and get knocked up and then take off again. After a while, my Pop got sick of it, and he didn't like how she was all over the place. With us getting to schooling age, Pop took over raising my brothers on a farm not far from here and me. I have two brothers Tom who's a doctor. He lives in San Francisco and Barkley." She gives me a weird look at Flick's given name. "Yeah, I know it's a fucked-up name. Barkley hates it. He goes by Flick in the club, and he's my enforcer. It's not widely known that Flick and I are blood brothers. There is no real reason for it. We just don't broadcast it" She nods in understanding. "I was in the service from the time I was 18 to 23, then got out and prospected for the mother chapter in Maine. I was there until I was put up as president of this chapter two years ago. I have never been married and have no kids, but both of those things will hopefully change soon." I wink down at her giving her a knowing smile.

She still has a look of shock on her face after I press the button to get the elevator going again. So, I lean down and kiss her lips. That has become my favorite thing to do. I always want to be close to her, kissing and touching her.

Ruined

I am fucking ruined.

"We have a lifetime to learn everything there is to know about each other. You and I are a forever kind of thing, so we have time. I know this seems like things between us are moving fast, sweetheart. I promise you that this– us– is moving as it should. Fate wrote it in the stars, and I am just following its path."

Something crosses her face. She nods at me, smiling her big beautiful smile that damn near brings me to my knees. Staring into her eyes, taking her in, I know I am one lucky motherfucker. I smile as she lifts on her toes and kisses me sweetly. And I can't help but tell her just that.

"Sweet and beautiful, I am one lucky son of a bitch. You are mine Vera James. I hope you are ready for a life filled with me loving on you, giving you the world, and treating you like a queen because around this place, that is exactly what you are and forever will be. So wear your crown with confidence and keep that fire I know you try to hide out and on display. Don't let anyone dim your light or have you questioning us. We. Are. Forever." I kiss her to solidify my last words, pouring everything I feel into the kiss. I slowly pull away, pecking her lips a few more times with my own before the elevator door opens. I turn as the doors slide open; I pull her to my side, keeping her close to me. Everyone needs to know that she is mine.

As we make it through the hallway, she stiffens. I slow my steps but don't stop. Instead of me giving in and addressing her change, she does what I knew she would. Because my girl is a motherfucking queen. Vera takes a deep breath, squares her shoulders, and continues to walk into the common room. Her head is held high as she takes everything in. She didn't get much of a chance earlier with everything going on and with me snatching her little ass up, making sure she didn't take off on me again.

Everyone stops what they're doing to watch us, and I know it's more than that. They are assessing her. I can almost guarantee that tongues have been wagging about what went down this morning. These nosey fucks are wondering what went down between the two of us after I set Darcy straight. Well, fuck them and their nosey asses. It ain't their business.

I pull Vera closer to me when I notice a few looks from my brother. Looks that make me want to punch them in their fucking faces. Especially after seeing that some of their eyes are locked on her tits. Letting out a growl with Vera startling slightly at my side, I'm sending a few death glares, and the fuckers quickly look away. I look down at her as she stares up and me. Damn, my shirt looks good on her, and it lets every last one of these fuckers know that she's mine and only mine.

"Are you going to feed me now, *my* big bad biker president? You know you worked me good and hard, and now I'm starving."

I can't help but chuckle because if that wasn't her laying claim on me, I don't know what is. All the brothers recognize what she did, and they start cackling and cheering my girl. I give her a wink.

"Yeah, sweetheart. Your ol' man is going to feed you. Let's go sit at our table." I start to walk over to my table. I hear a scoff, and I know shit…

These bitches will never learn.

"Look at her strutting and holding on to him like she's Queen B." There are a few cackles, and my body stiffens. I shake my head and try to ignore that stupid bitch, I've already lost my shit on her once, and if she keeps this shit up, I may have Magda handle her. Vera doesn't react. She keeps on her path like she didn't hear what I did.

"She's not even his type. He'll get tired of her and be back in my bed by the end of the week. That little display this morning was only so he could get in her pants and get her out of his system. He didn't mean any of it. That fat bitch doesn't have anything on me, no one she can keep a man like Brick satisfied with her fat, flabby ass." At that last part, Vera stiffens. Fucking Darcy, when the fuck will she learn. Without warning, Vera pulls away from me and spins on her heels. I know shit is about to go down if the fury vibrating off my woman is any indication. I am conflicted about what I should do. Should I stop this? Or let her handle it?

Tully stands from his seat and catches my eye. I can see what he's suggesting I do in his, and I know he's right. I have to let this shit play out. Vera needs to exert her authority over the club girls. She may not be my ol' lady just yet, but she damn well will be, and they need to show respect. So, right here and now is the best time to show these bitches who the Queen is. And because of what happened at the diner, I know my girl is fully capable of taking care of herself. I'll step in if she needs me, but I doubt she will.

I watch as she makes her way to the table filled with some of the club girls. She doesn't know who spoke. But I, along with every brother, know that if she gives these bitches an inch now, they will take a mile and show her no respect, and the first lady in any club should be the president's equal and is above all other females in the club ol' ladies or not. And these bitches need to respect the hierarchy or get the fuck out.

Everyone is watching this play out. You could hear a fucking pin drop. Once Vera reaches the table, I can see that she looks at all the girls and somehow knows it is Darcy. Her shoulders are back, her head is held high, and she's standing at her full height. Her posture's showing them she's not one to be fucked with, and I smirk. Yeah, sweetheart, you set them bitches straight.

"I'm sorry, what was that?"

I see Vera's stance shift; it becomes predatory, and then she tilts her head glaring at and holding the stare of the three main problem girls in the club. Fuck knows how she figured out that they are usually the ones that keep shit stirred up around here, but she does. Something or someone shifts, and Vera's head snaps towards Darcy. The other two are smart enough to look like they have good enough sense and look everywhere but at Vera when they realize what's really going on. Darcy, on the other hand, does not.

"Oh, shit," I hear one of my brothers say. I watch Vera slowly shift closer to the table, looking like the queen she's born to be. She points a finger in Darcy's direction.

"I am assuming it was you," she sneers. Oh hell. Darcy is now looking around the room. I see the moment she thinks she will put on a show. I know the moment she decides she will try some shit with my girl, I start to take a step toward Vera. Vera must sense me shifting in her direction because she looks back at me, shakes her head, and gives me a wink. I lift my hands and take a step back. I hear a few chuckles and a few whispered comments from brothers can be heard. Everyone is watching and waiting to see what will happen next.

Vera pulls one of the seats out and sits down. My goddess is so beautiful and graceful as she sits in the chair. Sitting back, crossing her arms, she stares at Darcy. Waiting for the woman to say or do something. I can see Darcy's wheels turning, but they aren't quick enough.

"You learned nothing from the little get-together earlier between you, your president, and the other whores?" I shift to a table nearby and signal the prospect for a beer. I positioned myself to see and watch my girl's face. I've only seen her lose her shit once, and I quickly learned that she is a master at keeping her cool until she isn't.

"Since you have so much to say, I will enjoy my meal with you. And you can explain to me why you are a woman who spreads her legs for anything with a dick and no real aspiration other than to lie on your back. Thinks that *me*.... a woman that works for *everything* she wants and needs is the lesser of us both?" Vera tilts her head and stares Darcy down with a raised brow.

Darcy doesn't even comprehend the insult as she huffs and puffs. She looks at the other girls sitting at the table, and they are both still looking at everyone but at her or Vera. She has no allies here, but that won't stop her from digging her grave.

"I... I have been Brick's main girl for years. He brought me here to be at his side. He made sure that I... me... his favorite, followed him from the mother chapter. He wants me here long term, not just for the night." She looks Vera up and down like she is nothing. And it is taking everything in me to stay seated and not go over there and lay into the lying bitch.

"I know what he *needs*, know what he *wants,* and I give it to him *gladly* and will continue to do so when he gets tired of you. I've watched girls like you come and go from his bed, but he always comes back to me when he gets tired of you. He *always* comes back to *me.*"

"Interesting" Vera sits up, putting her elbow on the table and resting her head in her hand, acting as if everything Darcy is saying is the most interesting thing she has ever heard and doesn't bother her. "That is good to know. Is there anything else?" Oh, she's *good*. My girl is damn good.

"You think he will be faithful to you; Brick likes things that only I can give him. He is very particular in the bedroom. He is too much of a man for a little… well," Darcy scoffs and starts to cackle. "Well… not so little, but you know what I mean. My advice to you is to enjoy it while it lasts. Because it won't last long." Darcy sneers and smiles, snickering in Vera's face as if she had just won.

Vera just nods her head and smiles at Darcy, and I know I just know she is not going to go easy on her.

"What's your name? I don't want to call you what I have been calling you in my head… You know cum bucket, slobber nobber… That sounds quite rude, don't you think?" There are a few chuckles in the room, and I can see Penny and Tina trying not to laugh.

Darcy doesn't answer, so one of the brothers yells her name. Everyone in the room is invested in this interaction, even me. Vera stares at Darcy for a long moment. She tilts her head a few times, making a show of assessing her.

"Well, Darcy. A couple of things, and then I will go and eat my dinner with my ol' man. I've changed my mind about eating here. Looking at you for too long may make me lose my appetite. I have to ensure I stay nice and healthy since he's trying to knock me up. And the bitterness coming off you is likely to spoil my meal" Well, I'll be damned. My woman is taking no prisoners, just as I thought.

"I can tell you from personal experience that I get it. Bricks, dick and kisses are coma-inducing and intoxicating, so I get how losing them can be devastating to someone as desperate as you."

Darcy whispers, *"He kisses her?"* as she looks down and backs up with fire in her eyes. That's one thing I never do with the club girls, and it's a hard limit for me. I would never let them kiss me. I know where their mouths have been, and it's too damn intimate for who and what they are.

"I never see him getting tired of me and returning to you. That's neither here nor there. Only time will tell, but I can guarantee time is on my side. As I said, I get it. He went from one whore to another for a long time and returned to his main whore. You are a beautiful woman and should rely on something else to get what you want. But here's the thing", She points to me. "That man has made me some promises. Promises that I know he plans to keep, and I will hold him to."

Holding my breath because I don't want her sharing our intimate conversations with the club, she turns me into a fucking pussy, and my brothers don't need to know any of that shit. Fuck. Like he knows what I am thinking, Tully looks at me with amusement, and I flip him the bird, fucker. He silently laughs from his spot in the corner.

"For instance, after we finish eating. We are headed to my place to pack it up. My ol' man *needs* me and *wants* me here with our family. I will be moving in with him, and he will continue to try to put his baby in me. He has plans to give me his last name and crown me his queen. These are just a few of the big ones. So, with all this planning, he won't have time to even think about you." Vera shrugs at Darcy, who looks at me with shock and hurt in her eyes, but she quickly recovers. She tries to speak, but Vera holds up her hand.

"Darcy... Darcy... Darcy. Recognize when you've lost and move on. You lost; you will never be in Brick's bed again. By the way, he is Prez to you. I may have said a few not-so-nice things, but let's be honest, honey, no one in history has ever turned a hoe into a housewife. If you enjoy sex, good for you. I'm not judging, but if you are doing it to trap a man into taking care of you. You need to reevaluate your purpose and goals in life. I am starving, and looking at you makes me a little itchy. Good talk." Vera taps the table, stands calmly, pushes the chair back in, and struts towards me with the grace she always has.

Before she gets to me, I hear a scream, and somehow Vera knows it's coming before I can stop it. A full beer bottle comes flying toward Vera's head, she shifts and the bottle whizzes past her head and my shoulder, shattering on the ground. I am fucking livid. My eyes narrow at the woman standing and making her way toward Vera.

This bitch has lost her fucking mind.

Nine

VERA

I knew it was going to come to this. I tried not to let my anger get the better of me, but come on. What did she think was going to happen? Did she think it was going to go her way? Unlikely. She thought wrong. Her not backing down wasn't a surprise or a shock. But I am sure my reaction is.

James may not have told me everything yet. But I know enough. He may not know I am from a similar lifestyle, where whores are whores no matter where you go. I get that these women want to be the one. Heck, I wanted to be the one. I'm all about matching energy, so verbal sparring should have been all there was between that bitter bitch and me.

The look on her face said it all. She wouldn't let sleeping dogs lie because she didn't like being put in her place. There was something in her eyes that leaned towards keeping this— whatever it is, going. If not now, at some point, she would come after me, try to get back into James's bed, and use any means necessary to do it.

My body, despite my relaxed outer demeanor, stayed on alert. I stood, turning my back to her, even though I knew better. I hoped she would let it go, but I could sense she wasn't going to wait. She was going to show her cards, and she was going to regret it.

You're not raised by a Soldier in the mafia to not know when to be aware of your surroundings. I'm glad for my sense of awareness. A loud screech comes from behind me. Damn, why do all of James's ex-lovers have to act like this?

Why are all of these women so crazy about his–

I don't turn around. I can see her through the mirror behind the bar, and the moment the beer bottle flies from her hand in my direction, I simply shift my body. The bottle whizzes past my head and James's shoulder, crashing to the ground.

Looking up at James, I can see the fury in his eyes. But this is not his battle to fight. This is for me to handle if I'm to be his ol' lady and first lady of this club. Faster than I've ever moved in all my life, I turn around, make my way back toward her, and I am up over the table in seconds. She doesn't have time to react before my hand is in her hair. She's scratching and screeching. I don't care, and she brought this on herself.

"I" punch. "was' punch. "trying" punch. "to" punch. "be" punch. "nice."

She crumbles to the floor with my hand still in her hair, but I am not done with her. I pull her back up onto her feet. Blood snot and tears run down her face as she screams for help. Her eyes dart around, looking for anyone to come to her rescue. I pull her so that she and I are face to face.

"You had to fuck it up. You had to be a stupid whore who couldn't take rejection." I bring her weeping face closer to mine and shake her head with the hand still holding her by her hair. "I will not allow you to disrespect me, learn your fucking place, And. Stay. In. It." I punch her in her gut, releasing her hair as she falls to the ground, wailing.

I look around the room and see the club girls' shocked faces and the brothers' pride-filled faces. I look over to James, and he has his arms crossed over his chest, staring at me. I can't read the look on his face. Did I read it wrong? Did I take it too far? Is he upset I beat this bitches ass?

Without a word, I step over the still-wailing whore and return to him. Our eyes stay connected; still, he shows no emotion, nothing. I'm not sure if he is angry or proud. Now, I know I should care, but I don't. She deserved everything she got.

When I reach him, my breathing is still heavy; I rest my forehead on his crossed arms. Suddenly I feel his body shaking. Taking a deep breath, I force my eyes up to his. My eyes meet his, and there is amusement in them; he has a massive smile and silently laughs.

"Well, that's one way to put a bitch in her place." He chuckles, uncrossing his arms and wrapping them around me. He bends down and kisses me. It is not a simple little peck on the lips. It's one of his intoxicating kisses. The one that always leaves me drunk on him.

Ugh, this man.

He pulls away from me and lifts my hand to inspect them, kissing my knuckles. Shaking my head, I finally returned to myself because everything in the room had disappeared for a little while. Now everything is boisterous and loud. There are a few catcalls and ribs towards James about his ol' lady being a badass and how no one should piss me off. At this moment, my embarrassment for losing my shit in front of all his brothers, the other ol' lady, and club girls make itself known. My face heats up, and I look down. I've got to stop beating people up in front of these men. They are going to think I have anger issues or am crazy.

Ok, maybe I do and am a little. But they don't need to know that.

I feel his hand on my chin, lifting my head, so I look up at him. He leans down to my ear. "You have nothing, and I do mean nothing, to feel embarrassed about, sweetheart. You have every right to defend yourself and put that bitch in their place. You are my girl... own it, and never let anyone step on you or in your way. Own your title and always keep your chin up." He winks at me. Stepping behind me, he puts his hand on my shoulder, squeezing them and kissing the top of my head.

Stepping to my side, he wraps his arm around me and pulls me to his side, steering us toward where I assume he wants to sit. I have no idea what that was, but as I look around, I see pride, amusement, and respect on the brothers' faces, and I smile a little.

Maybe, my brand of crazy is ok. It is all going to be ok.

- B R I C K -

I knew she had it in her. I didn't like how embarrassed she was once she returned to herself; I know what it is to see red and lose my shit. I want... I need her to know that no one here, especially me, would ever judge or hold it against her for defending herself, her man, or this club. We all respect her even more for it. Her putting Darcy in her place showed the brothers that she's not afraid to get down and dirty when need be. That shit goes a long way when dealing with outlaw bikers.

I signal for Doc to come over and deal with Darcy for now. I will have to decide on her future later. I am not heartless; I won't kick her out of the club for acting out the way she did unless my girl says otherwise. I may have to send her ass to another charter. I know she can't go back to the Mother Chapter in Maine. That is a worry for tomorrow. I am not stupid, and Darcy is not one to give up easily, even after getting her ass handed to her and being embarrassed in front of the club.

I look over to where Darcy is still lying on the ground. Doc helps the wailing woman and tries to shuffle her out of the common room. I signal a prospect over to me and tell him that I want him and a few others to watch over her until I decide what to do with her. I look back to Darcy and see she's milking this shit for all its worth as she's being pulled towards the club girl's quarters by Doc. I catch the scathing look she sends to Vera. She shifts her head, and our eyes connect. She immediately turns her face, and I narrow my eyes on her. Yeah, I need to deal with her ass soon.

Looking around, my eyes connect with my counsel, the brothers in leadership roles sitting around the table. I am, for now, the only one with an ol' lady, at least the only one that takes the title seriously. Tommy Boy doesn't count, no disrespect to Nancy, but she isn't a true ol' lady. He hasn't marked her, she just recently got her cut, and it was only because the club is clear in our by-laws about women. It may not be right by the world's standards, but women in or around the club must have a purpose.

And with Nancy not being a club girl, she had no purpose, so essentially, she was free game, which pissed Tommy Boy off, especially when a few of the brothers made a play for her. To prevent the brothers from continuing to try it on with her, Tommy Boy gives her a property cut but refuses to get her tat. So, I don't see Nancy as a true ol' lady without that last step. As long as she doesn't cause problems in or for the club, their weird-ass relationship is not my damn problem.

I key back into the conversation at the table as Vera and I are about to settle in for dinner. "Well, Killer, welcome to the club, darling. These girls heard loud and clear you are not to be fucked with." Tully chuckles along with the rest of the brothers. Vera buries her head in my side in embarrassment, and I find it cute as fuck. The fact that she can go from the sweet, kind-hearted woman to a badass in no time, that... that is how I know she was meant for me.

Tully stands and walks around the table towards us. My eyes narrow on my

VP as he snatches Vera out of my arms. He hugs her and kisses the top of her head. Knowing I'll want to rip his arms off his body for touching what's mine.

I don't even realize it, but my hands are balled into fists, but I know that there is murder in my eyes because, for my girl, I will, *in fact*, put a brother down. Vera must feel my mood change, and she steps away from Tully, smiling at him, wraps her arms around my torso, lifts her toes, and kisses me on the chin. Immediately, I calm the fuck down.

Staring at my brother, best friend, and VP for a second longer, relaying with my eyes the torture I will put him through if he does that shit again. I look down at her, and she smiles at me, and I can't help but smile back. I hear a few chuckles from my brothers, and Tully makes eye contact with me again, shaking his head. The fucker winks at me. He knows that shit he just pulled riled me up. Fucker

"Now, Prez, you know I didn't mean anything by it. Just wanted to Welcome *your* girl properly. It's nice having a *proper* first lady in the club." His smile is broad, and I have an urge to stab him. Maybe I should punch the smug fucker in the face; why the fuck is he smiling so damn much. All the brother's cackle like little hens. Tully lifts his hands as if he isn't asking for an ass-kicking.

"Fuck you, brother, don't do that shit again," I growl out, pulling his usual chair out and sitting my girl in it before I sit down. Tully sits on the opposite side and usually sits where I put Vera. The gesture shows the rest of the club her importance to me. It also shows his respect for her by keeping his trap shut. Once everyone is seated, I signal the girls to bring our food. Officers eat family-style, and the rest of the club has a buffet. I learned a long time ago; that these hungry fuckers won't leave a scrap if left to their own devices.

I appreciate Tully for not starting dinner without us. Usually, if I am behind or busy, he will start and make sure one of the girls saves food for me. But again, my brother shows that he respects my ol' lady and me even if it isn't official yet. Well, not completely I got her cut on order and need to get her to see Ink at the club's tattoo shop, Sinners Ink.

Vera smiles at me, taking everything in when a few girls bring the dishes and plates. Her eyes narrow on them as they scurry around the table.

"Who cooks the food, because if it's them." She hitches her thumb over her shoulder, not pointing at anyone in particular. I get her point, though. "We are going to have a serious conversation." She says with narrowed eyes on me. And at first, the brothers just stare at her, unsure what to say or how to react to the look on her face. Then her lips twitch, and I swear there is a collective sigh. Brothers around the table begin to chuckle.

None of us says much for a few moments as we watch her take stock of what the spread includes. And yeah, we are manly men, so we are pretty much steak and potato, kind of guys. I lean over to her, leaning in so I am a hairs breath from her ear. "See something you like?" Her response has me instantly rock hard. A shiver makes its way down her body, and I smirk when I see her shift in her chair, I love that I affect her this way.

Kissing her behind her ear, leaning back in my chair, I smirk as I hear an intake of breath. The look in her eyes makes me want to snatch her up and say fuck dinner. I have to be patient, though. I smile, thinking about how I was just between her thighs. I'm starting to hate making us come down here to make an appearance. Fuck.

We stare at each other; our eyes are saying everything. I lean down and kiss her lips, never looking away from her. She is the most intoxicating woman I have ever met or will ever meet. She has a hold on me, and I know for a fucking fact that my life is going to get a lot more interesting with her in it.

I'm fucking ruined.

"So, where you come from, Vera?" Hound our information man who is never really off the job knows exactly where she came from. "Sometimes I hear an accent, and other times I don't. You're not from around these parts?"

"No, I'm not. I used to live in San Francisco and have been traveling around. Before living there, I lived in Boston with my family" She gets a faraway look in her eyes and then there is a sadness that makes me want to punch my brother in the face. I give him a stern look saying to back the fuck off. He knows what she went through. He knows more than anyone. So, bringing up her family is…

Lucky for him, he does, and things flow easily from thereon. Everyone starts eating and enjoying the spread, Vera is tentative about the food, but she doesn't look disgusted. I never did answer her question about who makes the food. Yes, the club girls help out, but Magda is the main one that cooks for us.

"Just so you know, sweetheart, Magda has been cooking for us since we moved here. She's a young girl we took in. She was in a bad situation; the club took her out of it. She cooks and does other things for the club and is a good girl. She means a lot to me." Vera narrows her eyes on me as she hears the admiration in my voice. Oh shit.

"Magda is not nor will she ever be a club girl. She's like a sister to all of us, she's off-limits, and the brothers respect that. I'll introduce you later. She cooks and leaves and hates being around the club girls for obvious reasons. You'd like her. She beat a few asses herself." I, along with a few brothers who were listening in, chuckled and agreed with me about Mags.

Vera visibly relaxes. Crisis averted. Thank fuck.

Rocky gets in on the conversation, which is rare for him. Rocky doesn't talk a lot; I've seen him laugh and smile tonight more than I have in a long ass time. Rocky and I— like Tully and me, have been friends for a long time. Both of them followed me to the service. When we got out, they prospected with me at the mother chapter. To see my two best friends getting along with my girl is a good thing. Knowing my brothers like her fucking warms my heart. Makes me see that I made the right choice: not being a prick and ignoring our connection.

I look over to Tully, staring at me, and he nods. He looks at Vera and Rocky, who are deep in conversation about what? I have no fucking clue. I just nod and smile. I can see the approval in his eyes. He knows this is something. For her to pull Rocky out of his shell is not an easy task. I take a swig of my beer and enjoy this time with my family and my girl.

Tully and Slim catch my eye. We are sitting on the couches in the common room, and Vera is snuggled up on my side. I knew at some point my girl would lose the battle she's been fighting for a while now. I know she was trying to stay strong and hang with the big boys. Today was a lot for her. I wore her out, and then she did a little ass-kicking. So her conking out is to be expected.

Fucking cute

Doc came back down after dealing with Darcy and checked Vera's hand out, and surprisingly there were no broken bones. My little fighter knew what she was doing and only had a few bruised knuckles. As she snuggles further into me, I kiss her on the top of the head, and a warmth spreads through my chest as she snuggles even deeper into me. She fell asleep a while ago. Having her in my arms like this is not something I thought would ever happen. But I am damn sure happy. Fuck, I am a pussy when it comes to my girl, and I wouldn't change a damn thing.

Hearing a throat clear, I look up to see my brothers with shit-eating grins on their faces. I chuckle because I know they see how gone I am for her. I'm not even trying to hide it.

"I'm going to put her in bed, and I'll be back down. All of you look like you got some shit to say"

Both men nod, and I know they want to say some intelligent shit about me being so soft for my girl. I send them both glares.

I make my way up to my suite. My girl doesn't wake up for a second, not when I take her shoes off. Not when I undressed her leaving her only in her underwear. Fuck. Of course, my cock is rock hard, no matter how hard I try to think of anything other than sinking back into her.

I have some business to handle tonight with how Tully was eyeing me. I adjust her in bed after pulling the covers over her nearly naked form. I lean down, kiss her forehead and reluctantly step away. I never knew it could feel like this when you found your one. The fact that I hate letting her out of my sight and the ache in my chest is overwhelming the longer I've gone without laying eyes on her. Shit yeah, I am fucking gone for this girl.

Staring down at her, "You don't know it yet, but I am in love with you, Vera James. I am one lucky motherfucker, and I will spend my life making you happy." I lean down and kiss her pouty lips. I smile when she shifts into the kiss, trying to get closer to me. She whispers my name, making me smile even more, and wanting to strip down and lay in bed with her.

Fucking club business

Walking back into the common room, I see Slim and Tully sitting at the bar. Tully sees me coming, and he raises his beer to me. I nod at him. A few of the club girls watch me. I smirk at the wary looks on their faces, and their eyes shift behind me. I chuckle and shake my head; my girl has made an impression.

I sit next to Slim, who grunts at my arrival. I shake my head at the surly bastard. Like Rocky, Slim is not one for a whole lot of words. "So, what you got for me, brothers?" Tully looks around to ensure we don't have ears on us, and I see the action for what it is. It isn't good.

"Well, you were right. It wasn't a brother. You ain't going to like it, Prez."

"Tully listen… don't beat around the bush, man, just rip off the Band-Aid."

"One of the girls is a possible plant. Hound did another check of the newcomers and prospects. Anyone new within the last year…" I raise my hand to shut him up. I can already tell I am going to lose my shit. I stand and start walking to my office. Tully and Slim follow, neither speaking.

Entering my office, I take a seat behind my desk, and Tully and Slim take theirs; I nod for Tully to continue telling me what he found. I know I need to keep my shit together because Tully looks at me in a way that says I may lose it.

"Hound found a discrepancy with Penelope" I sit back in my chair, waiting for the bomb I know is coming to drop. "The girl is related to one of the Keepers. It didn't come up in her initial check because she is a distant relative. Hound only found out because he dug deep and used some of his local contacts. Not sure how she knew anything to do with our runs and routes. That part I am concerned about. If she is indeed the person passing information." He gives me a look that says a few brothers may have loose lips around the club girls.

Fuck. Shit. Damn it to hell.

"We need to keep an eye on her. We need to know for sure. It was her that passed on the information. If it was her, we need to know how the fuck she got it and how she relayed it. Everyone and anyone who isn't the three of us, Rocky and Flick, are under a microscope. We've had this conversation one too many times. A wet dick does not excuse loose lips. Fuck. We need to get the situation taken care of with the Italians. I'd like to get that run done with just three brothers. It should only take one truck, one driver, a lead and follow. Doing it quickly and under the radar would be best for now. I don't want to discuss routes with anyone or say shit about it to non-officers. I'll wait until the last minute to tell my girl I am leaving. Not saying she has anything to do with this, but she also doesn't know much about club life. I'd like to keep it that way as long as possible. I'll be driving the truck, so I can show my face and let them know that shit was a fluke. Slim, you and Flick can figure out what's what. Tully, I want you here to watch over my girl and the club while we get this shit done."

"You got it, Prez," they both say. Slim drinks his beer as he stares out the window behind my desk. He's always on alert, which makes him the best Sargent-at-arms I could ask for.

"So, that girl of yours is something else. She fits in good Prez, really good. She is going to be a good First Lady for this club. Happy to cover her back, brother." Slim taps the top of my desk, stands, and walks out of my office. I watch him go because coming from him, that's one hell of an honor.

Life can't be this easy, can it? I couldn't just find the woman of my dreams, have my club flourishing, my brothers happy, and club girls not trying to fuck us over.

Ten

I t's been a few months since Vera moved into the clubhouse. She's taken it upon herself to not only whip us old dogs into shape but become everything I ever dreamed of. I am proud to call her mine. Not ashamed to say that my brothers and I haven't always taken the best care of ourselves. We thought we were doing well, having Magda and the club girls cook three meals daily. According to my woman, the shit being cooked isn't always the best for growing boys. The relief on Magda's face said it all. Magda looked relieved as fuck that someone else was going to be in charge of feeding our asses. She's said she only does it because otherwise we'd starve or be as big as houses and she hates dealing with the club girls in the kitchen.

V has taken over the kitchen, and not a damn one of us is complaining. Magda still helps here and there, and she seems happier with my girl. And it's nice to know that Mags has someone she can hand with and talk to. I often catch the two of them cackling link hens in a hen house, and it makes me happy as shit.

V's got all the brothers wrapped around her finger. As the first lady, she has their respect because of me. My brothers respect me, but it's more than that. She's earned their loyalty because of who she is and how she is with all of us.

Currently, though, she is ignoring me right now.

Sitting in the bar watching my girl as she deals with a "situation" between my brother Tommy Boy and his ol' lady Nancy. Drinking my beer, I'm trying to hide my smile. Watching V, I can tell her patience is beginning to wane. I'd warned Tommy Boy to keep his exploits out of the common room until his shit was handled, but the dumb ass didn't listen.

Now he's getting his ass handed to him in front of a few brothers and club girls. Usually, I wouldn't, and as Prez, I shouldn't allow it. In this instance and with this situation, I keep my trap shut. Tommy Boy is in the wrong. It's fucked up how he's dealing with this shit.

Vera and I have our issues at the moment, and she's been ignoring me the last few days. And it stems from me explaining to her that things in the club are not as they are in the civilian world. We play by a different set of rules, and the women in the club should know that, of course, the way I said it didn't go over well. Our ways are set, as are the rules regarding how we treat our women. I don't always agree with them. But the brothers' personal lives are their own. As long as they don't affect the club, I tend to stay out of it. What happens in the club with the brothers and their ol' ladies isn't for anyone to judge or speak on. It's no one's business if a brother steps out on his girl.

And why the fuck did I say that shit.

To say V wasn't a fan was an understatement. My dumb ass then tried to drive the point home by saying that ol' ladies have no place to say a damn thing about what or whom the brothers do. Which caused an argument that has had her ignoring me. My balls are protesting like a motherfucker. She's pissed as fuck, and I get it, even when I tried to explain that that is not how I think or feel. She wasn't having it or listening to a damn thing I had to say.

She speaks to me when she has to, and it is pissing me the fuck off. I know our way of life isn't for everyone, but my girl is taking it too damn far, ignoring me, and that shit ends today. I need her too damn much for this shit to keep on the way it is. Especially when she's not willing to hear me out. I am not a man of flowery words; I say what I mean. But I'm quickly learning that choosing my words wisely and with caution and care should be a priority, even if it makes my balls itch and retreat to do so.

I'm all in with her, and I've said to her more than once that she is mine and I am hers and what my brothers do is not a reflection of what she can expect from me, *ever.*

"You fucker..." V has her hands on her hips as Tommy Boy sits stunned and staring at my girl. He just got off, which means the dumbass is still in a daze. My girl is taking full advantage of his blissed-out state by letting him have it. He is looking up at her like she has lost her mind.

Tommy Boy looks around, and our eyes connect. But fuck him... if he thinks I will save his ass, he's mistaken. I've got to get my ass out of the doghouse before I give a damn about him. I shrug as he stares at me for help. I take a swig of my beer and say nothing. He did this shit to himself.

Vera just got back from the hospital after visiting with Nancy. It's been a few days since we discovered that Nancy had had a hell of a time with her pregnancy. Neither of them told us all about it, whispered the conversation and argument between my girl and me the other night. After we found out what was going on, Tommy Boy made no move to go to his girl, which pissed my girl off.

Tommy Boy has been ignoring calls and pages from Nancy. Even I think that's fucked up, given the circumstances. Because of that dumb fuck, I am walking around rock hard and with aching balls. I know this is a serious situation, but why in the ever-loving fuck do I have to suffer because of that fucking idiot. This shit would be hilarious if I weren't suffering along with his dumbass.

"She has been there for five days, you dick. Five fucking days and your ass has been here getting your rocks off while she suffers a-fucking-lone. Did you know she almost lost it, you prick, Hmm? Did you? You are a piece of shit, and I hope your dick falls off you, asshole." She stomps her foot, shooting daggers at the confused brother. It's hilarious, and I don't know how he could be so fucking confused.

V doesn't give him a chance to respond, and the smirk I had on my face from the fire in my girl disappears instantly after hearing what V just said. Aww fuck. All her words penetrate my brain and every brother in the room. We stare daggers at Tommy Boy and realize that my brother fucked up, *really* fucked up. We are all about our own rules, but even that has a limit. And that dumb fuck reached it.

Damn it, man.

"What the fuck?" Tommy Boy looks around. V stomps out of the common room, making her way to the elevator, slamming her little pissed-off hand into the button, beating the shit out of it like it stole something. She's pissed, and I should go after her, but I like my dick. I will give her a bit to calm down and then try to talk with her.

Fuck

"Yeah, what the fuck, brother? I know you and Nancy have your fucked up thing going on. And as a club, we let it go, but she's pregnant with your kid, man. Your kid... At least show her enough respect to be there when she's going through shit. You should know better than that, man. You shouldn't be here getting your dick wet. I know we all have this whole thing about what happens in the club should be staying in the club. And that's what the fuck ever, it is not my call what you choose to do with your woman. I know we live by our code. This is different, she's in the hospital, and you should fucking be there for her. It's *your* kid, and she's suffering, and what? Don't you give a fuck? Well, if that's the case, I know a few brothers that would be more than willing to treat her right, and you do too. Get your shit together. Because if your shit keeps fucking with my shit, we will have a goddamned problem," I growl out. I can tell the fucker is pissed at me calling him out, but fuck, what does he expect.

I see movement on the other side, and I turn my head to watch. Flick throws his beer in the trash and stomps out of the clubhouse. I nod to Slim telling him to follow my brother. Flick and I are the same when it comes to the women in our lives, so I know he is just as pissed off as V is about this shit. He has made his thoughts known more than once regarding Tommy Boy and Nancy and how he treats her. I'm unsure if his feelings are platonic, but he cares about Nancy more than the man she hitched her cart to. That's clear as fucking day.

I look back over the Tommy Boy as he looks shocked, dumbfounded and angry at why everyone is on his ass about this. I know my brother has a fucked up, weird relationship with his ol' lady but both V and Flick are right. He should be with her right now. I stand and walk over to my brother as he looks around the room, shocked at what just went down. I can also see his narrowed eyes on the door Flick left out of. He's pissed off by Flick's reaction because I know he's thinking the same thing I am. Flick feels a great deal about Nancy. That's a fight for another day.

"I don't tell all of you how to live your lives, but it ain't right, brother. At least show her the respect to go and see her. V wasn't completely out of line on that. It was not ok for her to air your shit in front of everyone, but you have to see shit as we do as she does. Your girl is hurting and alone, and you haven't even been to see her since we got the call. That shit isn't right, and you know it. I'll talk to my girl. But you have to respect her for being there for yours, in a way you haven't. Get your shit together, brother."

I stare at him for a minute and watch all the emotion flick across his face. And then he hopes up and takes off. Hope he and that girl get their shit together. Because their fucked-up situation is affecting my relationship, and I can't have that.

"She, still ignoring you, Prez?"

I whip around and see Rocky staring at me with amusement in his eyes. My eyes narrow on him. He and V have become close, and he is the one that has been taking her to see Nancy at the hospital. So, they spend a reasonable amount of time together. I catch them in the kitchen when V cooks for us, chatting it up. I like that my brother is open with her, but I hate it at the same time. Because all of her giggles and smiles have been lacking toward me, and I don't like it.

"Yeah, but that shit ends today. I am not sleeping another damn night without her in my bed." V has been sleeping in another room in our suite, and I fucking hate that she's been locking me out. I growl out and stomp towards the elevators and only stop when I hear his last statement.

"She gets it, you know. Nancy opened up to her about her relationship with Tommy Boy. She gets it now." I look back at my brother; he has his back to me as he sits at the bar but looks at me through the mirror above it. We stare at each other for a moment, and I give him a nod.

I walk into our suite, and she is pacing back and forth in our sitting area. She didn't hear me come in. She is cute as fuck as she paces, talking to herself. She's full of fire because she is spewing rapid-fire Italian. I think it's cute that she only speaks it when she is pissed.

"Sweetheart, you ready to talk to me now?"

She spins around, looking stunned, as she holds her hand over her chest with wide eyes. "Shit, Brick, you scared the fuck out of me." My eyes narrow as I make quick strides to get to her. I snatch her little ass up and into my arms. She wraps her arms and legs, and I stomp to *our* room. She has ignored me for long enough.

Kicking my bedroom door open, I toss her to the bed. I get flashes to the last time I did this, and she didn't hear me out. I guess this is how I will have to deal with my woman from now on, and I'm ok with it. She stares up at me from the bed with narrowed eyes. But I'm not having that shit.

"Now, sweetheart, we find ourselves in the same positioned we were in not long ago…" With a brow raised at her, I take my clothes off, starting with my cut and shirt. She stares up at me with unsure eyes. Her eyes widen when she sees my hand go to my jeans, releasing my button and zipper. My pants fall to the floor, and my thick heavy cock springs out. I, more often than not, go commando. The first night we were together, I didn't, for some weird-ass reason, but since then, well…

"You have a bad habit of shutting me out when you don't get your way, or we have a misunderstanding" My knee connects with the foot of the bed, making my cock slap against my belly. I can see the heat in my girls' eyes and smirk at her. Grabbing ahold of her legs, snatching both of her shoes off of her feet and tossing them on the floor. She yelps when I unceremoniously remove her pants. She squeaks but still says nothing as she stares at me in surprise.

"You like for me to chase you, don't you, sweetheart? You like to get me all worked up and needy for you." I trail my hands up her bare legs making my way to her core. Spreading her legs, she is glistening for me, and my cock twitches. My finger grazes her core. She lets out a whimper, and my eyes shoot up to her, and I can see she's begging me. Smiling because I know she's been as needy for me as I, for her. I see all the looks of longing and need. None of them have gone unnoticed. Her pride and anger have stopped her from coming to me to deal with her ache and thirst.

"Oh, no, sweetheart, you've been a naughty girl." Smacking her clit a few times, and she gasps in shock. "You will be punished for not hearing me out about how we do things in my club." The lust in her eyes disappears, and the fire returns to them. Smirking at her as my thumb meets her clit, I slowly circle her nub. My cock is painfully hard, but I refuse to let her shut me out and not talk to me over shit she nor I can change about the club. She doesn't have to like it; she just needs to know that I, as her man, am dedicated to her and *only* her.

She whimpers, stopping my movements. Her face is filled with pure annoyance. I stared down at her with an impassive look, showing her that I may be playing at giving her pleasure. I hold back my smirk because I know I am pissing her off. She will not get it when and how she wants; my girl is about to learn a valuable lesson. I push both of her legs together, straddling her thighs. She stares up at me, trying to hold onto her annoyance. I remove my shirt staring down at her as I do. After a few moments of our staring at one another, my thumb goes back to her clit, her back bows, and I am relentless in my pursuit of punishing her. As soon as I feel her nub start to harden, knowing her climax is close, I stop. And boy, oh boy, does that piss her right the fuck off, that fire... Fuck, the fire in her eyes is a big fucking turn-on. I refuse to give her what she wants, and she still refuses to talk to me. So, we will stay at this stalemate until one of us breaks, and that sure as fuck ain't going to be me.

"You have been ignoring me for days, sweetheart. I'm not a man that likes to be ignored." I give her a stern look, but there is no real fire behind it. "All because you disagree with what the brothers may or may not choose to do with their women. Or what those women choose to accept. What did I tell you, Vera...? What did I say you were to me? What promises did I make to you?" I stare down at her with a raised brow. She continues with this silent treatment, rolling her lips into her mouth. She crosses her arms over her t-shirt-clad tits, turning her head away from me.

Oh no, that won't do. Now she's just being a stubborn little shit.

Narrowing my eyes at her, nodding my head at her defiance and stubbornness. Leaning over open the top drawer to my nightstand. If she wants to play this game, then we will play, and we will play *my way*. Smirking to myself. Feeling her eyes on me as I shuffle the contents of the drawer around. My smile widened when I found what I was looking for. I quickly palmed the item, sat back up, and stared at my woman. She looks at me with unsure, questioning eyes and a tiny bit of fear.

"Put your hands over your head, sweetheart. Wrap your fingers around the slats."

"Brick... I..."

"No, sweetheart, you had your chance to talk the easy way. Now... Well, you will do what I say and listen to me. Put them over your head V. And know that calling me Brick will not work in your favor. Unless we are around the brothers, I am James to you and only you."

I give her a stern look. My girl is going to learn tonight how I feel about being ignored. She lets out a huff uncrossing her arms, slowly lifting her arms, and grabbing ahold of the slats on the headboard. Once her hands are around the slats, I lean down, ensuring to keep my body weight off her as much as possible. My lips are close to her without kissing her. Oh, how I want to taste her luscious lips, but now is not the time for that. My hands go to her wrists as I slide the cuffs up. She jumps a little when the cold steel wraps around her wrists. But fortunately for me, I'm no longer seeing fear in her eyes but lust-filled darkness and fire. Good

"Tonight, sweetheart, I plan on teaching you a lesson. You have left me aching for you for *days; now* it's my turn. You *will* talk to me, sweetheart or your *punishment*. I will repeatedly bring you to the precipice of your release, never letting you feel the sweet relief. My sweet—sweet Vera, you need to learn that as your man, I will never do anything. *Anything* that will hurt you disrespect you, or have you doubting what I feel for you."

My voice is gravelly with need. I need to do this; she needs to know that this shit she's been pulling is not ok. As pissed as I have been with her ignoring me. I am also a little hurt, even if saying it makes me sound like a pussy. I made promises to her that I intend to keep, and she needs to trust that I will, regardless of what others in the club choose to do. I am committed to us, and she needs to realize and recognize that I'm not them. We just went through this shit. She spent a whole weekend hiding out because she refused to talk it out, and I'm going to ensure this is the last time it happens.

"Brick?"

Leaning down and kissing her to distract her from what I am doing works. Smiling into her mouth, I feel her trying to deepen the kiss, but I won't let her. Wrapping the cuff chain between the slats and clicking the other into place. When she feels them on her wrists, she tries to pull her arms and gasps when she realizes what I have done. I sit up and stare down at her.

"Brick?"

I would feel bad… But she did this to herself, and by continually calling me by my road name, she's only making it worse for herself. Seeing her eyes' lust, need and frustration only spurs me on more. She bucks a little but not much. She is more testing the cuffs. They are lined so they won't hurt her wrists.

"What… what are you doing? Brick"

"Well, sweetheart…" kissing her lips. "I am teaching my woman" I kiss her cheek. "My ol' lady," kissing her other cheek. "A lesson," and finally, I kiss her neck. "And the next time you call me Brick, you aren't going to like what happens" I nip her chin. She shifts, and I can feel her wariness, but she knows I won't hurt her. I sit up again, pull her shirt up, and place it so it is on her arms and covers her eyes. I kiss my way towards her erect nipples.

124

Take each of them into my mouth, lapping and kissing them. Fuck. Her breath hitches at the attention I am giving her beautiful nipples. I love how she never wears a bra, easy motherfucking access.

"My sweet Vera, my beautiful woman, my heart. I told you I would never lie, cheat, or betray you. You can't be mad at me for what others do in their lives. This is... we are not them. I am not them." I growl as I bring my hands down from her breasts to her hips, scooting my body down the bed.

"Bri... James please"

"No, baby... You need to hear me and hear me good."

I reach the foot of the bed, spreading her legs and staring at her beautiful pussy. I let out a groan as I see her glistening wetness. Fuck. I take a few breaths trying to calm my ass down. It's been too damn long since being inside of her. She needs to learn this lesson, even if my cock is aching.

My hands make their way slowly up her legs. Watching as goosebumps popped up while my fingers trailed up her body slowly. Making my way to her glistening core. I can see that she is fighting herself, trying to stay upset but overwhelmed by her body's response to my touch. She tries to close her legs. I stop her *before* she can squeeze them together to get the relief she's looking for. I won't allow it, and my sweet, beautiful ol' lady needs to learn.

"You were angry with me and refused to hear me out, sweetheart." I kiss her calf as my hands trail up and down her inner thigh. Her whimpers are becoming frustrated as I won't touch the place. She needs me most. Again she tries to close her legs, but I have had enough of that. I crawl up and onto the foot of the bed, placing my knees in the center of her legs, holding her legs open. I stare down at her; her anger and frustration are warring with the lust she's feeling. I smile down at her.

"How many times do I have to say you are mine? MINE. I know it isn't easy giving in to me, giving me your heart, trusting me with your soul. But I am not giving you a choice. I told you the moment I entered your body. You were mine. I will not have this conversation with you again. I will not allow you to ignore me when you are pissed or we have a misunderstanding. You will talk to me. You will never *ever* keep this beautiful body away from me."

My fingers trail from her knees to her inner thighs and her pussy. I slowly circle with my thumb, staring at her even though she can't see me.

"Are you mine, Vera James?"

She tries not to give in to me but the pleasure of my touch. Sucking her bottom lip into her mouth as her upper half twists and writhes, she can't go far because she's restrained. Smirking down at her, I speed up my thumb movements, leaning down, two fingers entering her and her whimper is music to my ears. I can tell she's close, but it wouldn't be a punishment if she refused to answer me. I am not above using her body against her.

And I do.

-VERA-

He's using my need for him against me. And as much as I'm trying to stay angry at him, he is making it damn hard. I know I am being ridiculous and getting upset with him about Tommy Boy and Nancy. But, come on... what woman wouldn't get angry that a man can do whatever he wants and a woman is supposed to take it? Not any woman I've ever met. It's not just about their arrangement or that he can do what he wants. It's the fact that she can't. Nancy told me that she was ok with it. I think she's crazy, but to each their own. No, what I'm mad about, is that these men don't hold each other accountable. I don't care if Nancy is ok with him sleeping around. I care that she's suffering alone, and not one man from this club has made an effort to check on her or make sure she was okay or needed anything.

My brain is a muddled mess, and losing my train of thought while James brings me to the edge for the third or fourth time. I am trying damn hard not to allow my body to succumb to my need. Am I being stubborn? Yes, I am. But in my head, I am doing this for the right reason. I refuse to let my body be used against me. I'm not saying I don't like it because I definitely do. I know makeup sex with us will be amazing. But I don't want to glaze over and forget my thoughts and feelings. I don't want to give into him physically if I can't emotionally. I don't want to feel like my voice is never heard.

This is not the time to take a stance because, oh my.

Yes, I thought that if I ignored my body response, it wouldn't be so hard to hold out for a bit longer. It may seem like the stupidest idea or thought process, but I just—don't know. I needed time to think. And I need him to realize orgasms won't fix everything. Probably not a good time to have this stance, being that we are both playing cat and mouse with my orgasms.

Damnit, He. Will. Not. Win.

He has had enough of me fighting him. I can feel it in his determination and his movements. And I am honestly tired of fighting him, but I need him to understand where I'm coming from. Sweat beads all over my body, my breathing is rapid and– shit.

"I am not angry that you would cheat, lie, betray or hurt me. I am angry with you because your brotherhood has the potential to destroy any woman attached to it." I say between pants trying to get my point across, but it comes out breathy, and my need is obvious. I stare into his eyes, or at least where I think his eyes should be. He still has mine covered with my shirt. His fingers leave my body, and I hear a deep inhalation of frustrated breath, and he shifts on the bed. The weight of his body is gone.

"None of you get it. You wouldn't because you haven't truly respected the women you and your brothers surround yourselves with for so long. And they don't require or demand your respect. What Nancy accepts, or what you all choose to do when relationships aren't the problem, in your perspective. If a man wants to cheat, he'll cheat. That's on him. My problem is that woman has been struggling, and not a single one of you men made any effort to check on her to ensure she was ok. To ensure she had what she needed, I'm angry with all of you." My anger is starting to bubble within me. And my breathing becomes erratic.

"If that is what I have to look forward to. If not a single one of you men would be at my side when I am going through something, I don't want this. I can't. I wasn't built that way. I wasn't built to be a good little woman who made excuses and grinned and bore it if I were to be mistreated or neglected. I wasn't built to give you my all; to be told, that's how the club is or its club business. I deserve more than that. Any woman attached to any one of your men deserves better and more than that."

The realization of what I have said seems to hit him. I can feel him lean over. I hear a shuffle, and then his hands are on my wrists. The cold cuffs leave my wrists. He messages my wrists and pulls my shirt off me so I can see him. What I see... Still leaning over, I see in his eyes that what I said registered with him. What I said makes sense enough to warrant my anger and frustration.

"I…" He stares down at me, and I can see the war waging within him. He understands where I'm coming from and is trying to figure out exactly how to marry the two perspectives.

"I never thought about it. My concern has always been this club and my brothers. None of us have had an ol' lady. It's all new to all of us. Until recently, I never paid much attention to how it all looked from the outside looking in. Nancy is an ol' lady by name only. That is a story for another time. It may be harsh, but that's the reality of their situation. But sweetheart…"

He stretches and lays his body next to mine; he kisses me on my lips and stares into my eyes.

"They are not us. We are in a league of our own. You are a priority, my one and only. You will be the mother of my children. You will have my name because Vera James already has my heart. I will make sure we do better because you are right. We as a club should have been there, we should be there for her, and we will be, I promise you that. You just have to be patient with us. We will make mistakes. And I know I will piss you off because club business is club business. But the women of this club are and will always be your domain, so from now on, instead of ignoring me. I want you to sit my ass down and talk to me, and if you need time, say that, don't shut me out."

We stare at each other for a time, and then there is a moment. A moment I know– I am sure of it. James Brick Masterson is my forever, and I must learn to trust and believe in him– in us. Let him love me as I him.

Even if I sometimes want to ring his and his club brothers' necks.

Eleven

After the little setback a few weeks ago between Vera and me. Things have been good between us; she still has moments when she lets her displeasure be known regarding what's going on in the clubhouse. For the most part, she's happy. And damn, if I'm not happy, she is happy. Tommy Boy continues to be wary around her after the tongue lashing he received. Have to say he is doing better when it comes to Nancy. The two of them are in a better place, thanks to my ol' lady meddling.

Though we are back to business, we were able to delay the Italians regarding their product. We'll be heading out pretty soon to get that shit handled. We are currently meeting about what has been found out about our mole.

"So, as I told Prez, Penelope is a snitch." I hear a few grumbles and raise my hand to get them to shut the fuck up so we can get on with Church. We have a lot of shit to go over.

"Over the last few weeks, I have had prospects on her discretely. Prospects have been watching her here and when she leaves the clubhouse. And they have reported that she is indeed meeting with one of the Keepers…" At that, the brothers at the table explode in anger. I hear a few what the fucks and why weren't they informed. Tully sits watching the brothers, letting them get their frustration out, and I do the same. Their faces went from angry to furious at the last part, and I get it. I'm bullshit about it.

We have kept this information close to the chest for a reason. We wanted to give Hound time to check all the brothers to ensure that none of them were a part of this shit. This is true and not so accurate at the same time; we were able to determine that a few brothers have been a little too loose-lipped around the whores, and I am going to address that shit tonight. Before he continues, I speak up as the grumbling around the table is annoying the fuck out of me.

"You have been told several times about running your mouths in the common rooms and outside the offices. She wouldn't have fuck all the share if you kept club business OUT OF YOUR FUCKING MOUTHS OUTSIDE OF CHURCH" I stop myself before I lose my shit more.

"We lost part of a shipment because those motherfuckers knew *exactly* where we would be and when. And that could have only happened because our now-known snitch got the information from one of *you* dumb fucks…"

"Prez"

"Listen, and fucking listen well. We are new to this area, *not* new to the game. Loose lips can get one of us on the wrong side of the grass. I, for one, am not going to lose a brother. We got lucky with that ambush, and you all know it. I'm for damn sure not willing to lose the contract with the Italians; we've worked damn hard to get it. I will do none of that because one of you can't keep their fucking mouths shut. I will find out exactly who was running their mouths, and I promise they will regret it. I WILL NOT REPEAT MY-FUCKING-SELF. You got me."

I stare all my brothers down; my body vibrates with anger as I accept their acknowledgment of my words. I look over to Tully to let him know to continue. Because if I say much more, I am bound to put a bullet in someone to get answers. I love and respect my brothers, but we've had this conversation one too many fucking times, and this most recent fuck up cost us our stock, time, and money. This bullshit could have cost the contract, and I won't be letting this shit slide. I know that Elijah Barone is only filling us out, and any fuck ups on our part could have him severing our relationship.

"Brick and I were able to talk with Barone and explain the delay. He wants to set up a meeting with the Keepers and was far more understanding than we thought he would be. He knew what went down and about those fuckers getting the drop on us. I have no fucking clue how he knew, and I sure as shit wasn't going to question the man on that. We are all some scary motherfuckers, but that man and stories about how he handles business makes my balls fucking retreat" He shivers, and I know he is trying to lighten the mood in this meeting. I respect my brother and best friend for that. There are a few unsure chuckles but chuckles all the same.

"From what Barone has said, he will contact the Keepers directly. H3e said that Pyro has been trying to work with him for years, so he's got a line of communication with him that we don't. Brick and I decided to let it play out." He looks to me and then the brothers to gauge their reactions. I see a few who seem apprehensive about letting someone else and an outsider take the lead on this. The reality is that the Keepers declared war when they partially succeeded in taking out shipment and putting one of theirs in our club to spy and inform on us.

We don't know Barone well, and even though he says he only wants to work with us, I know that we have to be cautious. We can only take him on his word for now, but I will be wary for a while until we know precisely where this partnership will lead us.

"For now, we have a snitch to deal with. We are not the kind of men that harms women, even though I know we have Magda. I want to put it to a vote. Do we kick the bitch out, or do we use her?" I look around the room to gauge my brother's awaiting reactions and comments. I can see they are unsure because of my earlier blow-up.

Rocky sits up slightly in his chair, and we all take notice. He begins to speak, which grabs everyone's attention, the quiet Treasurer is usually an observer, so when he says, we fucking listen. People think that because he's the clubs' Treasurer, he's less deadly and vicious than Flick or Slim, but that is not the case. He intentionally took his position; he and I knew that his bloodlust could get the better of him, and once you got him going, he would not stop until all the threats were neutralized. And when he gets into that state, he is a hard man to rein in.

"I vote we use her. She is a fucking snitch…" he snarls. "So let the bitch snitch. We don't know what angle Barone is playing at, so we need to keep our guard up even when doing business with him. We have to make sure that we keep all of our bases covered. I know all seems well with Barone, but I'm questioning *how* he knew about the shit that went down. Is it just Penelope we have to worry about? Or do we have someone else keeping Barone and the Keepers informed in our club?"

That has everyone, including me sitting up a little more. He isn't voicing anything that Tully and I haven't discussed. Hound has been doing his thing and has found nothing so far. Barone may have someone in with the Keepers that is keeping him in the loop; as Rocky said, he may have someone here. I am not going to let my guard down either way. Until I know for sure, I am leaving the possibility open, which no doubt will keep my brother's hackles raised and keep them cautious until we have all the information. I feel that Barone is not one to have underhanded and dirty dealings. He may be a Mafioso, but he seems to have a semblance of a moral compass, but you never know. Therein lies the issue of how much I should trust him with my club business and this brewing war with the Keepers.

"I am with Pres; I will personally handle you if I find out any of you fuckers are willingly feeding that bitch information about the club. We got ol' ladies here and a club kid on the way. We don't need an all-out fucking war if we can help it. So, I vote to use the bitch and boot her after this shit is handled." He states in his deep gravelly voice. Face stone cold and without emotion. He sits back, signifying he has said all he needs to say.

"Well, shit, man, that's the most I have heard you talk at once in all the fucking years I've known you." Flick chuckles, as do a few of my other brothers. It's true. Since my ol' lady has been here, we all have noticed that my brother has been a little more outspoken than he typically is. I smile a little at the thought. All my brothers are as in love with my girl as I am and consider her and her safety. Never saw it coming but damn, does it feel good. I look over to Tully, who has a shit-eating grin on his face as I am sure he is reading my mind. He chuckles and tunes back into the conversation at hand.

"All in favor of using her?" I asked with narrowed eyes.

All around the room, I get *Ayes*.

"All right, that's settled. We will use her. You can continue using her and all of her holes as you see fit. Unless you are told, any information you let *slip* out will be designated by myself, Tully, Flick, or Slim. Nothing fucking else. I goddamned mean that shit." I let them all see the seriousness of my words as my glare meets every one of their eyes. If anyone puts my club or my girl in danger, no one will help them or save them because they won't be breathing for long. I let that threat linger before I carry on with other business.

"I know it's been a while since I've received formal updates. What do we got going on regarding the businesses? Is the diner back up and running? Has Stevey boy been able to replace my ol' lady and that dumb bitch yet? How are things going with the strip club, tattoo parlor, mechanic shop, and grocery store? How are we doing on numbers, and are there any other businesses you think we should tap into? With this deal with the Barone's, we have a lot more money and need to ensure that shit gets handled appropriately." I know I am rapid-firing shit to them; I am ready to get the fuck out of here and get inside my girl.

"Aww, fuck yeah, Prez, we got a few new girls, and fuck me, those bitches are Betty's. Steve has been a dick about the changes your ol' lady wanted to see at the diner, but Slim and I set his ass straight." Flick speaks up again, and we all chuckle yet again; my brother is a fucking clown and only thinks with his dick. I shake my head and look over to Rocky to get numbers.

The meeting continues with us discussing our options, how we want to proceed with the business, and the new influx of money. We decided to add a gas station and rest stop to the mix as they are manly cash-heavy businesses which will help us to keep our less than legal business finances under the radar. We are new to the area and do not need the local PD or Feds up to our asses as we continue to establish ourselves.

Just as I am about to end the meeting, the door flies open, and the panic-stricken prospects. Cadence looks around the room with wild eyes, and when they connect with mine, they widen in fear and mine narrow.

"Prospect, What the fuck?"

He swallows hard, and I can see the sweat on his brow. He looks flustered as fuck.

"Cops"

That one word has some of the brothers up and out of their chairs, all except Tully, Slim, Flick, and I. One thing I don't do is allow brothers to keep anything here that could get us fucked over by the pigs. All weapons are registered and licensed on the premises. I don't allow hard drugs, and weed may not be legal, but we indulge. Mostly, the cops don't pay it much attention unless they have a hard-on for *biker scum*. The brothers that left know what the fuck to do. It's clear that the cops aren't here or at least haven't made it this far. This place is vast, and we have a few secrets regarding how we can get around this place unseen. Thank fuck for Hound and his paranoia. He suggested a few changes we hoped we would never have to use, but it looks like we may have to.

"Do we have anything?"

I look over to Tully. He shakes his head no. This makes me sigh in relief, we usually don't, as I said, but with shit with the Keepers, we had to store some shit close to get what we needed to be done. And for a brief moment, my body goes taught. My mind goes to my ol' lady. V went up for a nap, and she hasn't been feeling too well the last few days, refusing to have Doc check her out, saying it's a stomach bug or whatever. Fuck I don't need this shit right now. Knowing damn well, my ol' lady is not down with a stomach bug, but I'm trying to be patient with her. Trying to let her figure it out. I run my hand down my face as I look over at the prospect.

"Talk to me, Prospect."

"When I was leaving the store, after picking up the things your ol' lady sent me to get her, I saw a fucking shit ton of cops in the parking lot. They were all huddled together, and it looked like they were gearing up for some heavy shit to go down. At first, I didn't think much of it. When I was walking back to the truck, I overheard one of them talking about how the intel was good, and they were going to take care of the new biker scum, saying some other shit. I wasn't wearing my cut because we don't wear um in cages."

I raise my brow at that because we don't, but him forgetting in this instance works in our favor. So, that saves him an ass chewing he would typically get. We wear our cuts with pride, so walking around the club or town without them can be perceived as a slap in the face. I look over to Tully, who shakes his head, knowing what I'm thinking—also knowing that we will let the prospect off the hook because he was able to get back unnoticed.

"I hauled ass to the truck and got here as quick as I fucking could."

"Now, boy, you know you are supposed to be wearing your cut unless I deem otherwise. You are right. We aren't to wear them in cages. And thank fuck you forgot to put it back on. You may have saved the club one hell of a headache. Tully, give Jacobson a call and tell him I'm pissed the fuck off for not getting a heads up. He may be earning a larger portion of his sizeable retainer today. Even though his greedy ass is a brother," Cade looks at me oddly, so I decided to throw the kid a bone because outside of officers, not many know Jacobson as a brother, just as the clubs' lawyer. And that's how we like to keep it.

"Cade, Jacobson is a club brother who stays on the outs, not because of anything he's done, but because we decided years ago, we wanted him to be as clean as a whistle and stay legit in the eyes of the law. Doing that also ensures he can get info for when shit like this happens. But I'm telling you no one, and I mean no one outside of officers of this club, and now you know that." I know he gets it by giving him a stern glare to make sure he understands to keep his trap shut when he gives me a nod. The kid is a steel trap and will make an excellent brother. We should be voting on patching him in real soon. I'll be proud to call him brother.

"I need you to make sure that the bar is cleaned up, pack all the liquor you can in the storage room, use the second room, and secure the door. Those fuckers will try and destroy anything they can get their hands on, and that shit is expensive as fuck. Have a few of the other prospects help you out. Make it fucking quick; we don't know how long we got before they bust down our doors. Slim, I want you to stick like fucking glue to Pen. There ain't no telling if this is shit she's involved in. I want to make sure she stays in sight at all fucking times. Better yet, make sure all the club girls are in the main room but stick to that bitch."

He nods and takes off, as does Tully. I look at my brother; he seems as concerned about this shit as I feel. What the fuck is happening around here, and how did we go from flying under the radar to whatever the fuck this shit is.

"I need to go and check on my girl and get her ready for whatever the fuck is going down."

Flick nods and stares at me for a moment, and I can't decipher the look he's giving me. I'm not going to try. I walk out of church and make a B-line for my suite on my floor. I need to inform my ol' lady again of shit we will have to deal with in our lives. Since starting this chapter, this will be our first real experience with the pigs; we've had a few kick-ups but nothing notable. As much as I want to say this will go one way, I am not sure. This is going to be fuck of a learning experience for us all.

I take the elevator up to our room; this shit can go one of two ways. My girl can flip out or do what she has been and take this shit as it comes, which has been her norm. My head whips to the left when I see movement on the ground level as I look out of the window and see precisely what catches my attention.

"Fuck me"

I pick up my pace; it will be a while before they make it up here, at least that's the hope. Taking my key out and unlocking the door, I slipped in and quickly got to my room. When I enter the room, my girl is not in bed, but I can hear a gut-wrenching sound coming from the bathroom, and I don't like it.

"Sweetheart?"

I call out to her to let her know that I am in the room making my way to the bathroom. V is hunched over the toilet, and my eyes soften as she looks up at me.

"*Sweetheart*"

Tears are streaming down her face; if I didn't know better, I would think someone hurt her with how red and puffy her face and eyes are. She has definitely been at this for a while to look this cute and pitiful. I grab a rag and wet it and get her toothbrush, soak it, get her toothbrush, and load it up. Heading to her, I help her struggling body off the floor and start to wipe her face for her.

"Here, sweetheart" Handing her the toothbrush, she begins to brush her teeth and watches me through the mirror, she still has tears in her eyes, and I feel like shit because we have to be quick, and I know what this means. I am a man and have been unprotected with her for the last few weeks.

"I'm sorry," Vera says with a hitch in her voice and my brows furrow.

"Why are *you* sorry, sweetheart? You and I both know that we knew this day would come. I want this with you" I walk up behind her, placing my hand on her ever so slightly rounded belly. She leans over, spitting and rinsing her mouth. She stands straight, staring into the mirror and leaning back into me.

"Sweetheart, I wish we had time to take this moment…" I look away from her—

"But we don't."

- V E R A -

Ugh, I do *not* like this feeling. They say that pregnancy is supposed to be this beautiful, magical thing. That's a fucking lie. For days I tried to deny what I already knew, I was pregnant. And no, I am not a completely useless idiot. I know how babies are made, and the fact that we never once protected ourselves against it should not have me acting so surprised. I have no idea what the denial is all about. Yes, I am young. Yes, I am alone. Well, I–

Having him find me hunched over the toilet, throwing up and sobbing, seeing the understanding in his eyes. I know that from this moment on, our lives will change. But the set of his jaw and the annoyance in his eyes as I narrowed my own at him.

"We don't have– much time. I need to tell you a few things, and I need to be quick about it. But know that I am happy about this baby. You are mine Vera James, and so is my boy. But, for now…" Brick takes a deep breath. The annoyance transfer to worry and then to another look. And I have seen it, that *look* before.

I've seen this look on my father many times.

"Whatever it is, spit it out so we can deal with it and then celebrate." I smile at him, and I am sure it doesn't completely meet my eyes. But how I am feeling and how hard I am working to keep my churning stomach from continuing to revolt. He needs to know that I am here. I will always be at his side, whatever is going on.

James stares down at me, assessing me for a long moment before he speaks. Given my news, I can see he is warring with himself on how to be delicate with me. He needs to learn that I am made of stronger stuff. I wish I could tell him about my life and my family. But I can't, so I will have to show him. He leans further into my touch, closes his eyes for a moment, and takes a deep breath. And when he opens his eyes again, he isn't my James, he is Brick President of LSMC, and at that moment, I know whatever it is that he has to say to me, it is serious. Club business is serious.

"The prospect you sent out to get your shopping done came back. He came rushing into church, letting us know there were cops camped out at the Grocer. He said he overheard them talking as if they were coming for the club. Just before coming in here, I watched them pull up. Not sure how much time I have before they bust in here. But I want you to do everything they say when they do. I want you to stay by my side" He puts his hand over my stomach. "And only speak when spoken to, answer nothing. Our lawyer is on his way. They may rough the boys and me up, but this isn't our first rodeo. I don't want you getting worked up. You got me?"

He leans down, and my eyes widen when he kisses me on my toothpaste-covered lips. Once he releases me, I turn and rinse my mouth out. I quickly return to James and plant another kiss on his lips, mindful not to go too far. We got some *pigs* to deal with. I step back from James and look up at him as we stare longingly at one another. Yeah, these fuckers need to hurry up and go.

"You and the boys are free and clear. Nothing to find, right?"

And yet again, I have stunned my man. I do that often, it seems.

"No, sweetheart, we've got nothing stored here. We don't know the law too well around here yet. So we keep things legal around the club." I stare at him and smile, feeling marginally better, and nod as I step away from him, grabbing his hand and leading him to our door.

"Good, let's do this."

With a stunned looked and a slight chuckle. James and I make our way to see exactly what the situation is.

I can guarantee it is going to be a shitshow. I can feel it in my bones.

Twelve

BRICK

A fter explaining what may or may not go down with the pigs. V
didn't seem too fazed. She told me we would get through this
together, and she will be by my side. Damn, I love this woman. As
we make our way down the elevator, V clasps her hand in mine, silently
standing in her strength and showing me that she will be an excellent first
lady of this club.

I hate that today of all days, we have to deal with this shit. I would like
nothing more than to stay in our suite and worship my woman's body the
way she deserves. We're having a kid; my woman is carrying my son. And I
am truly happy about that. Before V, I wasn't sure if I wanted to share
myself with anyone other than my brothers and club. But with V, it's easy;
she makes me want to be a better man; she *makes* me a better man. With her
by my side, I know that the life we are building will be damn crazy but so
fucking worth it.

Like with all things, my girl gets it. She has been quick to learn and
understand that the man I am with her is not the same man I am to
everyone else. I can't be. For this club to be successful, I have to separate
my love for her and my love for my club. Not entirely, but just enough to
make sure motherfuckers know not to fuck with me and mine. I am a man
that will do anything to protect what is his, and V and my fucking club are
mine.

What I love most about V is that she respects and understands the
club's weight on my shoulders. And as much as I want to stop this elevator
and go back up to our room, she knows that I have my club and brothers to
deal with. Fuck I still haven't dealt with those mouthy bitches after V put

'um in their place yet again. I hope that shit doesn't come back to bite me in the ass later.

The reality of what we have to deal with comes crashing down on me as we finally make it to the ground floor. Hearing the chaos from the main room has my mind reeling. I don't want to deal with this sit today.

Fuck, Fuck, Fuck

V stops outside the elevator as she hears the hollering and shit breaking. She releases my hand and steps behind me. My brow furrows as I look back at her. Her face says it all, and at that moment, I understand. She is allowing me to be Brick and not James, and fuck, this woman is–

"I got your back; I will stay close…"

Before she can continue, three pigs come barreling into the mouth of the hallway, hollering for us to get down on the ground, and I know— I fucking know these fuckers are going to be dicks about this, so I do what they say. I'm not happy about it, but I don't want no shit going down around my fucking girl.

Two officers make their way to me, and one of the fuckers walks straight up to my woman. V's face is a mask of calm, and she attempts to do what they are hollering at us to do. The one focused on her snatches her by her arm, standing her up and in front of him before she even has a chance to get on the ground. My blood begins to boil as he pulls her body against his. V's still facing me, but the fucking pig has her side pressed against his front too fucking close for my liking. It's taking everything in me to keep my shit together.

V says nothing and gives nothing away; her eyes are still on mine. Holding onto her forearm, the pig begins to speak in her ear but not loud enough for me to hear. What the fuck is he saying to her? Whatever he is saying has my woman's eyes flash with fury, but she says nothing and reacts no other way. She doesn't try to get out of his hold, but it's clear that she wants to fuck this guy up. And I try to keep my face blank because my girl is a fucking spitfire, and her eyes say it all. I don't like it, but I am proud of her because she refuses to give him a response that he is goading her for, good girl. I give her a wink making her eyes flash with love and lust. The pig notices, turning his head towards me and staring me down. I pay him no mind as my eyes never leave my girls. I only watch him from my periphery. Taking a page from my girl's book, I will not give this fuck anything.

The pig doesn't like that my girl and I are keeping our shit together, mouths closed. Neither of us reacts to the taunting bullshit they are spewing at us. And these dumb fucks are going for maximum insults. I know they saw my fucking cut; they know who I am. Although I don't recognize any of them, one of them, the one holding me down, looks vaguely familiar.

My *club* may have only been in this area briefly, but the cops know *me*. A few of the guys on the force and I went to high school together. I was raised in this town; my father is known in this town. I was the star fucking quarterback before leaving for the service, for fucks sake. So, they fucking know me and know I am the President of LSMC. And if they had a clue, they know I do not take shit like this laying down, never have and never will, so these fucks better tread goddamned lightly.

It is clear that these three fucks are on a power trip by the way they are spewing their shit about taking my club and me down for our imaginary crimes. They want to show that they've got the power and are more than willing to use it to get to me and mine. Calling my girl and me all kinds of shit, but I continue to ignore them, as does V. Our eyes stay connected. So much passes through them. I can see her trust in me and her determination to show me and everyone else why she is the best woman to stand by my side, and I feel pride bloom in my chest. Nothing, and no one will fucking break us. Jacobson will be here soon enough.

I'm splayed out on the ground. My hands are being cuffed behind my back, and none too gently either. I don't struggle or say a damn thing. I'm focused on my girl. I can tell our lack of response is pissing the pigs off. Especially the one that's manhandling my woman. It's clear as day that my girl is a strong one. She is *everything*, and even though this shit is happening, my chest constricts for how much love and respect I have for her, for how strong she is being and has been for me.

I am hauled up from the floor, clench my jaw tightly, doing everything I can to keep my mouth shut. The pig holding V adjusts his hand and stance, staring at me with malice in his eyes. I know what is going to happen before she does, my blood goes hot, and my anger wracks up to a level even above what I am used to, and I see red because of what that fuck does to my woman next–

What the fuck? That mother fucker is dead.

141

V is unceremoniously slammed into the wall with a thud, and her arms are pulled behind her back. I hear a whimper come from my woman's lips, and that is all it takes for me to lose my fucking shit. With a roar, I push back on the fucker holding me, slamming him into the wall behind us, making him release me. The other fuck tries to get a hold of me, but I bang my head into him, and his nose explodes. Neither of them has any of my attention. Nor does whatever the fuck they are saying to me. It goes in one ear and out the other. My eyes are on their target. That mother fucker is going to get what's coming to him. I don't give a good goddamn what they do to me, but that *pig* crossed a line.

"Get. Your. Motherfucking. Hands. Off. Of. Her. SHE'S FUCKING PREGNANT, YOU *PIECE OF SHIT*." I roar out. V's head is facing me, her eyes are on me, but she seems to be in a daze. I can see she's trying to keep it together. Fucking motherfucker I'm going to end him.

"Get on the ground."

"Motherfucker, get on the ground. I *will* shoot you."

The fuck holding my girl thinks he has the fucking upper hand, as he smirks at me. I watch as he presses his body closer to V's. He brings his lips closer to her ear, taking his eyes off me as he says something to V, who stiffens. He doesn't realize that he is waving a fucking red flag, begging for an ass whopping. His body presses tighter to hers, and he begins grinding his lower half into her. The motherfucker doesn't know that he's signing his death warrant.

His head slowly turns towards me. His eyes are holding mine. It takes a moment, but he realizes he has made himself my fucking target, and his buddies are having difficulty wrangling my ass. There is a reason they call me Brick Shit House. Best believe that. At six foot four inches and two hundred and eighty pounds of pure muscle, I will destroy that motherfucker. My body moves, not feeling what the other fucks are doing to me. I only have eyes on the motherfucker that's hurting my girl.

Faster than they expected, I'm barrel towards the fucker who is smart enough to release my girl and step away from her. I slam my shoulder into his side, tackling him to the ground, and we both go down fucking hard. I hear a scream, but I am focused on doing the most damage.

"You motherfucker, you goddamned cock sucking son of a bitch. Do

142

you think these cuffs will stop me? I will motherfucking end you. You pencil dick little shit."

The cop under me is on his side, and I am on top of him, throwing elbows, knees, and headbutts for all I'm fucking worth. Who needs fucking hands? His partners are yelling and trying to pull me off of him. I'm not having it; I need to hurt him. I need to fucking destroy him. The other two pigs finally pull me up, attempting to reign my big ass in. But I'm not having it. I lift my leg near his junk and nail him between his legs. Sending a satisfied smirk. He yelps and whimpers. The so-called badass pig fucking yelps and whimpers like a little bitch, his eyes clench shut. Yeah, motherfucker.

I continue to struggle, kicking out a few times, trying to nail the pig in any part of his body I can. We are in an awkward position, but I don't give a fuck. This motherfucker needs to hurt. He put his dirty hands on my girl and rubbed his pencil dick on her. I hear V call my name, but I am in my haze, and all I can think about is destroying this motherfucker.

"Get this fucker away from me. Fuck shit, Jonson, Brooks."

Finally, the fucker gets the upper hand. Kicking out, he nails me on the thigh, only hard enough to stun me and give his buddies the ability to get a sturdy hold of me. I am yanked back by my cuffed arms, but I am not fucking done yet. My foot shoots out and nails the fucker on the side of the leg.

"You ever fucking put your hands on my women again…"

"Brick"

My head snaps over to my woman, and I see that she has tears in her eyes, and as quickly as the haze overwhelms me, it dissipates at the sight of her tears. My tough, beautiful woman is pleading with me to stop, calm, and not make this shit worse. Fuck.

"You are fucking *done*, James Masterson."

The fucker I tried my damndest to knock the fuck out stands red-faced in front of me. I ignore him and stare at my girl. Her tears are slowing but still swims in her eyes. She gives me a reassuring look and tries to smile. I can see that she has a knot forming on her forehead. I know what she did when she realized that fuck was going to slam her into the wall. I guess she did see it coming and decided to go head first. Fuck.

When she sees that I am about to go again at the sight of her. "JAMES, I'm ok," she shouts out. My blood is still pumping in my ears, and I am fucking furious. But, for her, I will try to calm the fuck down.

"Brick, I am ok, baby. *We* are OK."

She says again, giving me a small pain-filled smile. She is trying to get me back; I stare at her a little longer. The fuckers holding have been saying shit, but I don't give a fuck. My priority is *her* and our kid.

I am pulled towards the common room, but my eyes don't leave my girl. As they turn me, the fucker I want to end starts to walk towards my girl.

Fuck no.

"You motherfuckers better keep that piece of shit away from her. Or I swear…"

One of the officers shakes his head at my deadly tone; he looks between me and fuck face. If they haven't figured it out by now, if they ignore me, I swear I will lay them out right here and now and not give a fuck about jail time. The guy on my left releases me and walks over to my girl, and the dumb fuck narrows his eyes on him when he gently pulls V from the wall and starts to guide her towards the common room. The cuffs that were on her are now off. The other pig fucker holding me pushes me to follow, but I won't budge. There is no fucking way I am letting that fucker walk behind me. And the pig holding me recognizes that fact.

"Go ahead, Thompson. Captain, is going to have your ass for treating that girl like that."

The guy holding me says in a cold tone. Interesting. Thompson stares his buddy down but says nothing. So, Thompson is *that* guy on the force who won't be missed. Good to know. While the dumb pig Thompson grumbles his distaste, he isn't done. Like before, I see it coming and quickly sidestep him as he tries to shoulder-check me as he walks by.

Once he passes me, then and only then do I take steps towards the common room. When we reach the room, my eyes immediately search for my woman. And these fuckers are lucky because she is sitting with the rest of the women at a table. Her eyes, like before, stayed on mine, and I see her take a visible breath of release when I make my way out of the hall. I give her a wink and a smile taking my eyes off her to assess the room. All my brothers are lined up, laid out, and cuffed in a line in front of the bar. I hear a few chuckles as they see my disheveled state. They know their President well. They know I won't ever go down without a fight.

I strut in without a word and start walking over to where Tully is cuffed, and the pig tries to pull me in another direction. I growl, letting him know I'm not having that shit, and he gets it. I drag his ass over to where Tully is, and he's closest to the women like I knew he would be. Next to him are Slim, Rocky, and Flick. Their eyes meet mine, and I am sure my brothers can tell I am fucking pissed, even if they don't know why. Even if I try to show an air of confidence and nonchalance, they know.

I bend my knees, hitting the floor, assuming the position. The officer holding me tries to help me out, and my big ass appreciates it since I don't have use of my arms. Once I am settled, he lets me go and steps away.

"What the fuck happened? The Boss lady looked like she was crying, and that shit isn't like her. One of the pigs came out looking murderous. The guy holding you had a bloody fucking nose. What the fuck, James?"

My head snaps to my VP. He only calls me by my name when shit goes down or he's pissed the fuck off at me. Right now, I think it's the latter. He knows there is a possibility of V being pregnant, and he, the sentimental asshole he is, doesn't want me hemmed up for shit. Taking a few deep breaths, I look over to my girl, whose eyes are on me and smile at her.

"That fuck that came out before me, he slammed V against the wall. She just told me she was carrying my kid when I went up to get her. I fucking saw red and tried my damndest to beat the shit out of that motherfucker." I say loud enough for my guys to hear me, but not so loud the pigs will. They needed to know to keep an eye on my girl.

"Shut the fuck up, Masterson. You are already in enough shit."

The fucking pig Thompson calls out from where he's standing. He's got fury in his eyes and starts making his way toward me. The guy that called him out earlier puts his hand on his chest to stop him. His fierce eyes meet mine, and I smirk at him. Yeah fucker, cool your jets, little piggy. Your time will come. Understanding further that even his guys think he is a fucking dick and takes shit too far.

Before I can say some smart as shit to him, the front doors to the clubhouse open, and in saunters, our club *attorney* Markus *Law* Jacobson Esquire, can't forget that last part. I chuckle to myself. Tully looks at me like I am crazy, but I shake my head at him. Look back over and watch as Jacobson is stopped by the officer stationed at the door. Jacobson looks around, assessing the room, and his eyes narrow. I can't hear what they are saying, but it's clear Jacobson isn't happy.

Few know that Markus and a few of us were close growing up. They also don't know he prospected for the club the first year. Some of the brothers thought he was only a hang-around. And we will keep it that way for as long as we can. As I told Cade, we decided we wanted to keep our distance even though he is a full brother in the club. That decision was made for a good reason. He can stop shit like this from happening, more often than not. Keep us in the loop using his law enforcement contacts. When he catches wind that we are on anyone's radar, we are supposed to get a call. Sometimes like now, shit slides through the cracks. I get why he's legit and a very busy man. We will have words shortly to figure out what the hell is going on.

Jacobson scans the room again, looking for me, I assume. His eyes meet mine, narrow, and he says something to the pig he's talking to. The pig responds, but Jacobson is already making quick strides toward me. For a lawyer, he is an imposing man. He is nearly as tall as me, not as stocky. I have a good hundred pounds on him, but that fucker is a force to be reckoned with. He has taken down men twice his size.

Jacobson is the kind of man who always felt he had to prove himself in the neighborhood and farmlands we grew up on. He didn't, not really, not in my eyes. He was raised by two tough-as-shit parents that instilled in him to strive for greatness. Because he was black, he was taught and believed he had to do better and be better and damn if he isn't the best of us. I went to the service, and he went to college. A smile crosses his face as he strides towards my guys and me, and his eyes bore into mine.

"Aww, Brick brother, don't give me that face."

I glare at him, trying damn hard not to let a smirk across my face at the message I am reading on his face. He is bringing news, and his shit show has a purpose. That's a thing we are good at doing. We say a whole lot of shit without saying a word. He stares at me for a moment before standing up to his full height.

146

"Give me five brothers, and I'll get you taken care of." He steps away from me and makes his way to a cluster of pigs standing behind the women. I'm assuming someone in that little circle is the fucker in charge of this shit show.

My eyes return to my girl, realizing that her eyes are still on mine, brows furrowed as she looks at me with questions I may not be able to answer fully. I give her a wink. Fuck, this shit is uncomfortable as hell.

They are still tearing apart my club, looking for shit that isn't there for them to find. They're just being dicks. It's going to cost a fuck of a lot to replace shit, especially in the bar. Hopefully, the prospects could get as much as they could be stored away. Yeah, yeah, I know— Why are the booze so important? We're bikers. That shit's fucking gold, that's why.

The front entrance swings open again. I haven't been paying much attention to the shit around me. Focusing on my girl and making sure no one else puts their fucking hands on her. So when the main clubhouse doors open again, I ignore it and only look over when I catch a weird look crossing my ol' lady's face. I adjust myself on this disgusting hard as fuck floor so I can turn to see who the newcomer is.

Well shit.

Thirteen

V E R A

What a freaking day. I finally come to terms and acknowledge that James and I are having a baby, now the clubhouse is getting torn apart, and James nearly destroys the asshole pig who slammed my head, not so gently, into a wall. I can't blame him for getting bullshit. He had it coming, the guy's a dick, and that's being nice. I felt the shift when James looked at me, and the pig noticed. I knew something was coming.

The asshole holding me whispered vile nonsense in my ear. He told me that he was going to have some fun with me. He was pissing me off. I wasn't scared of him in the least, more like furious. I've taken on far worse than this prick. Knowing what he was doing, his goal was to taunt James. Refusing to let it happen, doing everything not to react or respond, I will not tolerate this pig fucker taking my man from me. There was no way I would let this dickhead, goad my man into doing something stupid.

Well, that went out of the window quickly when I was slammed into the wall. When my body began moving, my thought went straight to protecting our baby, my knee and head took all of the impact, and my head and leg hurt like a *bitch*, but I refused to show it.

After James lost it and damn near ripped the pig apart even with his arms at his back, that… that was not something I ever wanted to experience again. James was not even rational. I could see the change in him. Him becoming Brick president of Lucifers Saints Motorcycle Club, becoming bloodthirsty and ruthless. I actually felt bad for the pig because if he knew what was good for him, he would stay far away from me. James made it clear he didn't care that he was the law. If you hurt me, he would come for you.

Another officer pulled me into the common room after all was said and done. I am currently seated with Nancy and the club girls. And this is not a place I want to be, if I am honest. The club girls, for the most, serve their purpose, but as soon as they open their mouths, I want to shove my fist down their throats. I can hear the dumb bitches being dumb bitches, and although my eyes are on James, my hand is wrapped around Nancy's, trying to keep her calm, lending her my strength.

I hear the smart-ass shit they are saying as they try to figure out what they will do to get them out of whatever trouble the club is in. Fucking idiots, if these dumb bitches were smart, they would sit there and look pretty like the cum buckets they are and keep their mouths shut. Because if any of them turn on the club, James won't need Magda; I will destroy these bitches myself.

Where in the hell is Magda?

Looking around quickly to see if maybe they cuffed her with the brothers. If the pigs knew her story, they probably should. But she is nowhere to be found. Interesting. For now, I'm not going to worry too much about it. From my understanding, it's good she is not here.

My hand gets squeezed, and I look to Nancy, but her eyes are on the door. I was staring at James so in my head that I didn't hear it open. I squeeze her hand, giving it a gentle rub with my other, ensuring she remains calm. I know stress is bad for her and her baby. And she has been through enough.

Looking over to the door, my eyes widen for a moment. Standing at the door is a tall, dark-skinned black man who is impeccably dressed. He scans the room with knowing eyes, eyes that continuously sweep the room as he speaks to the officer at the door, and there is something about him that puts me at ease. He is tall and toned but, of course, nothing like my James. But even I can find his bald head, brown eyes, and square stubbled jaw sexy, which I will never say out loud because I've learned that my man is a caveman.

And tends to be all *My women, my dick, mine, mine, mine me no share. Me caveman.*

The man from the door walks over to James, speaking for a few moments. Questions filter my mind, taking in their interaction. James sees and stares into my eyes. He gives me a slight smirk only the way he does and wink. The assurance written on his face calms me a little. A slight grimace flits across his face. He definitely can't be comfortable on the hard floor. Better him than me. I know that's not nice, but I have lady parts.

Boobs, I have boobs. Boobs and hard surfaces don't mix.

Continue watching James, wondering who the man is, and momentarily get distracted by Nancy squeezing my hand. Looking over at her, she has a wariness in her eyes, and I know this is a lot for her. Her eyes bore into my own with a silent question; unfortunately for her, I don't have many answers. I know, being the president's ol' lady, I am believed to know more than I do, which in this case, I don't. I won't let that fact shake my devotion to James and the club.

"It will be ok, just stay calm, and I am sure whatever this is– it will be over soon."

She stares at me for a little longer, breaking eye contact and looking over to Tommy Boy, and like James, he gives her a wink and a smile, which has her relaxing a little bit. Her breath hitches as she leans over to me.

"I am not used to all this. I never thought this…" She waves her other hand I am not holding around the room. "I never thought this would be my life. To be in love with a man, be pregnant, and know that that man doesn't feel like I. I– I never thought this would be my life. But, what can you do when your heart decides for you?"

She looks down at our connected hands with a sad smile. The unshed tears glisten in her eyes, and I know she is fighting not to let them fall. One thing about us ol' ladies is we can never show weakness around the brothers or the club girls. They will see it as a and use that to try and destroy you. And that breaks my heart. Sadness envelopes me thinking about her situation. The fact that she loves a man so completely, and only to be seen in his eyes as he sees every other woman in his life, is a heartbreaking reality. I don't want to judge, at least not anymore. If this works for them and she is unwilling to demand more, I can only support her.

"You have to decide how much you are willing to take. I can't answer that for you, Nancy. I know the club will ensure that you and the little one are cared for no matter what. I'll make sure of it. You are not alone, even if the two of you don't work out. You have a *family,* even if that family doesn't include him. You have…"

A crash comes from somewhere, which makes her jump slightly in her chair and has me turning my head to see where it came from. And as I turn back to her, I see that tear slips out, and I know that she doesn't mean it to happen. Her eyes squeeze closed. Quickly she swipes at her face to get rid of the evidence of her overwhelming emotion. And I hear a few snickers from the club girls. Turning my head towards them, I give them a look. The look that says they will pay dearly.

A lump makes itself known, forming in my throat on its own accord and clearing it a few times to get rid of it. I can't allow my emotions to get the best of me. It is my job as the first lady to keep it together. It's my job to be here for the other women of the club. I know this is new, but I'm quickly starting to understand my role. I will do all I can to care for the club's women even if the men don't. Well, all the women except for the club girls. Those cum buckets are on their own. Half the time, I hope those dumb bitches fall down a flight of stairs.

With all this chaos around us, Nancy has to fight the emotions she is feeling, and my heart hurts even more for her. I squeeze her hand again to gain her attention. "You deserve happiness. True happiness, and if he isn't it, I will be here for you no matter what I will be here."

Her head bobs in acknowledgment. This is hard. I don't want this for her. This time should be the happiest of her life, and it's been nothing but turmoil and heartache. I honestly hope things work out for them, but I want her to be prepared if they don't. As I said, I will make sure of it.

As I watch as she tries to gather herself, I hear a few snickers from behind us. My head whips in the direction, my eyes narrow on the culprits and of course, it's fucking Darcy and the skank crew. I bight on my cheek, trying to keep myself from saying something that would undoubtedly cause a fight, and right now is not the time. My body locks up, trying to keep myself rooted to my seat as Darcy smirks at me. Her eyes travel past me, heating with lust fill. Shaking my head, I'm not playing these games with her. She wants me to react and look over to James, who I'm sure she's directing her slutty ass look toward, but it's not happening. My eyes scan her face lingering on the bruise still present on her jaw from the last time I kicked her ass.

The satisfaction I feel makes a smile grow widely as I look at her knowing that it will piss her off more than any other reaction I could give.

She knows I won't take her crap and made it clear a few times after our first *introduction*. But she is the type of woman who won't give up.

Never hated a woman more than I hate Darcy, And I had to deal with Claire for nearly a year. She serves a purpose in the club. Even if I hate her, she is outstanding on her back, and the brothers love using her. If I am honest, I get a sick satisfaction knowing she acts this way towards me because she wants what I have, and I know she will never get it. James 'Brick Shit House' Masterson is mine and always will be.

Funnily enough, I'm the one that convinced James to keep her around. It may prove a mistake, but we got into it after what she said and did the last time. She deserves the life she chose and the hell of living in the shadow of a woman she hates. Is it unkind of me to feel and act the way I am, maybe? But I don't feel bad about it. I am a mafia princess, and this life isn't far from the one I grew up in. So, some of those mentalities don't just disappear because I am no longer a part of that life.

The decision to give her yet another chance came with stipulations. James sat us down in his office with Tully and Flick and explained that she would not receive any more warnings. If she starts any more shit, she will be shipped back to the mother chapter, no questions asked. That warning isn't sticking.

In my time with James, one thing is obvious. The club girls serve their purpose, but they are selfish, self-centered women who think that because they spread their legs and are protected by the club, they can act however they want. They have another thing coming if they think they will continue to disrespect an ol' lady. I will keep making it clear that I won't stand for it.

James may be in charge of the men, but I am in charge of the women. My smile gets bigger as Darcy's eyes narrow on mine. I raise a brow at her daring her to say or do something. But like always, she tries to push as close to that line as possible without going over. She lets out a huff and turns away from me. Just as I thought she would. I turn back towards Nancy to check on her, and she has gotten herself together. I look over to James, but he isn't looking at me. His head is turned and facing the entrance. The entrance that I didn't hear it open yet again. The entry now has a man I know standing in it. A man that I know.

Don Elijah Barone

My face pales, knowing that if he is here. Oh my– oh g– Oh no– Nancy

152

must sense something is off with me. Seeing him, I try hard not to let my body react any more than it already has. I thought I was done with that life. I thought I was safe. I thought that this would be my home now. I am happy here. I am in love. I– I–

"You ok, Vera?"

I cleared my throat and took my eyes off Don Barone, looked over to Nancy, and plastered a smile. Hoping it doesn't come across as fake. I want to say no, no, I am not ok. I can't say that, though. I can't say anything at all.

Why is he here? I have been careful. I have not contacted or spoken to anyone from the *famiglia* in over a year. My mind raced, and my palms started to sweat. Pulling my hand from Nancys, playing it off as me wanting to check on my head. I don't need her asking questions I can't answer. Not needing her to feel my hands sweating and clamming up. I do not want her to feel or see my body's reaction to the man that saved me, but he is also someone I never, ever wanted to see again.

"Oh yeah, I just got a little dizzy. The pig slammed me against the wall earlier, and I smacked my head pretty good, fucking pigs," Chuckling, hoping that explanation is good enough.

She stares at me for a moment, and I hope the turmoil and fear I feel come off as pain and nothing else. I run my hand through my hair, pulling it away from the lump I received. Her eyes go wide, seeing that I am being honest. Or at least–

Shifting in my seat, peeking through my lashes over to the door. Don Barone ignores the officer trying to talk to him. With an air of confidence, dismissing the man with a few words and a wave of the hand. The officer's eyes go wide and bug out of his head. He sputters a few things and trails behind Don Baron as he struts across the room.

Elijah, the Don of the Barone *famiglia,* is not an overly large man. He is maybe six feet tall if that. Broad but not as large as James and his men. One thing I know, even if he is not built like a fighter, it doesn't mean he isn't one. He is a formidable man. He has a face and a smile that he uses to disarm anyone that comes in contact with him. The ability to make you believe that he wouldn't hurt a fly, which I and everyone in the *famiglia* knows, is far from the truth. Don Barone can make you comfortable to the point where you never see the strike coming. Not until it is too late.

Don Barone struts across the room, tailed by the still-sputtering officer. His hair is short and perfectly styled, and his square firm jaw is set, not in anger but in determination. Watching as he adjusted the cufflinks of his tailored suit as he continued to make his way to his destination.

We Italians are stereotypically supposed to have tan skin that looks sun-kissed year-round. Don Barone's Afro-Italian heritage has his deep brown skin looking like it glows. As weird as it sounds, it's ethereal. Many people don't know that we Italians come in many different forms and from many backgrounds. From our history, the Barones go back several generations in Italy. They continue to be the most feared and formidable within the families. Many in the mafia not only fear them but are in awe of all they've accomplished in the generations. Their *famiglia* has been a part of the mafia.

His dark eyes scan the room, stopping at nothing in particular for a brief moment, his eyes meet mine, and my breath gets stuck in my chest. His eyes move on quickly, and they do not show recognition. Releasing the air that was stuck in my chest and relief floods me. Maybe he's not here for me. He walks past all the guys on the ground, not acknowledging them. I don't dare look at James to see whether or not he saw my reaction. All the men watch Don Barone as he moves towards the grouping of officers and the black man that came in earlier.

My eyes close on their own accord, and I turn my head back to James to see that he and all the other brothers are watching Don Barone. Their faces are set in their LSMC masks, the stern look that gives nothing away. I don't know what they're thinking.

Why is Don Barone here?

His actions clearly show that he is not here because of me. Is he the reason the cops are here? Is he working with James and the club? Or is he working against them?

I won't settle until I know.

I can't.

This is my life now, and I will not give it up. This is my home and my family. The only family I will ever have.

Fourteen

W hat in the actual fuck is he doing here? I know we are supposed to meet this week to discuss what is going down with the Keepers. Hopefully, we'll get a plan to get them taken care of. Did he set this shit up? I will kill that motherfucker, mafia ties or not. I will fuck his world up.

All the brothers, like me, are confused as fuck. Barone doesn't look at us as he walks past, walking toward the group of pigs. Glaring, I watch as he shakes the hand of a few of them. As my fury rises, a malicious chuckle makes its way out of my chest. That motherfucker is *dead*.

"What the fuck is he doing?" Tully asks. Glaring harder, not taking my eyes off Barone when I answer. "I have no fucking clue, brother, but if he had a hand in this shit, he's *dead*. The pigs put their fucking hands on my woman. If he is the cause of that, he's a dead man walking." I say with mirth, my body is coiled tight.

"Calm down, brother. We don't know shit right now. We don't need a war with the fucking Mob. We are still new around here. Our connections aren't as strong as they can be. So, don't say shit until you get all of the facts. Got me?"

Fuck, I know he's right. More often than not, the fucker is. Shit.

"Yeah, brother, I am still going to fuck the pig up who put his hands on my girl. You ain't talking me out uh that shit, not a chance in hell."

He chuckles because he knows how I am about my girl. I know everyone is shocked as shit at how devoted and protective of her I am. She is never far from me or my thoughts. She goes out with Nancy every once in a while, but for the most part, if I don't have a prospect or a brother with her, she's by my side. If I could get away with her going into church, I'd have her there, sitting on my lap while my brothers and I handle business. Call me crazy, clingy, or whatever the fuck. I can admit that my woman is my obsession.

On more than one occasion, Tully and V have had to talk me down from taking her on runs. Club business be damned. I was more than willing to put her in a hotel nearby to keep her close to me. I didn't give a damn if it was an hour or a week. I like keeping my woman close. Is the love I have for her irrational? Sure as shit it is. Do I give a fuck? Hell fucking no, I don't. V is my world. I will protect and love her until my dying breath.

Fuck, when did I become this sappy pussy? My head swivels, my eyes connect with my girl, and a smile breaks on my face at how beautiful and full of light she is. Fuck I love the hell out of that woman.

I feel a kick to my side, and fuck me, that hurt. Motherfucker. I can't do shit about it but breathe through the pain. I hear a few of my brothers holler in protest as the fucker who kicked me kneels next to me. I'm doing all I can to keep my breaths even. Breathing through the pain in my ribs. This motherfucker is going to die. I shift my body to look up at... of-fucking-course officer dead man.

"What, you smiling at dirtbag."

The dead pig walking kneels next to me, speaking quietly as if it matters as if he has much life left on this earth. I will let this dumb fuck spew all the bullshit he wants because by the end of the night, he will have 'nothing, and I mean not a damn thing to say unless he's talking to Lucifer himself.

"I can't wait to take you in. You sweet, sweet girl will be all left alone, and I will be right here, ready and willing to console her and that sweet pussy. She will be my new plaything." The pig fucker says clearly, try to get a rise out of me. Not happening. He'll get his.

He runs his hand over his jaw and looks to where my girl is sitting with lust in his eyes. Oh yeah, he is going to die a slow and painful death. My jaw is tight. In this position, I can't do fuck all in retaliation, but this dumb fuck keeps poking the bear. When I look over, her eyes are on mine and shine with love and trust, not responding or reacting to the pig fucker, hovering over me. She is mine and mine alone. Good girl, don't give him what he wants. Damn, I love that woman. Her strength and devotion are what keep me grounded.

Our lack of reaction has the dumb pig fuck, red-faced with fury, and that has a laugh bubbling out of me fuck, that hurts.

My laughter is full-on and boisterous. I don't give a fuck. My brothers join in cackling, laughing, and chuckling along with me. They may not know why I am laughing my ass off, but they will.

"Oh, man…" I take a deep breath as I gather myself getting ahold of the pain in my side and chuckling. "You have no idea, do you? My ol' lady is way too much woman for you, man. She'll chew you and your little pencil dick up and spit you out. She will devour you in the worst fucking way. Do you think after what the fuck you did, she'd want fuck all to do with a power-hungry pencil dick pig like you? She'd rather sit bare-assed on the hot California road than be near your micro dick. Ain't that right, sweetheart." I look up to my girl, who gives me a wink. Her cheeks heat up, but my girl, embarrassed as she is, plays along.

"I couldn't imagine going from a big strong man like *you* to some overcompensating pencil dick. Call me crazy, but I kind of became rather fond of orgasms. Not sure a micro mini dick will have the same effect."

She says with a straight face. And all the brothers lose their shit, laughing their asses off. Little piggy Thompson sputters and leans further down towards me. But thinks better of continuing on his taunting as he looks around, realizing we've gained an audience. Oh yeah, fucker, I remember the warning you were given by your pal earlier. I can see in his eyes that he does as well. Good, this is going to be fun.

"Aww fuck, you did, didn't you? You thought that you'd hem me up and what? My girl would come to you begging you to let me go. Oh shit, you've been watching too many pornos, *Officer Thompson*. My ol' lady isn't going to come to you crying on your shoulder saying *she'd do whatever you want* to get me out of jail. Ohhh shit… fuck, you are fucking out of your mind. Does that shit actually happen? Oh, you sick fuck."

I laugh even harder. Damnit, this shit hurts.

"Oh damn, Prez. This dude is like them weirdos on those shows. What do they call them predators? Yep, that's what he is, a damn *predator*. Man, you are crazy. How the hell are you a cop? Praying on innocent women.

157

Somebody needs to take your badge and put your ass in one of those crazy hospitals." Blink hollers out, and all the brothers grunt in agreement. He isn't lying about that shit. Officer pig fuck ignores everything Blink says, but he isn't the only one who keyed in on this conversation. And this dumb ass idiot is playing right into my hands. Divide and conquer.

"Why? Why would a woman like *that* want to be with a low-life like you? Earlier was a misunderstanding when she found out you are nothing but a common criminal. I will have her. I *will* have her. And I will fucking destroy her snatch and make her mine."

"Oh *shit*. You are fucking delusional. Shit man. Who fucked you up like this? So you are going to what? Take my women against her will?" I say the last part loud and clear. And I know he knows I just goaded his dumb ass into saying shit he shouldn't have.

Fucking idiot.

"What? That— I didn't..." He stutters, stands and looks around the room. He realizes what he has done fucked up, and I try not to let the satisfaction show too much on my face. But I can't let that be it. Oh, not I am going to make sure this fucker destroys himself.

"What, that's what you said. You said, and I quote, 'I *will* have her. And I will fucking destroy her snatch and make her mine' or did I hear you wrong?" I quark a brow at him.

He stands stunned. His face is red as shit, and I know he is fucking livid my criminal ass just got the best of him in front of his cop buddies. Yeah, fucker. I wanted them to hear you talk your shit. It's clear as fuck that this dick is already skating on thin ice within his department. So, I have no problem pushing this pussy over the edge. It will be easier when he fucking disappears because he won't be missed. Even if he is, his fuck ups will make it hard for anyone to care to look too hard for him. No one will look too hard for a sick fuck like him, and he may not know it, but my brothers and I do.

"Fuck you, Masterson" He seethes and looks around frantically as almost all the guys in earshot stare at him with disgust in their eyes.

He goes to try and kick me again...

"You better step away *now*, or there will be problems," Barone says with a calm, even commanding voice before the blow connects. And even if I am pissed and think that asshole is why my club is being torn apart, I have to give him some respect for stepping up.

"Who the fuck are you?" Dumbass puffs his chest out, trying to look intimidating. It doesn't work, and I chuckle. His head snaps over to me, and he glares. I just smile up at him, ignoring the twinge in my side. We both hear a throat clear, looking over to Barone, my brothers, and the cops standing around him.

"Who I am, does not matter. The matter at hand is that you and your compatriots need to pack your things up and get out of here immediately. This isn't the wild west; you don't make the rules. This..." Barone's eyes narrow at the pig, waving a piece of paper in the air. "This is *not* a warrant; this is a poor excuse for a letter requesting documentation of ownership of this property. This property was recently sold at auction to the man you have unjustly handcuffed on the ground. You have no grounds or reason to be here. You and your department are destroying the property of these law-abiding citizens. And I, for one, think that your Captain should hear about your disgusting behavior towards these men and that woman."

Well, I'll be damned. Guess the fucker isn't why these shitheads are destroying my club. I guess I don't have cause to slit his throat.

"That's not— No, That— You were given the wrong paperwork. There must be a mistake. I..." Little piggy sputters.

"*Officer Thompson,* you mean to tell me that we DO NOT, in fact, have a warrant to search the premises. That someone, whether you or someone in your department, has the sheriff's department and me here unlawfully searching this property. Is that what I am hearing?'

Oh shit. The sheriff pig looks at his comrade Thompson, and he's fucking pissed. I guess no one thought to look at the paperwork before mounting up. This shit gets better and better. This guy is so fucked. I try to hold back my laughter because I know that as soon as I start up, my brothers will also. I'm relishing the fuck out of the fact that this prick is making it easier for me to get my hands on him. My smile gets wider as I stare at the fucker who thought he would get one over on my club and me.

"No, fuck that. We may not have the correct paperwork *right now*. But that is just a clerical error. It's coming, my office may have given me the wrong papers, but the warrant still stands. It was signed by the judge this morning. I was there. I saw it with my own two eyes."

Really? We are going with a clerical error. This prick. I am sick of this shit. Time to dig his grave a little deeper. I look over to V and give her another smirk and wink. I can tell that the stress and strain are getting to her, and I need this to get wrapped up so I can get my woman checked out. This shit and what that fucker did can't be good for her or our kid. The officers continue to bicker, but I have had enough.

"*Well*, unless you have the paperwork right here and right now, this shit is unlawful as fuck. You slamming my pregnant woman against a wall is *unlawful* as fuck. Someone better do something about it. And get my boys and me out of these fucking cuffs. And do me a solid, and GET THE FUCK OUT."

I stare with fire in my eyes at the lying sack of shit, looking around and arguing with the other sacks of shit that have been fuckin up my damn clubhouse.

"For the record, gentleman, the city and county will be hearing from my office regarding this unlawful and highly unethical search of this property. I will also be filing suit for damages. And if I am not mistaken, Mr. Masterson just stated that during this unlawful search, his woman…"

Jacobson looks over in the direction of V and Nancy. Even though they have not been formally introduced, he knows she belongs to me. My beautiful little pixie wouldn't belong to anyone but me. She is my light, the love I see in her eyes consumes me, and I loathe that she has had to deal with this shit. Watching her struggle to keep her mask firmly in place is hard as fuck. Knowing she is doing all she can to show everyone that she is the first lady of this club and that no one will break her, shining bright, showing her strength. I am so damn proud of her for being so strong through this shit.

Shaking her head a little, she looks over to Jacobson.

"Vera Ja…" She clears her throat, eyes turn to me, and my brow furrows for a moment. Then I realize what she is doing by the question in her eyes. She is looking at me for permission. Permission she doesn't need, but I understand why she is asking. She doesn't know him or his intention, regardless of the words he's spouting. I give her a nod and smirk. She relaxes and releases a breath. The tension in her releases from her shoulders, and she answers him.

"My name is Vera... Vera James," giving him a small smile.

He nods to her and continues. "Miss. James will need to go to the hospital due to the stress caused by this and any injuries your officers caused her. Your department will be held liable for her hospital stay due to this. And if *anything, I mean* anything, happens to her unborn child because of this fishing expedition. I will rain hell down on your departments."

Jacobson's usually calm and relaxed demeanor is no more. His body is taught, and you can feel the fury coming off of him, and it isn't going to be pretty when he blows. Unlike us, he uses the law to exact justice and revenge. I've seen it firsthand. He is a beast regarding the law, and his intelligence is unmatched. I guarantee he and Hound are going to dig deep into office Thompson. They will find all his skeletons, and we will slowly torture him, not physically at first. Then I plan on making his death slow and painful. I know my brothers will ruin him in the public's eyes. And as much of a pussy as it may make me sound, I am fucking giddy.

Officer fuck face is still sputtering and bitching at the other officers as a few of them start removing us from our cuffs. The other pigs are overruling him, and it is chapping his ass. My eyes stay on him. I let him see the amusement in them. He has a hard-on for us— more importantly, me. I have never seen the fucker a day in my life. None of us or our girls have had any run-ins with the cops, not seriously, so what the fuck is his deal? Fuck. As much as I want to slit his throat, we will have to figure out his deal before I destroy his life.

There are some severe glares, shaking heads and narrowed eyes pointing in his direction. I pull myself off of the ground when I am uncuffed. My ribs still have a twinge from the cheap shot the fucker got in on me. But I'll be damned if I show it, I know nothing is broken, but I will have a bruise. If I know my woman, I know she will lose her shit about it. I'll have to distract her later after all this shit is said and done. Fuck, it was supposed to be an easy day.

As soon as I make it to my feet, I am plowed into by my sweetheart, and I try to hold back a wince as she buries her head into my chest. She holds onto me like a lifeline, and it's clear as day that she is not as ok as she may have seemed. I wrap my arms around her, pulling her even closer. Taking in her scent of Citrus and Lemongrass always calms me and has since the first time I held her in my arms. I kiss the top of her head once I realize the tension she was holding onto was released, and she relaxes in my arm.

I pull away from her, look into her beautiful eyes and see the love, devotion, and confidence she has for me reflected in them. I narrow my eyes not because I am angry with her, but because I also see the pain she is trying to hide.

"Don't do that, sweetheart."

She knows exactly what I mean, so she breaks eye contact with me, putting her head back into my chest to hide from me. I am not having that, though. Releasing one of my arms from around her, I gently grasp her jaw and lift her eyes to me; I ignore all of the shuffling and arguing going on around me and focus on my girl.

"You are hurting, sweetheart. You can try, but you can't hide from me... I see it. I see you. As soon as these dumb asses are out of here, I am taking you to the hospital to get you and our little one checked out."

Kissing her lips, I stop her from attempting to argue with me because I know it's coming. My woman is the first lady, she takes that role seriously and will put cleaning up the club before herself, but now, she needs to recognize and realize it isn't just her anymore. She is carrying our son. And he comes first before me, her, and the club.

Our kiss lasts longer than it should when I hear a moan from my girl. I have to pull away. And fuck do I hate doing it.

I look around and see my brothers have already started to move around and get things situated. Jacobson, Tully, Flick, Slim, and Rocky stare at us with huge smiles. Despite the shit that just went down, they all heard the news about my girl and our kid she's carrying.

"So, we got the future Mr. President baking," Tully says, chuckling as he pats me on the back and sends a wink to V. She blushes and looks down.

Movement catches my eye, and I look at Barone, staring down at my girl, looking everywhere but at him. I am not sure what the look he gives her is. I clear my throat, and his eyes find mine.

Stepping closer, Barone makes his way to our group. I shift V to my side, keeping her close to me. As I said, I know my women. I know she's itching to help clean up the damn mess. It isn't happening. I want her close until I can get her out of here and our kid checked out.

"Well, Masterson, I am sure you were ready to rip me apart," he says with amusement. He's not wrong, but I'll never admit it. "Since a few things have come to my attention about you and your club, I can tell you that I will never have ill intentions for you or your club. I have a few vested interests in the area. You aren't the only one to find a slice of happiness around here. So you'll see more of me around these parts."

He smiles at me and then down at V. Looking down at her, I see her eyes widen at him. They stare at each other for a few moments before Barone's eyes return to mine. I don't know what that was about and am unsure whether I want to question it. I am sure with her Italian heritage V has heard of Barone and his reputation. I leave it at that because I doubt it can be anything else.

I am not sure when Barone and I got to this level of comfortability in our business relationship, but I will not decline to be on the right side of Don Elijah Barone. He is the Don of the Italian Mafia on the West Coast. The motherfucker is crazy as shit and feared by all those on the wrong side of the law. Nothing happens in the underworld without him knowing about it, whether in his territory or another, so I shouldn't be surprised he's made his presence known in my club's neck of the woods. And being that we were meeting soon anyways, I don't mind, and I'm not questioning it. Maybe I should, but I have priorities.

So, no, I am not going to contradict the clear statement he is making by being here, by stepping in and having my clubs and me back. I have questions on how he knew this shit was going down and when this man has his hands in everything, which could be good or bad for my club. That shit is for another time.

"Barone, if you want to stick around, you can, but right now, I need to get my ol' lady and kid checked out. Tully..." Both men look at me. And my little spitfire interrupts

"Make sure the club girls don't slink away. They better help clean this mess up. Also, I think Nancy should get checked out, and the stress can't be good for her or the baby either." She looks over to where Tommy Boy is holding Nancy, who is visibly shaken up, and Tommy Boy looks up at me and gives me a nod. Then my girl turns her head glaring toward the club girls, and I squeeze her to me. She hates those girls, but she keeps them in line, and now I know she is right. If given a chance, they will slink off.

"Your right, sweetheart. Tully, you will be in charge of ensuring the prospects get what needs to be cleaned up. V is right. The girls better be helping. Anyone who isn't, I'm not going to play games. They're gone. Everyone, including them, must pull their weight to get the clubhouse back in order. Who knows what shit they did upstairs or what they damaged. This place got fucked up pretty damn good. Make a list for Jacobson so he can do his lawyering shit. I don't want the club paying a dime out of pocket for any of this shit. If anything needs to be replaced today, ensure you get receipts from Rocky."

We all chuckle because this place will take a while to get back in order, and we all know it. Tully will have a hell of a time wrangling the club girls. Those bitches are bound to make excuses about why they can't help. I narrow my eyes as they stand around, snickering and cackling as they watch us. It pisses me off that they haven't got to it, but I am damn serious. If they don't put in work, they're out. And I haven't forgotten about our little snitch. I catch Cade's eye as he right's a few tables and chairs. He gives me a nod—he knows what I want. I watch him walk over to Penelope; he'll keep an eye on her.

"Jacobson, get with Rocky once we got everything cleaned up and tallied up. He will have all the receipts and prices and whatever you need regarding what needs to be replaced. He is the one to keep track of all that shit. I want Slim and Flick with me. Barone, you can either take a ride with me, or we can meet back here later to discuss business."

Barone gives me a nod, and something passes in his looking like approval, as he stares again at my women. Looking down at my woman, I squeeze her side.

"Let's get out of here and get you and our boy checked out."

Fifteen

BRICK

Snuggled in my arms, V is exhausted, and I don't begrudge her for it. She had one hell of a day. If I'm honest, we all did. With that prick slamming her against the wall, the stress of what went down was hard on my girl, even if she tried to act like it wasn't. The pigs and their fucked-up warrant put a wrench in our day. My jaw clenches and my arm tightens around my sleeping woman as I ponder today's events. My girl wiggles a little, and I try my damndest not to squeeze her to me too tightly in my anger and annoyance. But I'm still fucking livid.

Today was supposed to be a day of celebration. As soon as V came to terms with what I already knew, I wanted to ask her to be mine in all ways. Ask her to be my wife. Today we were supposed to be celebrating finding out about our son. That's what today was supposed to be. I'll have to be patient a little longer; it will all happen soon enough. She's already mine, and I'll be damned if my kid is going to come into the world and its mother and I don't share a last name.

I've got some planning to do.

Instead of celebrating, I am snuggled up with my exhausted woman as my brother drives us back to the compound. My V is tough as shit, but in the hospital, I saw for the first time her vulnerability. It had shone bright as day in her eyes. And I never want to see that shit again, not like that. I saw fear for our unborn child, and it damn near crushed me. I could tell she was trying to keep me from laying waste to every fucker at the hospital.

She tried to hide the worry in her eyes, but I saw it. She is tough'en, but she can't hide from me. I saw the relief she felt the moment our eyes saw the little one on that weird-ass screen and heard the words that our kid was ok. All the tension she was holding left her body, and the tears for both of us started. I am a dad; I am a fucking father. That moment was one of the best moments in my life. Then and there, I promised that nothing would ever take her or our boy away from me. I am going to give them the best fucking life.

Well, I'll be damned. I'm a dad.

I don't get the luxury of relishing what today meant for my girl and me. The instant we crossed the compound gates, my brain started running through everything that needed to be done. I have work to do with the pigs showing up and then Barone. Also need to make sure my love is resting.

She has already tried to scold me for carrying her everywhere from the time we left to go to the hospital to now. Her feet haven't touched the ground. If I have anything to say about it, they never will. She's going to have to get over that shit. My boys and I will ensure she doesn't lift a single finger until our boy comes into this world. I may get on her nerves and piss her off, but I never want to feel what we felt today, ever again.

After the truck comes to a complete stop, I look up to see Flick staring at me through the rearview mirror, and I know he knows. I will be a nightmare when it comes to my woman. He chuckles and shakes his head, and exits the vehicle. He can't be too much of a dick about it because it's his nephew she's carrying; he will be just as overprotective of her as I am, if not worse.

I may have grown a pussy, but I don't give a fuck. My girl and kid are and will always be a priority. If me being an overprotective prick who fusses over his women makes me a pussy, then so be it.

As I walk through the clubhouse doors, holding my exhausted woman in my arm. Seeing that my brothers have everything in hand, they could get the shit those pig fucks destroyed in order for the most part. I did see a stack of broken tables and chairs and other shit outside, which I am sure will be replaced soon enough. I look over to Rocky, whose standing near the door, and I tell him quietly that I need to get V settled and that we will have church shortly.

Movement catches my eye, and I look over to see Barone staring not at me but at my woman, and that has my hackles rising. Why the hell does he keep staring at my girl?

166

With my brows furrowed, I stare down at Barone. I know I need to get to the bottom of whatever is going on with him. Because I don't like the feeling I get when I see his eyes on V. I was going to let it go, I really was. It's happened one too many times for my liking. Barone notices my glare, and his face transforms from the soft assessing look, reverting to the impassive hard one he's known for. I shake off whatever I am thinking and make my way to the elevator. Tully follows me, looking at him. My brow creases. I know he cares about my girl and all that shit, but I can take her to my room alone. Neither of us needs a damn babysitter...

"Calm your ass down."

Shaking his head at me, not for the first time, I hated that my best friend could read me. Can't help that I'm on edge. With the pig putting his hands on my girl and now Barone eyeing her up. Maybe I'm being a dick about other dicks being around my girl. If I'm honest, I don't give a shit that I'm being overprotective of my girl, she's been through enough, and I will protect her, end of.

V shifts in my arms, calling out my name. I look down and see that she's still sleeping, realizing that even in her dreams, she looks for me. I smile a little at that. Kissing her on the top of her head and tightening my arms around her has her settling deeper into me.

Tully and I don't speak as the elevator doors close, nor do we talk about the ride up to my floor. And I'm grateful, my mind is reeling, and I need these few minutes to get my thoughts in order.

Once in our suite, Tully helps me open the doors but doesn't follow me into our room. The fucker knows better. Walking over to our bed, I softly lie V down and start undressing her. One thing I've learned about my woman is that she is not a fan of having a lot of clothes on when she sleeps. According to her, clothes are too constricting, and she gets hot. I chuckle because damn if it isn't true. I don't know why it is, but she turns into a damn blazing inferno when she sleeps. It's the craziest shit. But the killer thing about it all— is that she has to have a blanket or sheet covering her no matter how hot she is. Weird shit, but I love her little ass anyway.

Once I have her settled and undressed, I cover her up with one of the sheets, pulling it to her chin. She shifts onto the bed, pulling my pillow into her chest and cuddling it. V has been through so much shit since giving me a chance, even though she doesn't talk about it. I know her past weighs heavy on her, not having her family and being in this world alone, she keeps a brave face, but I know it affects her. Staring down at her, I vow not for the first time, not only to her but also to our little one, that I will make sure every day from now until forever that she doesn't regret letting me in her life— or letting me love her. She will be my wife, the mother of my children, and the queen of this domain. I will cherish her, protect her and love her.

Sitting next to her on the bed, I stroke her cheek lightly. I hate to disturb her, but she needs to know I've got to work. Damn, she's too beautiful for her own good. Slowly she shifts in the bed, her face leaning into my touch, turning her head, her eyes flutter open to meet mine. Giving her a full-on smile, dimple and all. Her eyes are heavy with exhaustion, and I don't want her to wake up too much. I lean down with my lips close to hers.

"Sweetheart, I am going to be gone for a little while. I've got to handle some club business and have church with the brothers. I want you to stay up here and get some rest." She goes to say something, but I stop her with a peck on her lips. I know V, as much as she is concerned about our baby, she is as worried about our club, our family. Doctors' orders were simple. She needed to be off her feet and take it easy for a few days. Shaking my head, I continue. Giving her a stern look, and I can see her conceding.

"Doctors orders, sweetheart. I'll have one of the prospects in the living room. If you need anything, let him know he'll get it for you. I mean it, Vera James. You stay in this bed and let us take care of you for a change. Our little one needs you to keep him safe and healthy."

Staring down at her, I watch the war wage in her eyes. She knows I will not change my mind about this, so she gives me a sleepy nod and a small smile. I know her. She will disregard everything to take care of everyone else. And I am not having it. My following words could have been at a better time, but I am tired of holding back and holding it in. And I know it will help her to understand where I am coming from.

"I love you, Vera James, and today you made me the happiest man in the world. Happier than I have ever been in my life. You and our boy are everything to me, and all I want to do is deserve you. Let me do that. Let me do all I can to deserve, protect and provide for you. Please, my love, let me do what I was born to do. Please listen to what the doctors told you and rest for me, for him."

Her eyes begin to shine. She sees everything I want her to, and a gasp leaves her lips after she finally completely processes what I just said. Hearing me tell her I love her for the first time is a shock to her. It's true and has been for quite some time. I smile and kiss her lips. A tear slips from her eye as I stare down at her, my hand is still on her cheek, and my thumb wipes it away.

"You love me?"

I ask with emotions clogging my throat, staring into her eyes. I know she does, but a man's ego needs to be stroked every now and then.

"You know I do, James. I love you so damn much that it hurts sometimes. You and I were meant to find each other. We were meant to be the other half of each other's souls. Thank you for taking care of me and peanut. Thank you for loving me… us. And thank you for giving me a life I never thought I was good enough to have"

She chokes up, and the tears start to fall a little harder, and I'm man enough to say that I shed a few myself. Only she will see this side of me; only she and our children will ever know James Masterson, the man. Her eyes clench shut for a moment as she takes a few breaths, she lets out a little chuckle, and it surprises me. I look into her eyes and shouldn't be shocked by what she says next.

"Go do manly Presidential ass-kicking stuff and be extra badass. I need sleep. We need sleep. Your little devil child is sucking the life out of me. I am so glad you're here to put it back in. Love you, not go. Shoo."

She pushes at my chest a little. I chuckle because my woman is the damn best of me. Even exhausted and overwhelmed, she is just… amazing. Kissing her lips again, I sit up, and we stare at one another for a little longer before a knock at our bedroom door. I know it's Tully, and as much as it pisses me off, he's right to hurry my ass along. It doesn't take much for me to want to strip down and climb into bed and lay with my woman.

"All right, sweetheart. I'm going to go. Remember, the prospect will be out there and get you whatever you need. Don't leave this suite till I get home, got me." I raise a brow at her.

"I love you. Vera James."

She smiles, agreeing. Hopefully, she will do as the doctor and I say and rest. She tells me she loves me as I stand from the bed. Taking a few breaths, I prepare myself for what's to come and leave the room.

Time to get to work.

The prospect is waiting at my front door when Tully and I exit my suite. I make sure to let him know to get V anything she needs and not to disturb her if it's unnecessary. He's a good kid like Cade. Jasper will be patched in soon. He is one of the few prospects I trust with my girl. And also one that my girl trusts implicitly.

We have a shit ton of business to handle, and with V pregnant, I don't need shit kicking back on the club like it did today. We could have lost our son if that pig took it too far, and I can't let that shit go. My blood begins to boil thinking about the fucker who put his slimy hands on my girl. I silently seethe, thinking about everything I want to do to him.

Tully and I walk to the elevator, knowing he has something to say. I can feel it. He wouldn't have followed me up to our floor if he didn't. He's protective of my women, and I get that, but that wouldn't have him following us.

"Spit it out."

We get into the elevator, and he is a little pensive for a moment. I can tell he is trying to gather his thoughts, which means he's trying to figure out exactly how not to piss me off.

"When you were gone with Boss Lady…" he pauses, rubbing the stubble of his chin.

"Fucking Christ, Tully. Spit. It. The. Fuck. Out."

"Damn man, all right, James. Cool your shit. When you were out, Barone was asking a lot of questions. A lot of questions about Boss Lady. Asking about how you treat her? Is she happy? Shit like that, and I didn't like it. He seemed too interested, and it was rubbing me the wrong way. I know you. I know how protective of Boss Lady you are. So, I am telling you this so you're prepared. Because I know that man has no filter and will ask you flat out the same shit. And for fuck's sake, don't blow a damn gasket. He's Italian, and she's Italian. They may not have rolled in the same circles, but he may have known her people and her past. So, don't think of any of that depraved shit I know is floating in your head. He may be

170

genuinely interested in making sure she's good. Your woman affects people, and people want to put her in a bubble and take care of her. Don't read too much into it just yet."

Tully stares at me, trying to gauge my response or reaction. And if I am honest, I'm conflicted. For some reason, thinking back, I haven't felt that Barone was a threat to my and V's relationship. He seemed more like a concerned older brother than a prick wanting to steal my women. Breathing through and allowing my thoughts to process. I'm trying to remain rational. With everything going on, I don't need a war with the fucking Mob.

"Fuck, I don't need this shit right now. But I get you. And if I am honest, I don't think his asking around is malicious. The shit that went down with her family happened in his backyard. I know he knows about it; the fucker knows every damn thing. How much, and why, who knows? But like I said, I don't think he's asking all that shit for any other reason but concern. Because if it's otherwise…" I wipe my hand down my face. "Right now, I just want to get the club girls handled, get this place cleaned up, get the Keepers situation taken care of, and kill officer fuck face. Is that too much to ask?"

"Um, about that…"

"About what? For fucks sake," I say, annoyed.

"Two girls, Penelope and Darcy, went missing while we were cleaning shit up, and Cadence is gone. I know you had him on Penelope, but no one has seen or heard from him or them for hours. Something doesn't feel right about that."

"Fucking, shit– damnit when it rains, it pours. Why? Why does today, of all fucking days, does shit have to hit the fan? Get everyone into church, including fucking Barone."

Stepping out of the elevators, I make my way toward church to await my brother's arrival, and I need time to calm my ass down. Tully heads in the direction of the common room, where I know the brothers are all waiting for their marching orders. Damn, I just wanted an easy damn day. Now I got two club girls and a prospect missing, a pig to kill, and a mafia Don to question his intentions towards my woman.

171

Sitting in my chair while all my brothers get settled in church. Looking around the room, I notice, not for the first time, that we will need more space. We started this club two years ago with only twenty brothers. Now we are at nearly fifty, with the transfers from other clubs, nomads wanting to settle down in one place, and the prospects we've patched in. So, we are bursting at the seams. I'll have to get with Tully and Rocky soon to see about expanding this room or maybe making one of the outbuildings into a chapel for full club meetings. But, right now ain't the time. I'm brought out of my thoughts when Tully sits next to me. I look around, ensuring everyone is situated and they are being boisterous as ever.

"All right motherfuckers, right now is not the time to be talking over me." I slam the gavel down, signaling church has begun.

"We have a shit ton to talk about, and my patients are fucking thin. So, please keep your shit talking to a minimum and relevant because I would hate to have my temper cause me to put one of you down. I'm serious, brothers. Today has been a shit-filled day. Even after finding out my girl is carrying my kid..." The rooms erupt as not everyone heard the news earlier. As all the club brothers were here for that shit show, I reluctantly let them have their moment. Afterward, I banged the gavel a few times to get everyone to calm down.

"All right, *all right*. Thank you, brothers. We are pretty fucking happy about the news. But we got shit to handle, and it needs to be handled A.S.A. motherfucking P."

Looking around the room, I see my brothers understand that their Prez is running on fucking fumes, and so are my patients, despite the happy news. Looking over to Barone, I get this shit out first and foremost because the more I stew on it, the more I question my resolve to not think too hard about it. He is standing near the door staring at me, and for the first time, I can read him. He's assessing me in the way he does.

"All right, Barone. I hear you have some questions about my women and me. Let me here, um?"

For a while, we just stared at each other. I'm pissed the fuck off at the challenge I see in his eyes; his audacity is astounding. But I'm not having it.

Vera James is *mine*. Mafioso or not, I will slit his throat to ensure that he and every other motherfucker on this planet knows it. I glare at him as he leans back into the wall, his arms crossed, and he smiles.

"I will allow it."

What the fuck, allow what? I don't have time for this shit, and he can see it written all over my face because he stands up and starts to walk toward me. All my seated brothers sit up, and Tully and Flick begin to stand. I wave them off. Quirking a brow.

"Allow *what* exactly?"

"I will allow you to marry Vera James" He smiles an amused smile but quickly sobers. "Know that she is very important to me. No, I do not know her personally. No, I will not tell you how I know her. No, her family is not in the *famiglia*. And no, I never have and will never want your girl. I will tell you this, James Masterson and we Italians stick together. If you hurt that girl or make her unhappy, there will be dire consequences. There will not be a place where I can't or won't find you and every member of this club or your family. I respect you enough to say it to your face, as I am sure you will say to mine. I have no problem slitting your throat. Now, let's talk about your two little birdies that flew the coop and the little lion cub that followed along."

He stares at me, and I him. I have so many questions. But know that I'll never get answers. One thing I have learned in the months I have been working with Don Elijah Barone is... the man is a titanium vault. He will only let you know what he wants you to. He has eyes and ears everywhere in my club, other clubs, and streets. Regarding my club, at this point, I am not going to look for the snitch just yet, I know they are here, and as long as they're not a threat, I'll let it be for now.

Barone says what he means, and means what he says, end off. And at this point, we have bigger fish to fry. So, I give him a glare for good measure and a nod in understanding. For now, we will have to let sleeping dogs lie.

"One thing that I will say is, I respect you. Barone, my woman, is off-limits even to you. You say you don't have a past or history, and I'll accept that. I will even give you the concession of knowing that I nor anyone else in this club would knowingly hurt V. They would sooner cut out their hearts. Everyone here loves and respects that woman and would lay their

173

lives on the line for her and my kid. Now with that being said. If I see you staring at my woman in any way that makes my trigger finger itch, your threats won't mean shit. I protect mine."

We stare at one another a little longer than we need to, our eyes saying everything and coming to an understanding. He knows where I stand, and I know where he stands, and we will move on.

"So, now that the pissing contest is…"

Snapping my eyes from Barone. I cut Tully off and look over to Hound. "Hound, what have you found on the pig?"

Hound clears his throat and sits in his chair as he takes a few papers from a binder. The man gets information faster than anyone I know. Whether from the streets or his new computer acquisitions, he is a good Information Officer. I know computers are new to regular folk, but as soon as Hound got his hands on one, the man learned that shit faster than anyone thought he would. I think he uses them in ways I don't think an average person could or is supposed to. But as long as he gets what I need, I don't give a shit how he gets it. Hound clears his throat.

"Yes, I was able to get info from the streets and do a little poking around my other sources. That pig is a piece of fucking work, Prez. He's definitely on someone's payroll. He has been cited more than once for losing evidence, not properly handling suspects, and other shit like that. On top of that, a few incidents with women subsequently get swept under the rug. The chicks disappear or recant their stories. All and all, my thought is because he's not well-liked and his reputation proceeds him. The fucker won't be missed if he disappears. I vote we take him out" Hound crosses his arms, knowing he did damn good in the few hours he's had to look into the fucker.

I chuckle, nodding my head. "Well, brothers, I don't think we need a vote. He put his hands on my woman, and according to Hound, he's a class 'A' douchebag that needs to be put to pasture. My Pops pigs ain't had a good meal in a while." All my brothers chuckle and give words of agreement.

"Any objections." I look around the room and get none. "Well. all right, we misplaced V's favorite prospect and can't have that." There are a few chuckles because it's true. If I didn't know she sees the kid as a little

174

brother, I'd be pissed, but I've gotten used to their closeness. And, of course, I threatened body mutilation if he crossed a line. I band my gavel again to calm the room. "And yes, the two whores Penelope and Darcy, went missing as well. I can't say them bitches will be missed. My only concern with them is that the timing is suspicious if it is a play by someone. So, what do we know?"

The door to the chapel flies open, nearly taking Barone out, and I swear to all things that if church is interrupted again for some bullshit, someone will get their ass handed to them. Granted, last time, it was because my woman almost maimed a hang-around who was talking about riding my dick a week or so back at an open club party. Yeah, my woman goes a little feral about my dick. Come to think of it... It always seems to be my woman getting into trouble. My face pales at the thought of something happening to V. I go to stand as Tully yells out at the prospect. The room is on alert as it always is when church is interrupted.

"What the actual fuck, Prospect."

Jimmy the Geek, our newest prospect, is looking around the room wildly, connecting his eyes with mine. A chill runs down my spine, and I'm already on my feet, charging toward him.

"Speak"

"Um, well, Prez, you might want to come out here– Uh, we have some visitors at the gate, and *uhh*, It's the Keepers, Prez."

He looks around the room, eyes wild and wide as he hears brothers shouting and cursing angrily. It's bad fucking form to show up in another club's territory, let alone their gates, without permission or notice. That shit is disrespectful as fuck and grounds for war. Them, being here now puts me on edge. I make eye contact with my officers. They know what to do.

Everything in me goes tight as the gravity of what I know will most likely go down hits me. Someone is going to lose their life tonight, and it sure as fuck ain't going to be my brothers or me.

The stuttering prospect keeps talking, and I block him out. I scan the room and find my brother Flick, and he gives me a nod. As much as I know, he will want to be in the thick of whatever this shit show is going to turn into, and our priority is to make sure V and my boy are protected. He takes off out of the room before I can even say thank you. My eyes momentarily connect with Rocky's, and I can see the indecision on whether or not to protect V or protect me.

"It's up to you, brother."

Staring at me for a moment, he nods a few times. "I will be with you, Prez, and I'll stick close to the clubhouse. I'm sure Slim will be by your side, and we need to ensure someone covers the back entrance."

And damn, if he isn't on his game. We keep a cache of weapons in this room and space off the Common room. People wouldn't notice it there if they didn't have prior knowledge, and it works in our favor as everyone starts to strap up.

"Ink, Phoenix, Bandit, and Zero, I need all of you to cover our asses and the back entrance. Don't care how you do it. Just get it done."

I look around for the trigger-happy trio and our little club mouse finding them, and I yell out. "Fox, Ripper, Scout, and Mouse, I need you up on the roof. Keep an eye out for any surprises. I don't know what these fuckers want, but whatever it is, it ain't good." They acknowledge me and take off to their posts.

"All right, brothers, let's go see what this shit is about. Stay on alert and do not let anyone who ain't supposed to be in my clubhouse in. If it ain't a Saint, make them one, got me?"

Around of got you Prez's hit my ears.

Everyone files out of church. I'm in no hurry, and it's not that I don't care. I know I need to give my brothers time to set up and get where they need to be. Also, I need to provide a few more orders to the prospects and club girls. Once I am in the mouth of the hallway leading to the common room, I bellow out.

"Prospects"

Like the good little cubs they are, they come running. They feel it too. They know shit is about to go down. The club girls that were milling around froze at my tone. Whatever they were doing was no longer a priority. They look over at me after hearing the tone of my voice. They, too, know something is going on by the way all the brothers are hightailing it out of church.

"You need to round up all the club girls and get them to the safe room. Tike, you know where it is. Make sure they bolt the door. Dice and Frank, I need you two on the elevators. They should be locked down. By chance, if they aren't, *do not* go up to my floor. Flick is up there with my girl and Jasper. He's liable to take you out if you come up unannounced. Make sure you lock both stair accesses and stay on guard. The rest of you, I want you to check your designated entry points and guard them with your life. You know your posts. Make it happen, boys. Shit just might get real tonight."

I get a few wary looks from the club girls and prospects. But they start to scurry around to get where they need to be.

Let's get this shit show on the road.

Sixteen

VERA

My eyes fly open when I'm woken up by pounding on a door, still groggy. My body's automatic response is to hop out of bed quickly to find out what the hell is going on. But moving so fast proves to be a bad idea because of my rushed movement. After being hit with a dizzy spell, I have to grab ahold of the nightstand. After a few moments, the pounding and my dizziness dissipate. James said he'd have Jasper up here with me, so I can only assume he got the door and handled whomever it was. At least, I hope he did. I stand still for a moment and listen for anything.

I let out a breath when I hear Jasper's voice, and I think it's Flick, but I am not sure. They speak in low, hushed, and rushed tones; I can't quite make out what they're saying. Since neither of them has come for me, I don't feel like I need to be in any rush to find out what's going on. If it were an emergency, I can guarantee Flick wouldn't give it a second thought to bursting into my room and waking me up, naked or not.

I make my way to my dresser on the other side of the room. James would spank my ass and end Jasper and his brother if I walked out of this room to investigate dressed or undress the way I am. I realize I'm in my underwear and have no bra. James knows how much I hate sleeping in clothes. I smile at myself, knowing how considerate he is and how careful he has been with me since having to go to the hospital earlier. I know he was freaking the hospital staff out with his overprotectiveness.

It was all worth knowing that our little one is safe and tucked in, nice and warm. I rub my hand over the barely-there pooch, thinking about James and how much things have changed and grown between us over the last several months. Before we were— us, I lived each day looking over my shoulder and feeling nothing but sadness and regret. I didn't dare hope to

178

have anything other than a sad, lonely life. For a long time, I thought that was what I deserved. But I know better now.

I know my family would want me to live, love, and be happy. I don't talk about them often to James. When we talk about what happened to them and that they were murdered. I left out the details about my involvement with the mafia. But the best parts. The parts I will remember. The pieces I will cherish. The details that I will pass down to my children I loved talking about those parts.

I know not being completely forthcoming with James may come back to haunt me at some point. Keeping a part of my past a secret is for a good reason and by order of Don Barone. I made a vow of *omertà* to the *famiglia,* and that vow cannot be broken. No matter how much I love and trust James, it is the way of our people. I trust Don Barone to protect me as I do James. And I hope and pray that I will be lucky enough to stay here, to live and love in this life with my man and our family for as long as I live.

Reaching the dresser, I grab one of James's shirts and a pair of my shorts. Once I am dressed, I slip on a pair of socks and head to the door. When I step out of my and James' rooms, all conversations between Flick and Jasper stop, and they stare at me warily. And that– the way they look at me makes my hackles rise.

"Nope, whatever it is, tell me. I can tell by the look in both your eyes that something is going on, and it isn't good. Spit. It. Out."

I stand staring at both of them, a hand on my hip; my face says it all. I want the truth. Usually, Flick would make some joke about me being a demanding first lady, and we'd have a chuckle, but he would tell me the truth. That's not what happens. He just stares at me, so wary and unsure. He looks so conflicted yet angry.

"Tell me... Is it... is it Brick..." I stumble forward as if my legs can no longer hold me up. The thought of... No. No... nothing has happened to James. Flick, is at my side in a flash and is guiding me to the couch in our living room, and he's yet to say a word. Jasper continues to stand, staring at me as if in a daze.

"*Please...*"

I don't know what I'm asking. What I do know is I need to know— I *need* to know if James is OK. I *have* to know that James is OK. Settling me on the couch, Flick kneels in front of me, taking a breath. He holds both of my hands in his and stares at me, searching for something. After a few moments, he nods as if he has decided.

"You *can't* lose your shit. My brother will have my ass if anything happens to you or…."

"Flick, just tell *me*…"

"Shit, all right, we were in church. You know, discussing club business and the like. All of a sudden, the prospect comes barreling in. At first, we thought it was about *you* as it usually is…" he chuckles because lately, it *is* usually about me. No one can keep my anger at bay or calm me like James can. I've been a lot quicker to want to rip a bitch to shreds, and a few times when it came to my man, I damn near did. So— yeah, he has had to step in a few times to calm me down and prevent me from going to jail.

"And what?"

"The prospect informed us that the Satan's Keepers MC is camped out at the front gate. And from our experience with them, things are never as simple as a sit-down talk with those pussies. Those fuckers have no morals and think brute force will win them a fucking medal. They're bullies and think they can push us out of town. Knowing that they never have good intentions. My brother, your ol' man, is being proactive. Brick had me come up to you to help Jasper keep an eye on you. Keep you protected. And keep you calm. Your calm, right?" Flick squeezes my hand, trying to reassure me. "Brick put the club on lockdown and is going out there to see what the fuck they want."

"Who is with him, Flick? Who all has his back?" I stand up and start making my way to the door. But Flick isn't having it. He jumps in front of me with his hands held out in a stopping motion.

"Whoa, whoa, whoa, little Boss Lady, where do you think you're going? Brick has this shit under control. Every brother that was in church has his back. He's got brothers surrounding the clubhouse on the roofs, every entrance point, in the front and the back. The entire clubhouse is protected. Everyone is here except…" He cuts himself off as I stand staring at him, and then it clicks. Except who?

"Who?"

He stares at me and says nothing. He rakes his hand through his hair.

"Except *who*, Flick? If you don't tell me, I will rip your dick off and feed it to you *slowly*. This is my family; every one of you means something to me. Everyone but the whores can take a long walk off a short bridge." I glare at him, and he stares at me in shock. "I know how fond you are of your dick, so tell me WHO. IS. MISSING.? Or I swear…."

He starts to pace the room, mumbling under his breath. I look over at Jasper, and he won't meet my eye. And suddenly, I hear him say it.

"Cade"

"Oh hell no, what if…. What if they have him? I mean– he goes missing, and they show up. That is no damn a coincidence, Flick. No way in hell."

I charge towards the windows that overlook the forecourt and front gates. My eyes widen. I can't believe what I'm seeing. There's a wall of men and bikes on the road outside the gates. Two men stand out in front of fifteen to twenty bikers. I'm assuming it's Pyro and his VP or Enforcer. Understanding clubs like I do now. I know James never takes meetings without his VP or Enforcer.

My eyes scan the men from head to toe. They are holding someone at gunpoint. Squinting, I focus on the person kneeling whose head is down, but it doesn't take me long to suspect who it is. You don't have to be a damn rocket scientist to figure it out. Slowly, as if he feels eyes on him, his head lifts, and he looks up in my direction. His eyes are unfocused. He is bloody and bruised. My hand goes to my mouth.

"*Cadence,*" I whisper.

Fury like I've never felt courses through my veins, heating my body. I know the club has this under control, but that doesn't mean I don't want to do something. That doesn't mean— I focus on the flurry of movement going on below. I see the club brothers moving around, using the cover of darkness to conceal their activities. Something or *someone* catches my eye, and I focus on them.

Brick leads a group of his brothers down the gravel drive toward the gate. I can see him turning his head now and then, speaking to someone. He doesn't seem fazed or worried. He looks relaxed, which strangely has my shoulders relaxing slightly at the sight, but his being relaxed doesn't diminish my anger. My eyes return to the gate for a moment to check on Cadence. He is still in the same position he was in before; by the tilt of his head, I know that if I were up close, I would see fury and defiance in his eyes.

With all the movement, my eye momentarily gets caught by the brothers who rode ahead of Brick. The brothers on bikes parked them in front of the gates. Brick is determined, and his commanding steps eat up the distance to his destination.

I feel a presence on both sides of me. Both Flick and Jasper stand looking out the window. I don't know when they did it, but the lights are now off in the suite, and we all stand stunned as we watch what is happening below us.

When Brick, his group, and Don Barone reach the gates, Don Barone refrains from stepping out of the shadows. The reason he is doing so is apparent, this situation is club business, and he is showing Brick respect by not getting involved, yet. Brick and the men at the gate speak to one another. The man looks angry. He doesn't seem to be getting what he wants. He says something to Brick which makes Brick start to laugh. Flick chuckles beside me, mumbling something about his brother, seconds away from exploding. And I would have to agree. Brick has this weird thing that he finds humor in situations ordinary people wouldn't. He will laugh and smiles, and then... in the blink of an eye, a switch flips, and he loses his shit. I've seen it happen more than once, so I know the signs.

Whatever was said has Don Barone stepping out of the shadows, which lets me know things are about to get real. Quickly, I step away from the window and make my way to my front door. I don't know where I'm going. That's a lie. I know that I can't go down there. Brick would lose his mind, be distracted, and worry about taking care of me rather than handling business. So, that leaves only one other option, the roof.

My escape to the door goes unnoticed until there is a loud click, which makes me freeze. Hearing a low growl, I take a peek over my shoulder and Flick, and Jasper stare at me with narrowed, annoyance-filled eyes. Their arms crossed, and I could see the challenge in their eyes. Before either of them says a word, I do.

"One thing I'm not and never will be is the little woman sitting on the sideline waiting for the big bad men to defend her honor or home because my family means *everything* to me. I know some things are out of my control. I know that outside of these walls and those gates, I have to leave it to the club. But we are not outside these walls or those gates. We are in our home; *my* home and I *will* defend our family." Flick goes to cut me off, but I stop him. "I'm not going down there. I am going to the roof. And you will not stop me. You can either come or not. I don't care. You don't know a lot about me, but you will learn."

I leave it at that, walking out of the suite and to the stairs that lead to the roof. It's only one flight, thank goodness. But the door doesn't open when I press on it. I tried a few times, and nothing. And I growl out.

A hand slides around me, Flick puts a weird-looking key in a slot, and the doors push open. I make my way up to the roof without any issues, and as soon as I open the door, a gun barrel is at my head, and I freeze.

"Oh Shit, hot damn boss lady, I almost took you out. Shit, Shit, *Shit.*" Mouse steps back, raking his hands through his thick curly dark hair. He looks up at me with his pleading brown eyes. "Don't tell Prez about this. He'll kill me– *dead.*"

"Mouse," I try to cut off his ramblings.

"MOUSE"

He snaps out of his ramblings of apology when he hears Flick's loud and commanding voice. Flick steps around me and through the door, followed by a silently chuckling Jasper. I would be laughing myself if things weren't so crazy right now. Mouse tends to be a little too excitable, but he is a damn good man.

"It's cool, brother. You did what you were supposed to do. Just glad you didn't take Boss Lady out. Prez would have both our asses." He chuckles, patting the still but mumbling Mouse on the back.

Shaking my head at them, ignoring anything else they have to say, I make my way over to Scout, who's focused on what's happening below. I can guarantee that he knows it's me sliding next to him. Scout, to those that don't know him, seems to think that his lack of acknowledgment means he is aloof and isn't paying attention. I know for a fact that is not the case. He is just good at making himself seem like he doesn't care. That attitude is why they call him Scout. He watches, hears and can get information no one else can.

My options were limited when I decided to kill the Don that murdered my sister. I thought to walk up to him at close range, get it over with, and shoot him. Eventually, I thought better of it because there was no way I would have walked away if I had done that. So, I got smart and sought out a man connected to the *mafia* but not related to anyone who would suspect what I was doing. That man taught me how to shoot, not just shoot... but be good at it, deadly. What I learned stuck, and at this moment, I'm glad for that.

I step up beside Scout and lay next to him on his perch. He doesn't startle. I know he heard the commotion when I came up here. He is simply doing what he does, which I am grateful for. I don't say a word, and neither does he.

He doesn't say anything when I slide the gun from his grasp.

He doesn't say anything when I set myself up and look through the scope.

He doesn't say anything when I gasp.

He doesn't say anything when I take the shot.

He says nothing, but he does look at me in shock as I continue to take shots that protect my man and this club.

And now they know.

- B R I C K -

Since the shit went down with the drop months back. Also, knowing that pussy they call a president put a snitch in my club, we've taken precautions. One of them is having two Prospects on the gates at all times. And right now, I am glad about it. Because of that, I'm able to put the club and my brothers on alert and get ourselves and our club covered for whatever is about to go down.

When I step out of the main doors of the clubhouse, what I am greeted with has my blood beginning to boil. Off in the distance at my goddamned gates, I can hear a good number of bikes revving their engines. I and the brothers, not currently occupied, make our way down our gravel road. Barone is slightly behind me. Turning my head slightly, I look at him from the corner of my eye and see his mask firmly in place. And I know he is ready for whatever the fuck this is. I can pretty much guess what this is about. I don't understand why those fuckers thought this would work in their favor.

Once we make it down the gravel road and closer to the gate, I see that some of my brothers are lined up on either side of the gate. They strategically have a few bikes in front of the entrance and between them. I smirk while I take in the sight before me. A good amount of Satan's Keepers are lined up to make themselves look intimidating. Pyro the Prez and his pussy of a VP Demon are standing on either side of my Prospect Cade, who is looking worse for wear, but the kid's face is a mask of anger and a hint of resignation. I don't acknowledge them yet. I signal and let the boys know what I want to happen.

"Snipper and Deadshot"

"On it, Prez."

My two brothers take off, and no one says a word as they discretely back out of our grouping of brothers and head where I need them to. This isn't our first rodeo dealing with hostiles. And I have a feeling that this isn't going to be pretty by the way my prospect looks.

With night already fallen, we tend to keep the gates darker than some expect for a biker compound. I have a reason for everything I do. One, I keep the lighting down as I don't want to draw curious eyes or unwanted attention. Two, if we need to move around the area, it's easier to do so under the cover of darkness.

I step out of the grouping of men glaring at Pyro, who has his gun trained on my prospect's head. He didn't notice my companion or anything going on around him. He and his sidekick smile at me like they've won the lottery. Like tonight isn't going to be their last night on earth, most likely.

Barone stays back, but in the cover of my brothers and the darkness, I notice from the corner of my eye that he does something with his hand. I look over, and my brow creases, but he smiles and shakes his head. Neither of the idiots noticed our interaction or who I was interacting with. They are so fucking dumb that they don't even realize the man they are dying to get in bed with is witnessing their stupidity firsthand.

I step closer to the gate, taking in exactly what I'm up against. And it's clear to see that Pyro wants to show force. But he doesn't realize that he is setting his club up to be taken out. Because of this strategy to puff out his chest and line his brothers up for slaughter– I shake my head at the idiocy. He may have gotten one up on us with that single transport, but I am the kind of man that lives and learns. This dumb fuck will never catch my club with our pants down again or me.

I can see his little minion Demon taking stock at the number of men lined up man to man or my men to their one man. I know he sees it. They are outnumbered; this isn't even my entire club standing here. I shake my head as my eyes return to Pyros.

"I hear you had some visitors today. It's a shame ol' Thompson couldn't follow through." Pyro says.

Clicking his tongue, rubbing his hand through his beard. This is the first time I can take this man in. He is not a bad-looking guy, just looks rough. Hard living has taken its toll on him, he and I are around the same age, and you wouldn't know it. His lifestyle has given him a head full of greying hair and a patchy beard. He's a few inches shorter than me. His roundness makes up for his lack of height. He is looking a little soft around the middle. Don't get me wrong, he seems like a formidable opponent, but I know I can take him without breaking too much of a sweat.

He can see me appraising him and his men. He tries to puff out his chest and look intimidating. It takes all that's in me not to roll my eyes. I just stand there and cross my arms, giving him the floor to say what he needs to.

"If he had done his job right, I would have had that sweet little thing of yours in my bed tonight. Heard she's a real looker and a firecracker. I love breaking little bitches like that in…" He licks his lips for a dramatic effect or some shit. Pausing to stare at me, waiting for a reaction. He isn't getting one. If he knew what I did, he wouldn't say a damn thing about my woman. But I'll let the fucker dig his grave. Don't get me wrong. I want to rip his eyes out, cut his tongue out of his mouth, sew his lip shut and watch as he chokes on his blood. I just smile at him; I want him to dig this grave deep. And I want to relish in his demise.

He doesn't get the response he was looking for from me, but he does get a few growls from my brothers. I just smile and shake my head at him. And he thinks my nonresponse is his cue to keep talking. "Welp, you know I paid that fucker damn good. All he had to do— Well, no matter. I got a few of your people and am tired of this little game of cat and mouse. I want you out of my town." He growls out, trying at his version of being intimidating.

I can't hold it in. I start laughing my ass off. This fucking guy can't be serious. He can't, and there is no way he is coming to *my* town, standing outside *my* gate telling me, *me*– that I need to leave town. Aw fuck, this is good. He can't be this damn dumb. It takes a minute to get myself under control. My brothers and I sober up when Demon strikes Cade, knocking him to the ground face first. Oh, he's fucking dead. Cade may be a prospect, but he's my fucking prospect. And nobody fucks with what's mine.

I growl and try to rein in my anger. Lifting my hand to my jaw. I know it's been enough time for my boys to be set up. Pyro has a gun still trained on my unconscious prospect, so I have to play it right. I can almost guarantee that they also have the two missing club girls. If I'm honest, I don't care about those bitches, one is a traitor, and the other is a pain in my ass. Don't want them dead, just don't give a shit about them.

"Shit, man, you're serious?" Pyro glares at me. The guys that came with him are off of their bikes. Some have their weapons drawn, and some don't. They stand behind their president, trying their damndest to look intimidating. In reality, they are all a bunch of pussies.

"You damn right know I'm serious, you fucking prick. You and your club full of pussies rolled into town, started encroaching on *my* territory and taking money out of *my* pocket. That. Brother is a problem that needs to be remedied. So get your group of wannabes and pack it in. Or things..." He waves his hand, and his men aim, while mine do the same. "Or tonight, you will find out why they call us Satan's Keepers. We will reap your souls and not feel an ounce of regret."

"Well, shit, man. Why didn't you say that? I didn't know we were putting *you* in the poor house by running legitimate businesses in a town *you* don't live in..."

"Fuck you, you pussy bitch. Legit my ass, I know your running guns for the mob boss. You ain't fooling me, me and Barone got business, and your pussy ass club is in the way of that."

At that, Barone steps into the light next to me. And if I could, I would have loved to record that moment. The moment they realized that they were fucked. Pyro's smile falters at the sight of Barone, but he is quick to fix it, putting a smug but unsure smile back on his face. I chuckle to myself. Yeah, this is all bad for this idiot.

"First of all. Robert Casey, son of Adrian and Mark Casey, sister to Bridget and Michel Casey, father of… Well, far more than you think. Let me make myself clear" Barone stands staring Pyro down, fixing the cuffs of his jacket, giving off an air of nonchalance. "I don't work with men who sell and trade women. Oh, yes, gentleman" Looking at both Pyro and demon. "I know all about what you are trying to get into. I know all about you and your so-called skin trade operation. I know what you are looking for. You have already begged for my involvement and protection. You should have taken my refusal to meet as a sign that things wouldn't go your way. I see you are a stubborn man, Mr. Casey, so let me clarify this. My *famiglia* does not trade in skin. Firearms? Yes. Drugs? Occasional. Unwilling and stolen women? Absolutely the fuck *not*. You have two options, gentlemen. Pack up and leave…" He pauses because why not be a little dramatic? "…or *die*"

Barone watches the Prez and VP of the Keepers. You can tell that they weren't prepared for this. They either received the wrong intel about who was here or thought *that*. Fuck knows what they thought, but it's not going the way they expected, and I smirk at the idiots. Neither of them says a word. They look at each other and then at Barone. I am tired of standing here. I want to get back to my woman, who I hope is still sleeping. Who only knows what she would do if she knew this shit was going on.

"You have to be really damn dumb to come at me like this. Take *my* prospect, put your hands on *my* prospect, and have the nerve to demand shit from *my* club and *me*. So…" Standing at my full height, I stare them down. "…like Don Barone said. I am going to put it in a way you will understand. Here is what is going to happen. You and your merry band of misfits will get on your bikes, and you will do it quickly. And you are going to ride off into the sunset." I take a step closer to the gate. "This is not going to end the way you think it is. Cut your losses, Pyro. Sacramento is mine and *always* will be. You never had it and never will, accept it and move on. Or…"

And that does it. Pyro loses his shit. He puts a bullet in Cade's back, and I see red. Oh, this motherfucker is dea… Before I can take the shot, a bullet hole blossoms in the middle of Pyro's eyes, and he goes down.

Talking is done. Four club trucks come barreling towards the gate to give us more cover. I take off like a bat out of hell to get to cover behind the bikes and trucks. I see that the Keepers have abandoned their bikes and are pushing the gate open. A few, including Demon, make their way in my direction. Demon is searching the grounds, and I know who he's looking for. His eyes catch mine when I stand slightly, letting him know I am not hiding from him. He goes to raise his arm, but before he does, he catches a bullet to the shoulder. He looks around at the few Keepers still standing, and the realization hits him.

Whoever is snipping is taking the fuckers out left and right, covering me and my brothers' asses. We have quite a few former snippers in the club, and at the moment, I am grateful as fuck.

After we have been returning fire for a little while, I hear it. Engines are revving but not bikes. It sounds like big ass trucks. My curiosity gets the best of me, and wanting to make sure shit isn't about to get worse for my boys and me. I peek out from my location behind a truck's wheel well. And damn if what I see doesn't have a huge smile break across my face.

I stand to my full height and watch as several Jeep Scramblers come barreling up the road, headed straight for the Keepers and my gates. I look to my right and see Barone standing with a broad smile.

"How in the fuck?" I question.

"*Mio amico*, I was not just swatting at flies. I am a man of great means. I do not go unprotected *anywhere*, even if you think I am not. My men have been around," he waves his hand around.

"Well, I'll be damned. You're a sneaky motherfucker. Thanks for the assist, but the brother and I had it under control." I give him a grin and look around.

Demon's eye and mine catch, and I know this shit isn't over. But right here, he has no choice but to run like the pussy he is, as do the remaining members of his club that are still breathing. Their bikes are bobbing and weaving, trying to avoid the onslaught of gunfire and the vehicles coming at them.

Well, I'll be damned if I had known then what Demon and his club would put my family through years from now. I would have shot him dead.

189

Seventeen

W ell, fuck me running. She's a whole lot more than I expected her to be. To be honest, I didn't expect much. I didn't see it when I accidentally ran into her at the diner over a year ago. Vera has always been so unassuming and sweet— too sweet, too kind, and too soft. I was given this assignment to watch the club and then the girl. I never expected this, not in a million damn years. Hell, who would?

Over the last year, I watched her, protected her, and did my damnedest to point her in the right direction as I was directed to do so. Vera is a good girl who deserves the life she's building. She was dealt one shitty hand, so I get why he has been so damn adamant that she remains protected and watched over. The damn girl is a gem, a sharp little thing that will cut you deep if you handle her wrong, but a gem all the same.

When Don Barone tasked me to come out here to see what this new club was about, he knew I was looking for something. I'd been wandering for years, not finding where I fit within the *famiglia*. I did my job, but there was no joy in it.

Don Barone has that thing. That thing that makes him *know* you. He can tear you apart and look deep into your soul with one look. If you are someone worth a damn, he will rebuild you and give you your purpose. He will do all he can to ensure you live a happy, healthy, and productive life. I chuckle to myself. Of course, he'll do all that in a way that benefits him and the *famiglia*, but all the same, he helps those he deems worthy.

Staring at the girl I was tasked to watch over. She is steady as she picks off Keeper after Keeper from her perch next to me on the roof. The girl that was dealt a shit hand in life. I can finally see it. I know the fierceness, the determination, and the hunger to protect those she loves. I see the

190

Mafia Princess that has become so effortlessly an MC Queen.

Valentina Tomasi was built, born, and bred for the outlaw life.

- B R I C K -

Well, I'll be damned. As I thought it would, shit went bad real, damn fast. Watching the tail lights of the still-breathing Keeper's retreat has me in a daze.

What. The. Fuck?

The last twenty-four hours have been a damn roller coaster, and I'll be damned glad to get off. Once I see the taillights of those pussies disappear over the horizon. I look around at the destruction that surrounds me. Luckily there is no real structural damage done to the clubhouse. We didn't let the fuckers get that damn far. Looks like we lost two out of the four club trucks, and as for the bikes that have either exploded from being hit or torn to shreds by stray bullets, I'm happy. Not because they are damaged, just because my brothers were smart enough to ride the spare bikes, we keep in the garage here instead of their own. Smart shits.

I breathe a sigh of relief when I don't see any LSMC cuts among the dead scattered around on the gravel between me and the road. My brothers did real good containing this shit and keeping their asses alive. Don't get me wrong, brothers are cursing, moaning, and groaning their asses off, but I ain't see nothing fatal yet. Now we have to hope the pigs don't catch wind of what went down. There's no way in hell to explain this shit show away. Doubt they'll accept self-defense. I chuckle to myself.

"Looks like your men are in good spirits, and no one thought that death would be easier than clean up" Barone chuckles as he speaks to me, simultaneously giving his men orders in Italian. I look over at him and shake my head. This fucker loves this shit. His eyes glitter with excitement, even knowing that, for now, the fight is over.

"My men will help you with clean-up. Our vehicles took no damage…" He walks over to one of the Scramblers, staring at them with pride. The hunks of metal indeed seem untouched. I don't see the appeal, and I probably should since my ol' lady isn't going to be riding on the back of my bike for a long while. She'll need something sturdy to ride in with our kid. I smile, thinking about V and our little one. I scratch my stubbled chin and, not for the first time, hope she was none the wiser about what has gone down. Broken out of my thoughts.

"We will dispose of this…" he waves his hand around. "It was good to see that you and your men can handle business so efficiently. I am glad I chose you and your club over those disgusting mongrels. We will indeed have a long and industrious partnership. I would suggest you do a little more growing, yes." he growls out, turning on his heels and walking away. Leaving me dumbstruck as I stare after him. I hear a chuckle from beside me. Looking over, I see Tully and Slim doing what I was, surveying the damage.

Tully looks like he may have caught one to the leg, seeing how he has a bandana wrapped around his upper thigh and is favoring his other. Slim looks unharmed. Thank fuck for that because Slim hurt is like a five-year-old girl. The whining tends to get out of hand. And people think he's a badass biker. Before either of them can say anything, a realization hits, and my head snaps to the front gate.

Fuck

I take off running, and my brothers follow. Before I know it, my knees connect with the gravel road. Cades' unmoving form lays still, and my breath stalls in my chest. Thank fuck Doc had the foresight to get to him as soon as possible. He doesn't spare me a glance when he starts talking to me.

"This kid is one lucky fucker Prez. From my vantage, it looked like a direct shot to the center of his back, but this little shit must have moved because it got him on the side. Don't get me wrong, Prez, it got his ass good, but other than losing some blood, I think he will be ok." doc shakes his head.

I can hear audible sighs and grunts of relief when we hear that. I see Tully, Slip, Recker, and a few other brothers standing around watching Doc work. Usually, I would get in their asses telling them we got work to do, but right now… Right now, it's about the kid. I stare down at Cade and remain uneasy. He's too damn still. I know Doc said he was as good as expected, but for him to be so still and not moan out in pain as Doc digs around his side is jarring.

"Damndest thing, the bullet went straight through. The kid was smart enough to play possum, weren't you, you little shit?"

"Yep"

A tired, nearly whispered response could be heard from the kid. He tries to shift his head to look at me. I put my hand gently on top of his head, stopping the movement.

"Sit still, you little shit."

"Yep"

I look up at Doc, quirking a brow in question.

"He's high as a kite, Prez. I thought shit might go down, so I grabbed my bag with the good stuff fully stocked." Doc pats his old-school black doctor's bag. "As long as the kids talking, I'm happy. Need to get him up, though. I got a few gurneys in the back of my truck. Need a few brothers to help me get him up and get him to the infirmary. I did what I could for now, but I will have to clean him up better. I don't want the kid getting an infection. I also need to check out what the front of 'um looks like. They did a number on the kid." He shakes his head angrily. I know. I'm pissed as fuck too. I need to ask the kid some questions. I know now ain't the time, but soon. We need to find out how he was taken and where the club girls are. And whether or not they are still alive, the club needs to decide if they are worth rescuing or if they need rescuing.

"Holy shit, that shot going off scared the shit out of me. Fucking fuck, you know my woman will have my ass if something happens to you, know that right. She will take my balls to a cheese grater. *Fuck me*" I hear a few audible winces. And the damndest thing, I see his shoulders moving lightly, and Doc's head snaps up, giving me a glare for making the kid move. I hold my hands up, but he knows it's true. V is protective as fuck when it comes to *her* prospects, as she calls them, and we all fucking know it.

"Sorry, Doc" I hold my hands up, placating the man.

I hear some shuffling behind me and "Goddamnit woman" being yelled out, and my head snaps up, and in the direction of the voice I know well.

Flick

"Shush it, Flick. You are not the damn Boss of me. Your *brother* is barely

193

the damn boss of me. And I only let him think he is because sex is ten times better after I get in trouble after I'm bad. So, move your ass. I didn't shoot all those fuckers to go back and hide in the suite to wait for you men to do your manly crap. Nope, not happening."

I stand up, moving out of the way as a few of my brothers make their way over with a medivac stretcher in hand. I turn my head and watch as my little spitfire of a woman stomps her way through and around debris and bodies. She pays none of it no mind. Her eyes are determined. Even from here, I can see it.

Once she makes it close enough, her eyes connect with mine, and I can see relief flood hers.

Wait?

Did she say she...?

My eyes narrow on my woman's flustered form. I watch her as she gets closer and closer to me. I'm an impatient man and start stomping in her direction. Her steps falter but do not stop when she sees the look on my face. It is clear to her and everyone I pass that I am indeed going to handle her little ass.

I stop short of snatching her little ass when we reach each other. I know I, along with everyone else, heard what she said. And I'm sure as shit not happy. Because—

WHAT. THE. FUCK?

"Ohhh...You are in *trouble,*" Flick whisper shouts to V, and she whips her head around to give him an evil glare and the finger. He chuckles, shaking his head but saying nothing else as he stares between V and me.

"You Vera James soon-to-be Masterson will get that damn ass spanked. What the fuck do you mean you shot them? When, where, and how the hell? I swear to all things. Do not give me that *look.* Nope, I am not falling for it...." I stare at her as she looks up at me with her beautiful eyes. I know if she was involved in this shit, she had to have been worried out of her mind. But that is not an excuse to get involved. My eyes bore into hers. "I'm damn serious, woman; you are not getting your little ass out of this. You got my kid in your belly and are acting like Billy, the damn Kid. Nope. And you..." I turn to face my brother.

"You had one job, Flick. One damn job to do, keep my woman safely tucked away and away from this shit." I wave my hands around, looking to see that the cleanup is nearly done. But it doesn't make me feel any better.

"Explain" I give them both stern glares.

Flick says absolutely nothing. He crosses his arms and stares down at V. He's not the only one giving my girl a questioning and curious look. Rocky, Tully, Slim, Tommy Boy, Scout, hell damn near the entire club, and Barone and his men are surrounding us, staring at my women, waiting for an explanation.

V looks around at everyone staring at her in awe and disbelief. She crosses and uncrosses her arms looking down at the ground. She kicks at the gravel before speaking in a hushed tone. It takes every ounce in me to focus on and hear her words.

"So, ok. Maybe I kind of have a little bit of training with shooting rifles, and I kind of maybe went to the roof and took one and possibly used it to cover you and the guys." She looks up, and I see the stubborn jut of her chin as she stares into my eyes.

"I knew Flick and Jasper wouldn't dare let me come down here, so I did the next best thing. I am not going to apologize for doing what I did. I love you and this club. You are my family, and just like I told Flick. I have every right to defend my home within these walls and gates. I will not be the good little woman and hide away. I won't ever put myself in danger. I won't do that, but I won't hide, either. When I saw that man hurt Cade, I couldn't just let it go. Because if I would have waited just one second…" She puts her hand over her belly. Her head shakes back and forth. "I knew I wasn't in danger being up there and could help and stay safe. So I did what I had to. And I refused to lose you or anyone else ever again." She chokes out, and I can tell she's holding back a sob by the glistening of her eyes and shaking her hands. Her bottom lip starts to tremble, and that does it for me.

When she looks up at me, begging me to understand where she's coming from. Damnit, I do. I get it, and I'm pissed as fuck. But I get it. I have learned over the last year about my V that she is fiercely loyal and protective. When she loves, she loves hard. as I look around, this is our family, and I can't begrudge her for what she chose to do to protect it.

I step closer to her and pull her to me. She buries her head into my

195

chest, and a small sob breaks out as she clings to me. I know this was a lot for her, but I knew this reaction might come. I wanted to protect her from this and the thoughts of losing anyone else. That is why I had hoped she slept through it. But it is what it is now. It is about reassuring her that I am ok– that we are all ok.

Hell, as I said, the last twenty-four hours had been a shit show. Her head snaps away from my chest, she looks around me towards the gate, and another soft sob leaves her lips. I turn slightly as we watch Doc and a few brothers maneuver Cade onto the gurney. He is going to be okay because I wasn't kidding when I said she would have my ass if that kid didn't make it.

"Boss Lady, your prospect will be just fine. I'll sew him up and make sure he got the good stuff, and in a week or so, he will be good as new."

Doc pats V on the shoulder as he and the brothers carrying Cade walk by. They are slowly making their way to the clubhouse. Rocky steps up next to me with assessing eyes staring at V's watery ones.

"So, you just happen to be an expert marksman? Hmm? How did that happen…"

And that is how we found out that V had training in hand to hand because of her father. And she went out and got firearms on her own, saying she thought it would be fun. But there was something in her eyes that said the opposite of that. Barone gives her a look but schools his features when I lift a brow at him. I don't have the time nor want to read into either of their responses to V's clear lie.

To say my brothers were floored would be an understatement. When everyone came out of shock, the brothers ribbed her about being a tiny terror. They also gave Scout shit about V being a better shot than he was. And he took it in good fun.

It took a few days to get things back in order with the club, but we did. We still don't know what happened to the two club girls. But I am not pushing the issue too hard. We have other priorities now.

One week later

"All right, you bunch of ingrates, Church is in session. Sit your asses down" I bang the gavel down and look around the room, watching as my brothers settle in. Surprisingly, things have been almost back to normal after the shit went down with the Keepers and Barone assisting in cleaning up. We still have not heard about or located either club girl, and it doesn't seem much care. But as my woman says, they are people too, and we, as in the club and me, should at least make sure that they aren't being held against their will and all that. So here we are.

"So, shit's been moving along this last week. Looks like that showdown with the Keepers has made its rounds, and it's clear we are not ones to be fucked with 'round these parts." I say, looking around the room for confirmation, and I receive it in the form of nods, grunts, and smiles.

"With the Keepers going to ground, things with Barone and our alliance have been running well enough. The shipment made it to its location. I know it's only been a week, so I made sure all the businesses were checked out. I wouldn't put it past those assholes to go poking and fucking around with our shit, looking for payback for us taking out their Prez. Money is looking flush, and the businesses are running as smoothly as they can. But there is one issue. And you all know what it is. Darcy and Penelope."

I say the last part getting a few groans from the brothers. If I'm truthful, things around here have been quiet and drama free. Penelope may have been a traitor and a snitch to the club, but she was a good girl and didn't cause problems, unlike Darcy. "I know we don't care much for the girls. And I get why most of you fuckers are giving me the stink eye, but my woman is right. We need to ensure that they don't become a problem for us later. And I also guess to make sure those bitches aren't being used in nefarious ways." At that, everyone grumbled, letting me know they don't care about them. I get it, and neither do I. I let them say their piece before moving on.

"I want to bring Cade in today. One, because he has the information that we need. And two, because he was on Penelope's watch. Also, we still don't know how the Keepers got ahold of him. And lastly, we don't know if she and Darcy were involved in what went down. Since he has been so out of it and drugged up, we couldn't get the information we needed until now. Brothers, I also want to bring it to the table to vote him in. The kid is a Lucifer's Saint through and through, and we never had issues with him. He works his ass off, does what he's told, and never complains. It's time. So, let's get this shit out of the way so we can get to the good stuff."

I see nods of agreement, so I push forward. "All in favor of patching in a new Brother, say, Aye?" A round of eyes can be heard, I am assuming it's unanimous, but you can never be too sure. My eyes narrowed at the next question. "Any Nays…" Not one. The room is completely silent.

Good

Looking over to Slim, he stands and walks out of the room wordlessly; I know he will hunt down Cade. The kid can only be in one of two places, his room or my ol' lady, because she hovers around him like he's her little cub. I guess the momma bear in her is coming out already. I let a smile slide onto my lips, thinking about her and all the changes we have had in our lives and the changes to come. We may have gone through some shit, but we are on the other side, and I will enjoy it.

Cade walks in behind Slim stiffly; he looks unsure. Knowing Slim, he probably walked his scary ass up the kid and told him to get his ass to church and nothing else. So, Cade is looking like a dear caught in headlights. Is it a dick move to want to let him sweat a little? Even though I probably shouldn't.

I've gotten my ass handed to me on more than one occasion this week because Cade keeps trying to do shit, knowing he's still healing and my woman is not having it. She finds every excuse in the book to have him with her, *helping her* do things around the clubhouse. One day she had the little shit peeling damn potatoes in the kitchen, and we haven't even had a damn thing with potatoes in it in weeks. So, what the hell were the potatoes for, fuck knows. She finds the most remedial jobs possible, so he stays busy and off his feet. I know he knows what she's doing, but he humors her, and I appreciate him. The two of them have gotten a lot closer over the last few weeks, and surprisingly, it doesn't bother me as I thought it would. If any other brother gets too close to my woman, I still lose my shit, which gets an eye roll every time from my woman.

"Prez." The kid looks a little green. He's healed up pretty good, Doc says a few more weeks, and he'll be back to normal. I observe him. With this being his first time in church, I can see the nerves kicking in. But he does everything he can to keep his head up and a stoic, nearly unreadable expression on his face, and I try to hold back my smirk.

"You know what— I thought I wanted you in my club, kid…"

He gives me a questioning look and then looks around the room. His eyes get wide, and his stoic façade cracks.

"Brothers, Cade has been prospecting for the club for more than a year. He is, in my opinion..." I pause and look around at all the stoic faces in the room. I let the kid sweat it out just a little longer. I know if my woman finds out about me fucking with him like this, she'll be fit to be tied. But damn, if it isn't fun watching him sweat it out.

Scratching my jaw in fake consideration, "I think he's worth the patch" I hear an audible breath being taken, and I look over at Cade and give him a wink. "Kid, you are not just wanted in the club. You are needed. So, everyone, I would like to introduce our newest patched member of the LSMC brotherhood, Kid. And don't give me shit about your name when you have a baby face only a momma could love." I look around the room, and everyone looks at Kid, many giving congratulations and atta boys. Seeing the emotion, he is trying to hold in lets me know that Kid is a young man that wants this, and I am damn proud to call him brother.

Standing, I walk over to Kid, signaling Rocky to present Kid with his new cut and patch. I stare Kid down and watch as he becomes the brother. I knew he was always meant to be. He stares at the cut I placed in his hand and then back up to me, he looks around the room, and without a second thought, he rips his prospect cut off, tossing it on the table, and slides his newly earned patch over his shoulders. His eyes get big and a little misty. He hasn't spoken yet, and I get it. We all do. This is a moment every brother in this club worked our asses off for, so emotion is natural.

Kid rubs his hand down the front looking at the patch with his name on it, and a huge smile breaks across his face. He looks up at me, and I can see the respect and appreciation in his eyes.

"I just want to say, since I was young, I wanted to find family. I never had that. I wanted what other people had, and I found that here. I won't let you down, brothers. Prez, I will walk with you. I will fight with you. I will die with you. I will be a Lucifer Saint until my last dying breath. Thank you for allowing me to be a part of your family." He gets choked up at the last part; no one says anything because we are a family. I step toward him and give him a man hug and let the gravity of this sink in before going back and taking my seat at the head of the table.

"All right, Kid, take a seat. Let's get down to business. Congratulations, *Brother*. So, now you are healed up and a little more lucid, not on potato watch. Talk to me." Chuckles are heard around the room.

Kid looks around the room for an empty chair, finding one next to Mouse. Taking his seat, I watch as he lets out a visible sigh of contentment and looks up at me. Squaring his shoulder and begins telling the brothers what went down and how the Keepers captured him.

"Prez, you had me keeping an eye on Penelope, and for the most part, she was boring as shit. She didn't go to many places and didn't talk to anyone when she was out. I felt like maybe she wasn't involved in the way we thought," he says, looking around the room with a hint of unsureness in his eyes. And I understand what he means. If a snitch is indeed a snitch, they would at least do some snitch-like shit.

Kid continues, "As I said, she was boring until that day. After the cops came and we were cleaning up, I caught her and Darcy talking in a corner in hushed tones. I didn't catch much of anything that was said. Other than Darcy asking where she was going. By how they were acting, I knew something was up. The way they were whispering and looking around, I knew they would either do some shit or get into some shit. Long story short, they snuck out a few hours later. Both had a bag in hand. Everyone was busy, and I didn't think much was going to happen, so I didn't let anyone know I was leaving. I decided to follow them as I was tasked to do. They met up with a Keeper at the backside of the diner, and I assumed he was alone. I watched him pull in and park next to Penelope's ride. I tried to stay in the shadows and get as much information as possible. Fortunately for me, they didn't have the same thoughts about keeping it low profile. Darcy, Penelope, and the Keeper started arguing, then, out of nowhere, two creeper vans pulled up. Something knocked me pretty good in the head. And sometime later, I woke up getting the shit kicked out of me." He shakes his head. I know it burns his ass, getting caught unaware and by surprise.

"I was tied up, and when I looked around, I noticed that Penelope and Darcy were watching the Keepers beat my ass. Neither of those bitches seemed worried, concerned, or upset about what was happening. Neither of them bitches spoke up or asked them to stop. Penelope was hugged up on some guy. And Darcy was being her usual self and acting like she didn't betray the club chatting it up with the Keepers."

A round of fucking bitch, fuck her, and if I ever's are slung out around the room. But Kid has more to say, and it makes my blood boil.

"While they were knocking me around, they were questioning me. They wanted to know about runs, what we run, our business, how much we bring in, and whom we are working for and with. I answered none of it. I just hung them tied up in the middle of their clubhouse. I tried to stay conscious as much as possible, but there wasn't much going on in their common room. Everyone, including the woman, seemed to want to be there, including Darcy and Penelope. Those two bitches were drinking, giggling, and carrying on. After a few hours, Pyro and Demon returned to the main room. Pyro looked pissed, and Demon looked determined." Fuck, we didn't even know the kid was missing for hours. For him to go through that and still be so dedicated and loyal to the club, damn, my respect for him skyrocketed tenfold.

"They were dumb enough to tell me their plans. They are talking to another mafia family from the east coast but prefer someone closer to deal with their skin trade needs, as they called them. I didn't get any names; I'm assuming because the common room had a mixed bag of brothers and club girls, the two didn't want the information out. They said I would be a dead man by the night's end, so they didn't care if I knew they planned to kill all the brothers here and take Vera and Nancy, selling them off to the highest bidder." Both Tommy Boy and I let out vicious growls at that information. Over our dead bodies, would those motherfuckers ever get their hands on our women.

Kid scratches his jaw in reflection, and a look of pure anger and hatred crosses his face. "Darcy cackled when she heard that, and at that moment, I wanted to slit her fucking throat. I still do. I lost my shit, was knocked out again, and woke up at our front gates. All of you know the rest. As far as the two girls were concerned, they seemed like they wanted to be where they were. I don't think we as a club should care fuck all about them or what is happening to them; they chose their paths. It was clear that neither of them was being forced to do shit." He growls out.

"So, what you're saying is fuck those bitches, and we need to let karma handles those two. Which no doubt it will" Kid gives me a nod. "Well, all right then, as a club, normally we vote out club girls. But there is no need; both women are banned. We don't know what Darcy thought by being a temper tantrum-throwing club-switching whore, but I am washing my hands of her; she's banned. I'll let Mad Dog know up at the Mother Chapter. Need the prospects to pack her and Penelope's shit and dump, donate, or sell it. I don't give a fuck." I look around the room and receive sounds of agreement.

"Now, we know that the Keepers aren't going to take us taking out their President too well. I want eyes and ears on the streets. We took out quite a bit of their club, so I don't think they will come at us again, but you never know. I don't want to go on lockdown. Need all brother, ol' ladies, and club girls to stay alert and aware. And someone needs to keep an eye on Magda. You know she doesn't take traitors well. She's likely to hunt the bitches down. And I don't want anyone riding alone."

"Including you, Prez."

I look over to Tully because he knows me and knows I like to take long rides to clear my head. Being president is hard work, and sometimes I need some damn peace. I nod at him.

"Also, I want to keep eyes and ears out for any girls that go missing. I, like Barone, will not have that shit happen anywhere our family is, especially with V and Nancy being ol' ladies and pregnant. So, those two need to be protected at all times, even if there are walking around the yard. Also, before I say this shit, I don't have a pussy. But V brought up a valid point about her and Nance being pregnant. I want to build something close to the clubhouse. A place that will serve as a daycare of sorts for our kids and any other club kids we have in the future. I know Nancy works, and V has been on my ass about getting a job, so having a sitter in-house, someone we trust, would be ideal. And before you suggest one of the club girls as a sitter rethink that shit, you say it too loud my woman is liable to remove your balls." I receive a few chuckles from my brothers. I'm growing a pussy if I am bringing this shit up in church. "Anyways fuckers, I'll get with whom I need to get with to get shit planned out. Vera will be in charge of the staffing shit. Cause I like my dick and love my girl ain't jeopardizing shit, to interview bitches that only want to get in my or y'alls drawls."

The room explodes out in laughter because it's true as fuck. We continue talking about club business and things that need to be replaced and repaired. We talked about business, money, and runs. We also talked about replacing the two club girls we lost.

Shit's finally calming down and coming together.

Now all I need to do is roast a pig and marry my girl.

Eighteen

V E R A

Nine months pregnant

Who would have thought that this would be my life? Two years ago, I lost everything, and now... now I have everything I could ever want or need. I've made many mistakes in my life, and I thought I knew what I was doing. I thought that evil and pain wouldn't touch me. I was wrong. So— so wrong. But even though sometimes it hurts to breathe when I think about my old life and my family. Here is where I was always supposed to end up, where fate sent me and knew I was needed.

Here is where I'm supposed to be.

Here is where I found love.

Here is where I found family.

Here is where I found happiness.

Here is where I found the strength to forgive myself.

My hand goes to my belly, rubbing it, thinking back to my talk with Don Barone. At first, I felt that... that was it, thought that my time being happy was over. I thought he would make me disappear again, take me away, and I would never see James or my new family again. Fortunately for me, that is not what happened. He explained that he did indeed send me here for a reason and that he had a feeling that I might get involved with the club in some way. The way he said it made me believe that is what he hoped for. I chuckled when he scrunched up his face, saying he was glad I was smart enough not to be one of the loose-leaf women. Saying I was smarter than that, which I am. He reassured me that I would always be under his protection, with the threat of the Salvatores still very real. He did say that he has made people believe I left the country and has someone making sure it stays that way. I don't know what that means, but I trust every word he says. He may be a Ruthless Don, but he is my Don, my savior.

A few weeks after the incident, James told me that the two missing Club girls made their choices of their own free will and are, according to Cade, alive, well and spreading their *love* freely. They don't know what role Darcy had in all this; James says he thinks she jumped ship to get attention and see if the club would come running to *save her*. Which, of course, didn't happen. James was pissed, thinking about how selfish and fucked up she was. The fact that she went to that extreme because she was not getting what she wanted is ridiculous. The club is not looking to retaliate any further or go after either of them, and I don't blame them one bit. Let them bitches lay in the beds they made. From what I hear, they are lumpy, bumpy stinky beds.

I shudder at the thought of those men. To say they are nothing like the men of LSMC is an understatement.

The other day I was trying to get a little rest in my room because this kid loves sleep, and if I'm honest. I'm not mad about it. I had the television on for background noise, and it just so happened to be on the news. There was a breaking story about an SPD officer found dead in his home of an apparent suicide. They noted that his house looked like it was ransacked. They explained it away, saying that he did it out of anger. They also stated that there were visible injuries on his body, again explaining that his home was ransacked and that that is how he got them because he was so angry and didn't feel the pain he was causing himself while destroying his home. Not likely, but if that's their conclusion, then— I scoffed at that.

According to the news report, Officer Thompson was investigated for taking bribes and mishandling evidence, among other things. They said that he had become increasingly paranoid at work and kept talking about *them*, visiting him. He was said to have gone on rants in the days leading up to his suicide, saying that *they* were out to get him and that *they* were going to kill him. His fellow officers just thought he was acting out to try and get out of the shit he was in. Of course, I didn't believe any of that. A cocky officer who thought he could get away with anything would try his damndest to escape any trouble he was in. He didn't seem like the type to give up. It all seemed a little too bizarre to me.

I asked James if he knew anything about what happened to Officer Thompson, and he looked me dead in my eyes and said *Club Business*. I didn't talk to him for nearly a week. Oh my, did I get it when he was tired of me giving him the silent treatment. Of course, I was being a brat, I know club business is for my good and protection, so I'll blame my extreme emotions on my pregnancy. But seriously, I felt I had a right to know. The guy was an asshole and deserved what he got. Also, I am learning that *club business* is quickly becoming my two least favorite words.

A few months ago, we got confirmation about the sex of our little one. James, who called it, is ecstatic that he was able to bribe a doctor to show us in an ultrasound what we were having.

And yes, it's a damn boy.

Standing in our room, I stare at myself in the bathroom mirror. Today is the day. This day would have happened months ago if it were up to me. James and I wanted everything to be perfect, this was going to be my only wedding, and even though I didn't have my blood family here, I knew they would be watching. I smile at myself, thinking of them and how my father would feel about me being pregnant and getting married to the president of a Motorcycle Club. I would hope that he would be happy for me and proud. I know my mother would fuss over me, as would my sisters. I smile fondly as I close my eyes. I swear I can feel them around me, and my little boy gives a soft kick, and I rub my stomach.

I hear a knock at the door, and my eyes snap open. I look over and smile. Don Barone refused to let Brick pay for the wedding or any of the brothers to walk me down the aisle. I knew the long-standing tradition that if a daughter of the Mafias' father could not walk with her, the *famiglia's* Don or his representative would do the honors. And the other reason is that Don Barone has a soft spot for me. He brought his future wife with him today. Rebecca Saunders is a beautiful black woman who was raised here in Sacramento. She is soft to his hard, light to his darkness, and sweetness to his sour puss ass. I giggle because I would never say that last part out loud. But Rebecca is not someone I thought would end up with the Don. She is such a kind woman, and I love her for him. I learned that she might seem like a sweet, gentle, soft-hearted woman, but she can get sassy with the best of them. And has no problem putting Don in his place, even in front of others.

Don Barones' eyes soften when he sees me in my three-quarter sleeve white dress that flows softly to the floor. I wanted to keep it simple. I have my hair down and curled, and a crown of baby's breath is in my hair. I didn't want to fuss with makeup. After all, I knew it would look like a mess because I would no doubt be crying by the night's end. Don Barone smiles after he appraises me. His eyes light up, and if I am honest, they look a little misty, making *me* a little misty, and I refuse to let a tear fall. I have to get down the aisle first.

"Are you ready, *piccolo?* Your groom acts like a mad man and his moments away from stomping up here, so we must get a move on." He winks at me as I set my brush down, which I wasn't using in the first place. Stepping out of the room, I see Nancy, Beebe, Mona, and Rebecca, all of whom are near tears.

Seeing them makes me want to cry again, but I hold it in. My hand goes over my rounded belly, and I take a few breaths as the women in my life fawn over me. Nancy, Beebe, and Mona are bridesmaids. I didn't choose a maid of honor. I left that position open in honor of my sister Vittoria, even if no one knew. Nancy will stand in that spot. All of them look beautiful in their yellow spaghetti strap knee-length dresses. I couldn't be happier to see my friends and family. I never thought I would have this. Never thought I was worthy of it until James and the club. All of the women have their bouquets of sunflowers and baby's breath. Of course, theirs is much smaller than mine.

"Yes— I am ready."

We all make our way out of the room. And as we walk to the elevator, I see Flick standing at it, holding the doors open. He looks so handsome in his get-up. I didn't expect it, but James wanted me to have the wedding of my dreams. So, all the guys except for James are wearing a soft yellow button-down shirt, brown suspenders and dark jeans, brown bowties, and brown loafers. All of their boutonnieres are sunflowers and baby's breath. The only difference is that James' shirt is white. I was surprised that all the brothers were ok with me dressing them for our wedding, not one eye roll or argument, just a bunch of 'Yes, Boss Lady' and 'Whatever you want, Boss Lady.' I smile at the memories of how they tried to hide the disgust on their faces for me having the audacity of wanting them to wear dress shirts. They may not have said a word or complained, but I know better. Unlike me, the next woman to marry in this club may not have an easy time. But then again, tears do the trick every now and then, even when they aren't necessary.

"You are looking very dapper, Sir."

I smile and step closer, leaning in and kissing Flick on the cheek, and he blushes—he freaking blushes, the cutest brother-in-law ever. According to James and Flick, their brother Tom will be here as well as their father. They aren't sure about their mom, but James somehow got a message to her. According to James, Tom and his wife had twins, so I didn't meet his father until a few months ago. He was with them in San Francisco, helping them to acclimate as parents. His Pop is an amazingly wise and welcoming man. I am so honored to be marrying his son. And he hears it from me almost daily and tells me that it's his boy that is honored.

We walk to the elevators talking about everything and nothing. Flick racks a few jokes about how he nearly had to sleep on top of James last night to keep him from coming to our suite. He said he tried and almost made it because he ordered the prospects with the threat of not patching in to get out of his way. But Tully and Rocky were ready and stationed at the Elevator doors. They had a rotating shift and ended up having to lock the elevator and stairs because he wouldn't stop until they got him piss drunk and passed out. I giggle a little, but lucky for James. He's not one to be tortured the day after drinking, so Flick said he was just fine and didn't remember the shit he did or tried to do to get to me. We all had a good laugh.

When the elevator comes to a stop, I take a deep breath. Stepping out, we all make our way to the doors that lead out and into the backyard, where our wedding and reception will take place. I wanted everything outside, it was spring and warm, and I knew that even if the evening got cool, we would be ok with all the dancing, drinking, and carrying on.

Flick walks ahead of us and over to Tully, Rocky, and Kid, standing near the door. When they turn, all of their eyes connect with mine. They all have huge smiles; I dare not say they look a little misty-eyed. Each man walks up to me, giving me a kiss and an encouraging word complimenting me. It takes everything in me not to cry.

Because there are three girls and four girls, they are all walking separately. Before I completely lose my shit, the back door opens, and Pop comes through, smiling his huge contagious smile.

'Well, girly, you are a sight for sore eyes. The most beautiful woman I have ever seen. And I tell you what, if that son of mine doesn't do you right, you call me, I'll set him straight." Pop gives me a wink and pulls me into a hug, it's a little awkward with my belly in the way, but I take it, anyone. "Let's send these ingrates down the aisle to signal the boy you're coming. Cause if we don't, we are going to have trouble soon. That boys been hell on wheels all damn day, and it's taken an act of God to keep his ass down here." Pop, along with everyone else, chuckles.

Don Barone growls and steps in front of me, and everyone stops laughing. I look up at him but his big barely back is in front of me. With the door open, I look around his shoulder and see why he's growling and cursing in Italian, as does everyone else. James is done waiting. He is making his way down the aisle and towards us. His father and brother Tom cut him off, arguing for a minute before I see him clench his fist staring at the open door. He eventually turns around to stomp back up to where we will be saying our *I do's*.

Pop makes it back to us with an apology in his eyes. But I know, my man, it was bound to happen. He has never liked me far from him since that first weekend. I give Pop a wink and shake his apology off.

"All right, everyone, let's get this show on the road before I have to sit on my son," Pop chuckles.

Everyone chuckles along with him, and then we hear *In your eyes* by Peter Gabriel playing out, and everyone starts walking towards my man. Don Barone stayed in front of me until James and my song started to play, *Heaven* by Brian Adams, and as much as I tried to keep the tears from falling. My eyes connect with James; like me, his emotions have gotten the best of him. And I can tell he hates waiting for me, his hands clench open and closed, and he's bouncing on his feet. Just as he was going to take a step toward me, Flick and Tully put hands on his shoulders to stop him. The looks he shot in their direction would have other men shrinking away.

I shake my head and speed up my waddle, one I make it to him, he snatches me up and tries to kiss me, but Don Barone is quicker and slides his big brown hand in front of my face, and everyone laughs.

He stares James down and then looks at the priest Don Barone brought with him. We may be a bunch of criminals, but we are Catholic, at least I am, and this whole thing is for me. Don Barone gives me a wink after the priest asks whose giving me away, he answers, and after another stern look and a warning to James, he steps over to his waiting wife-to-be.

James and I chose to say our vows during the ceremony. Well, that's a lie we did, but we decided to write them only for each other. We also gave each other gifts. James gave me a beautiful necklace with two circles connecting, signifying our lives intertwining. I gave him a leather cuff engraved with the date of our first kiss, the day we found out about our little guy and today's date. I debated adding the date of our first time together but thought better of it. That moment is for us and us alone. Because those memories are what began our lives together so that we could get through the ceremony without me breaking down into a blubbering mess, being an emotional trainwreck, I could barely get the two words *I do* out of my mouth. There was a small splash, widening eyes, and a few gasps before all hell broke loose.

When the priest realized what was happening, he quickly pronounced us husband and wife. James refused to let my water breaking mess up the moment, and before the pain could shoot through me, he laid a very sexy, claiming kiss on my lips. Before I could even recover, James scooped me up and ran me to the club truck that had been sitting in front of the clubhouse with our bags and things ready to go, and it even had the keys already in the ignition.

James doesn't say a word to anyone even though everyone tries to talk to him. He gets me to the truck before shutting the door. He turns around to the crowd and yells.

"I don't care what you fuckers do, drink, enjoy the party, fuck. BUT MY WIFE IS ABOUT TO HAVE MY BABY" Everyone cheers a few brothers run to their bikes. James' smile gets bright, and he runs to the driver's side of the truck and peels out like a bat out of hell. Yes, he and the brothers had practiced this very thing multiple times, in the middle of the day, the middle of the night, when they were all in different places and working. He was hellbent on being prepared. My husband wasn't leaving anything to chance.

Looking over at me, he grabs my hand, kissing my knuckles, but doesn't speak. He is completely and utterly focused on the road. A contraction hits, and holy mother of— this is the devil's work. I am glad he loves me because I genuinely am crushing his hand. I breathe through the pain as we make our way to the hospital to have our son.

Nearly twenty-four hours later, with countless threats of violence,

James, his brothers, and the club were almost thrown out of the hospital. Our son Brian Victor Masterson, the namesake of our fathers, made his way kicking and screaming into the world. And I am the happiest, albeit tired woman in the world. I have my husband, my son, and my family.

After all, was said and done, we asked that Don Barone be Brian's godfather; no one knew why I was so adamant about it, and surprisingly no one through fits about it. But that could be because Don Barone dared everyone with a look to say a word, and they didn't.

James is a fantastic father; if I am honest, he is a little too clingy for my liking. I have to wrestle Brian away from more than anyone else. He gets so annoyed that our son has the nerve to get hungry and need me. When he pouts when I come to feed Brian, I laugh at him every time because he is ridiculous.

Everyone, including the club girls, has calmed down, and we don't have much drama. Again it may be because anytime anyone gets out of line and the baby is around, James threatens to *put them on the wrong side of the grass.*

Tommy Boy and Nancy had their son a few months before I had Brian, and they are doing well. I'm proud of Tommy for stepping up and being the man his family deserves, even though he still hasn't made Nancy his ol' lady officially in the club. But that is none of my business. I've learned that I need just to let them be who they are.

James and Don Baron have become pretty friendly, and they have *meetings* which is boss man speak for dinner and drinks away from the club a few times a month. Don Barone also ensures he spoils Brian from afar as often as possible. My baby boy is so damned love. I am so loved. I am truly happy.

Epilogue

V E R A

Four years later

I can feel the sweat pooling at the base of my back, the sheets under me are wet, and yet I'm cold. I feel overwhelmed more by my shivers than the pain. Why? Why did I think doing this again was a good idea? I said it once, and I'll repeat it– contractions are the devil's work. And to think I have to push two humans out of me this time. Freaking two.

I let out a loud moan and clenched my eyes shut.

I glare at my husband, who has apologies written in his eyes. I'm not having it. He did this to me again, not just one baby but two giant big-headed babies. Two babies are hell-bent on tearing me apart and making me suffer as much as possible— while I try to bring them into this world.

A relaxing, calm washes over me as another contraction has passed and gone. There is a flurry of movement, and people are shuffling around in the room. Apparently, twins are a big deal around here. Or maybe it's because my husband grunts, growls, and threatens anyone and everyone he can. Everyone is scurrying around to get the room ready for me to push. I squeeze James' hand, and he winces, which makes me smile. Cruel… maybe, but he's a big bad biker. A smushed hand is the least of his worries. Over the years, I've learned a few things, and paying my husband back for his wrongdoings is one of them. So, I will obliterate his hand and any part I can while I suffer the joys of giving him two more sons. Don't get me wrong. I don't want to hurt him, hurt him… But a little payback is so worth the pain.

Several hours later, I successfully tore my lady bits to shreds and gave birth naturally to our two grey-eyed black-haired boys, Sean Michele

211

Masterson and Mathew Rocco Masterson. We kept with the tradition of American first names and Italian middle. I stare at my husband as he rocks both of our boys in his big arms. Like with Brian, James will be a pain in my ass, and I know it. But I wouldn't have it any other way.

Even with the club being so busy. James always has the time or makes time for our family. And boy, oh, boy, is it a family. Brothers started falling like dominoes finding their one, and for the most part, I love the ol' ladies and wives that have joined our family.

Yes, I said wives because there is a difference. Some brothers saw what I did, and even though they may have knocked up a woman and wanted to take responsibility for their kid, they knew as well as I did that some women were not meant to be a part of the club. So, the brothers do their duty, and I respect them for that.

The wives that are not so club-ready or worthy live cushy lives outside the club. Am I a bitch for not caring, maybe? But as my husband told me many years ago, he is in charge of all of the brothers, and I am in charge of the women, and I make damn sure to let brothers know what I think about the women they bring around. I have seen things go bad on more than one occasion, and a woman scorned can leave a trail of destruction in her wake. And I, as the first lady, can't have that, our men work hard, and they don't need to come home to stress and drama. So yes, I am a little judgmental and protective of all of the men in my family. And I will never apologize for that.

The door to my room flies open, and my eyes go wide for a second, but then a tired smile makes its way to my lips at the sight before me. My little terror has come barreling in and bearing gifts. We no longer call our eldest son by his birth name. Oh no. He is forever known as Talon, the little boy who shreds everything in sight when he's having one of his *moments*, as his father calls them. I tried calling him Shredder, but apparently, that is a name for a bad guy who picks on turtles, so that was out, and Talon was in. And believe you me, it was a fight not to call him Shredder. But he said he loves turtles and refuses to be a bad guy and hurt them. I giggle, thinking about that conversation.

I stare at my little guy, who has a pinched look on his face and squinted eyes. He is not looking at me. Oh no, he's looking at his father and what he has in his arms. We tried our best to prepare our little man, but the look on his face says we may not have done a good job of it. James sees our son's gaze and beckons him over to meet his little brothers. Ever so slowly,

James kneels so that he's as close to eye level as Talon. James shifts while holding the babies so they can meet their big brother.

Talon narrows his eyes on his father and puts his little hands on his hips. "You and mom said they were brothers; you didn't trick me, did you? Hmm? Because they don't look like big boys to me. Mom said that they were big boys, and they aren't. Did you lie?" he glares at his father, and I am trying, along with everyone else in the room, not to laugh. Because he is earnest, he made me and James promise that he was getting brothers because there were too many icky girls in the club.

Yes, we had an influx of babies, and there are a few more girls than boys at the moment, and Talon hates it. For a minute, James looks stunned at the words that came out of our son's mouth, but I'm not. This is what he gets for including Talon in so much of the club, for letting our little guy hang out with him and the brothers every chance he could. Granted, Talon is only four, almost five and not involved in much of the *big boy stuff* more than any other club son, but it's enough for him to be very smart and smart-mouthed.

"Buddy, look at them. They are boys, Promise. You know your daddy and president wouldn't lie to you" I roll my eyes. That's the new thing. My son has been calling his father Prez and telling anyone who listens that the club will be his one day. And he makes sure all the club kids know who's the boss, and the kicker is– the kids listen. We all get a kick out of it. I'm sure we're going to pay for it in the future.

Talon stares at his father a little longer and then nods. He steps closer to the babies, gently touches both cheeks and smiles. Talon turns and looks at me with a massive smile on his face.

"You did good, woman."

And that is when everyone in the room loses it.

I couldn't have asked for a better life. Yes, I still have regrets and wish that the family I was born into was here to be a part of the family I chose. I miss them daily and will tell my children all about them when they are older. The threat is still there, I still have a price on my head, and James doesn't know about any of it. But it doesn't matter. I know that Don Barone has it all under control.

My husband is a fantastic man, father, and Prez. Watching him grow the club and lead makes me so very proud. I am so lucky that he loves me just as much now as he did the day he had that skank in his lap at the Diner. I still, to this day, don't know what happened to her. We never saw or heard from her again—no one has. I chuckle to myself as I think about those early days.

I look over to James, who is pouting and empty-handed. The babies have been stolen from him. I'm sure it was an ordeal because, for a man who shares life and his club, he's not very good about sharing. He walks over to my bedside and runs his hands through my hair. I stare up at him from my hospital bed.

Leaning down, he kisses me.

"I love you, sweetheart. Thank you for giving me a chance. Thank you for giving me this life, and thank you for giving me our children. You and our boys are my world, Mrs. Masterson. I would burn this world and the next to the ground to protect and provide for you. I am grateful for your love, kindness, and guidance. And I can't wait to make more babies with you. And live a life filled with laughter and love, and make all the good memories you can handle. In and out of the bedroom" I shake my head at that last part, this man. But I also know he is being honest, and I wouldn't have it any other way. James kisses me again, and my eyes get heavy. I smile, thinking about my beautiful life and family as sleep takes me.

"Sleep, sweetheart. I got you and our boys."

-BRICK-

Two years later

If you would have told me eight years ago that my life would be turned upside down by a little spitfire of an Italian woman. If you had said to me that I would find the love of my life and the mother of my children when I was trying to get away from a clingy club hang-around that worked in our diner. I would have laughed in your face. But here I am.

Husband, father, and president of one of the West Coast's most respected and feared clubs. That year that V and I met was one for the books. She and I moved at lightning speed, and I wouldn't change a damn thing about it.

The club had one down and dirty skirmish that had us coming out on top that year and solidified our alliance with the Barone *Famiglia*. It also made people sit up and take notice. We have grown a lot over the years. Brothers have started settling down and having kids of their own. Our businesses have expanded and are doing well. Up until today, we were the happiest we could ever be. Excited for the future– our future– the family's future.

Looking down at the love of my life, the woman who has made it all worth it. I hold her in my arms as she shatters. Holding her close to me as I whisper to her about all the good stuff we have in our lives, our boys, our club, our family. Telling her this isn't the end of all, just–

All she does is sob and apologize to me. She doesn't need to do that— this wasn't her fault. The doctors told her as such. There was nothing she did or didn't do. It is just the way of life. Our angel Grace Victoria Masterson was not meant for this world. She was meant to be our son's guardian angel. I have to believe that. I need to believe that otherwise, I will–

I feel all her anger, frustration, and, most of all, sadness. I know that no matter what I say, no matter what the doctors say or do. From this day on, V will blame herself for losing our girl. Even after being told repeatedly by medical professionals that there was nothing she could have done.

And she did. It took months for V even to get a little close to the woman she once was before our loss. They call it postpartum depression and survivor's guilt. After we lost our little girl, V was a shell of herself; neither our boys nor I could break her out of it. She was still my wife, mother and first lady, but not like she used to be. She was going through the motions.

One day, Rebecca, Barone's wife, showed up, and the entire day, she locked herself and V into our room and suite. And the next day, V seemed to look almost like herself. She was smiling and laughing. I still saw a little sadness, but I also saw the determination in her eyes to come back to me… to come back to us. Neither I nor anyone else could believe that change and I would slit anyone's throat who said a thing about it.

One day I broke down at one of our meetings, and I asked Elijah what his wife did to mine. Barone said his wife had a gift and left it at that. And I wasn't going to look a gift horse in the mouth or ask questions. So, I left it at that.

I did my best not to treat her differently for fear of her returning to her dark place. But she never did, she also didn't want any more children, and if I am honest, I didn't argue because I didn't either. We don't know how it happened, but neither of us wanted to go through that again. And so we didn't.

We have our three boys, each other, and our club, and we are happy. I couldn't imagine my life without V, she is my light in the darkness, my voice of reason, and the only one willing to put up with my shit.

My father was right when he said, "Love isn't something to be searched for. Love finds you and, if you are open to it, has the ability to be the best thing that will ever happen to you or the thing that ruins you."

I think my love for my wife is the best thing to have ever happened to me. And know that she has ruined me for anyone else. And I wouldn't have it any other way.

I will happily leave this world ruined but loved.

Extended Epilogue

VALENTINA

56 Years Old

S itting in the back of the clubhouse, my family is enjoying another warm California summer. We are celebrating my grandson Sebastian's patching into the club. It was one hell of a road for him and his father to get to this point. I smile as he laughs at something Talon says to him. I am honestly in awe of my boy and his family. We didn't know how things would turn out when they first showed up, but here we are.

A little sadness clenches my heart, but I try not to reflect too long or let the memories drag me too far as I sit here. I will always live with regret and pain, but my family, my life, and my husband lessons it a little, and I am truly blessed and happy.

I look around at the family that my husband and I built. And again, I am in awe, and tears threaten to spill down my face as I watch the families and children interact and run around. I catch the eye of my husband, who is surrounded by the new generation of the club. He is enjoying himself. I never thought I would see the day where he would be happy to sit back and let the youngins handle the club. But he is doing it reluctantly at times.

He gives me a big dimpled-filled smile and an air kiss. I giggle and blush like I am that 21-year-old girl he met in the diner all those years ago. The diner we still owned. Blushing, I look away from him and...

Something or, instead, someone catches my eye. A girl is standing at the edge of the yard, looking nervously around with wide expressive eyes. She isn't fully facing me, her head moves so quickly that I don't get a really good look at her my eyesight isn't as good as it once was, so I couldn't tell if

I recognized her from her. She continues to look around, unsure of where to look or where to go. That much is clear. And then…

Her head turns in my direction, and I can finally get a good look at her. Our eyes connect with mine, and my breath hitches because this can't be. She has my eyes, my hair, she looks so much like my mother… So much like me. They told… I stand, and my body begins to move of its own volition—Tears stream down my face.

I know her.

I loved her.

I lost her.

She's not real.

The look in her eyes says she knows me too… But how? I hear my name being called, but I refuse to take my eyes off her. for fear of her disappearing. Fear of her not being real.

She is so beautiful.

A mother knows her child.

A mother knows.

I feel someone trying to stop and talk to me, but I swat them away and continue on my path. I have to get to her. I need to know how? Once I reach her, I am so close I could reach out and touch her. But standing here, my body is frozen. My mind is reeling.

We stare at each other, and neither of us speaks. I can feel James' presence; like me, he is too stunned to speak. I hear the questions of my sons asking their father what is wrong with me and who this woman is. They seem angry, and they shouldn't get mad, not now. Not when–

I hear a gasp, unsure if it came from me or someone else. My tears never stop falling. I take a step closer to her, uncertain if I should. But my body moves… A mother knows. Her face crumples even more, and she begins to sob. I wrap my arms around her, holding her as close as possible. I hold my baby girl like my life depends on it.

"You're my mother."

It is said over and over again as tears fall from bother of our eyes. And my baby girl's sobs become even more gut-wrenching. I look over at my husband, and he nods at me. Because he heard her, he saw her, and unlike anyone else, he knows too because he feels it.

This girl is the daughter that we were told we lost.

"WHAT THE ACTUAL FUCK?"

Author Note

Dear Readers,

Phew, don't kill me for that extended epilogue.

Thank you for reading Bricks Ruin. Brick and Vera's love story. This was not a story that was going to be written initially. But there was so much that needed to be said; this book allowed me to lay the foundation for the future of LSMC Sacramento Chapter books. I knew what I gave you in this story would provide context for future books, so I hoped you paid attention.

Secret Sinner is the next book in this series. This book will focus on Talon as the President of the LSMC Sacramento Chapter. As the oldest son of Brick and Vera, he isn't quite the old chip off the block. You will see his tumultuous love story in the Sinners Duet. You will see some old characters come to light. There will be traitors and old rivalries returning. You will love some and instantly hate others.

Please note that the extended epilogue in *Brick's Ruin* happens after *Secret Sinner* Book 1, but at the beginning of *Sinners Redemption* Book 2 for context. Book 2 and *Hounds Promise* Book 3 will run simultaneously regarding the timeline. And because of that, you won't get all the answers until Book 3. I know… I know you want to know now, but you can't, but you will. I will spill all the beans on who, what, when, where, why, and how. And I promise you; you may only have half a clue.

The future is very interesting for the men and women of Lucifers Saints MC. The men of LSMC will continue to contend with strong-willed and fierce women. Some of those stories will be intertwined. You may fall in love with some characters and hate others. But in the end, their accounts will have you feeling some kind of way.

Until we meet again,
Tonya Ink

Stay Connected

If you are interested in signed copies and Book Swag, check out
www.tonyaink.com

If you are interested in works that are not yet published, being a part of the
story, live Q & A's, and receiving free swag for subscribing to my Patreon.
Sign up for my Patreon
www.patreon.com/tonyaink

Stay Social
TIKTOK | @AuthorTonyaInk
TWITTER | @AuthorTonyaInk
INSTAGRAM | @AuthorTonyaInk
FACEBOOK | @AuthorTonyaInk

Join Tonya's Inklings Facebook Group

www.facebook.com/groups/tonyasinklings

Made in the USA
Middletown, DE
08 October 2022

12130188R00135